Give Me
Thy Vineyard

A Novel of
Faith, Hope & Inspiration

Guy Howard

Author of *Walkin' Preacher*
of the Ozarks

OGDEN PUBLICATIONS INC.
Topeka, Kansas

———————————

Published by Ogden Publications
1503 SW 42nd St., Topeka, Kansas 66609

Publisher: Bryan Welch
Editor-in-Chief: Donna Doyle
Editor: Bruce Beggs
Project Manager: Laurie Cox
Cover Illustration: Carolyn Lang

ISBN 0-941678-62-8
July 1999 reprint
Printed and bound in the United States of America

———————————

For more information about Ogden Publications titles,
or to place an order, please call:
(Toll-free) 1-800-678-5779

Fireside Library

Other books by OGDEN PUBLICATIONS

Give Me Thy Vineyard
Contents

And Ahab spake unto Naboth, saying, Give me thy vineyard, that I may have it for a garden of herbs, because it is near unto my house; and I will give thee for it a better vineyard than it; or, if it seem good to thee, I will give thee the worth of it in money.

– I Kings 21:2

Foreword

There is no Wooded Lake in the Ozark Mountains. Clear Springs, Oakridge and Lake City do not exist.

The locations and characters as portrayed in this novel are characteristic of many areas still existing, unspoiled by the inroads of greed, selfishness and the rush of our modern civilization.

The conflict between two ways of life has existed in the Ozarks too often. Railroad right of ways have been taken and graded, and lake beds cleared of all life back of man-made dams. There is no United Electric Company in name, but there is in deed.

Although it is a work of fiction, let me state that this novel, its plot and many of its scenes had their conception and birth in historical fact.

The author wishes to thank Bill O'Toole and Ruth Parkay for their kind interest and helpful suggestions.

He wishes also to express appreciation to his friend, Steve Miller, for the care, research and art that went into the illustrations appearing herein.

Give Me Thy Vineyard

Chapter 1

WHEN ROSE GURNEY was 10 she had put away her
dolls and taken on the responsibility of housekeeping
for her father, widowed since the day she was born. When
she was 13, she had fallen in love with Hiram Jackson, and
although in the intervening three years she had gone out
with almost every eligible young man on the ridge, and had
had almost as many proposals as dates, it was still Hiram
who had the privilege of tying his horse to John Gurney's
hitching post whenever he liked.

She and Hiram made a fine picture on one particular
afternoon in May, as they sat talking together on the step of
Rosie's cabin next to Gurney's Mill, which her father owned.
Both glowed with rugged health, which is a blessing of
young people of the Ozarks, and both were as well favored
by nature as the colorful hills and mighty trees which
surrounded them.

Rosie had the kind of face which made you turn around for
a second look and kept you looking. Her skin was that rich
light-olive color which is characteristic of the oldest English
stock, and the blood often showed crimson through the clear
texture of her cheeks. Her thick hair was so dark brown that
it could have been taken for black except when the sun shone
bright upon it and revealed the russet glints of the lighter
shade. Her nose was small and straight, and her mouth was
small, with a full, moist lower lip which seemed almost to

contradict the girlish sweetness of the rest of her face.

It was Rosie's eyes which reflected her personality. They were large, black and brilliant, with flashing yellow glints that were warm when she was peaceful and fiery when she was angry.

Now as she sat on the step with Hiram, they talked eagerly about their engagement which they were ready to announce.

He was a sun-bronzed 6-footer of 21, with hair the color of freshly churned butter, and bright blue eyes. Hiram was a farmer and a good one. On the 160 acres which his grandfather had left him, he grew tall, golden corn and substantial crops of hay, tomatoes and tobacco. His cows, pigs and chickens were the envy of his neighbors.

But Hiram was a mountaineer, too, powerful and boiling over with energy that even the strenuous life of the woodsman could not absorb. For several years it had been his habit to go down to the still kept by Tobe Alton, who sold him corn liquor at special rates because he liked him, and burn up in the blaze of alcohol most of the money he made from farming. Then he would ride his madcap brown mare crazily up and down the narrow, twisting Ozark trails, usually accompanied by the wild McGonagle brothers or the Harmon boys, all of them yelling at the top of their lungs, forcing other riders into bushes and trees and raising clouds of dust that didn't settle for hours.

But Rosie Gurney had made him stop all this and keep his mind on his farm, and on her. It happened this way.

For three years Hiram had gone out intermittently with Rosie. But it was just last year when he noticed that she was more beautiful than the rest of the girls he knew. He became doubly interested when he heard Clark Harmon talking eagerly about how he was going to get her. Hiram knew Rosie was in love with him and it made him feel important. He could take his time, he thought. But Clark's persistent attempts to attract her and the fact that almost all his other friends had proposed to her, too, made him decide that maybe he'd better not wait any longer.

So one night he put on a clean white shirt, slicked back his hair and proposed to Rosie. But she turned him down. He would have to stop drinking first, she told him firmly. He blustered at that. It was an insult to his manliness. Any girl on the ridge and even beyond the ridge would be only too glad to marry him, drinking or no drinking. But Rosie shook her head, and her black eyes flashed glints whose meaning baffled him. He stormed out of the house and rode away.

But in six months he had stopped drinking and Rosie became his steady girl.

Yet now as they sat side by side on the porch talking, their handsome faces turned serious and they did not look like people whose wedding day is not far off.

"I tell yo', Rosie, I jest cain't see yer pa's side atall," Hiram was saying impatiently. "Here we is engaged right and proper, an' he wants us ter wait two years afore we kin git hitched. What do he think we'uns is?"

Rosie's low voice poured silk over him as she answered.

"Now, honey, we has gone over this a hun'erd times. Yo'uns know why Pa wants me ter wait till I is 18. An' hit ain't really a bad idea. We kin git ter know each other so much better whilst we is a waitin' an'–"

"I know yo'uns jist as good as I ever could 'thout bein' married ter yo', Rosie," he interrupted. "Hit hain't like we war strangers jist a meetin' an' a fallin' in love. We has knowed each other good fer three years. Yer pa an' his ole-fashioned way o' thinkin' nohow!" Hiram leaned back to mimic John Gurney's gruff bass. "'Rosie's maw war only 15 when me an' her war hitched up, an' she war jist past 16 when Rosie war borned an' she died. So I 'low a gal o' 16 hain't ol' 'nough ter start raisin' no family. I shore hain't got nothin' agin ye, Hiram, but I 'low as how it'd be a heap sight better iffn yo'uns wait till she's 18.'"

3

Give Me Thy Vineyard

Hiram paused for breath and then continued. "I shore has heard that air kind o' talkin' a thousan' times. An' I'se plumb sick o' hit. Yo'all is older than most gals yore age, Rosie, an' yore pa knows hit. Yo' hain't giggly er silly. Hit jist hain't right ter make us wait."

In her heart Rosie agreed with him. She loved Hiram passionately, but still she did not feel strong enough to disobey her father. John Gurney was a good, kind man and this was one of the few things he had ever demanded of her. The two years would pass quickly, she rationalized. Time just tore by when you were in love. And then they would be married and there wouldn't be any fussing or arguing and everybody would be satisfied. She longed to comfort Hiram, but she knew almost any reply except assent to his argument would cause him to explode violently. She remained silent and a shiver ran up her arm at the touch of him.

"I'se worried about the farm, too, Rosie," he said. "The way things is now, I don't even know where I'll be at in two years."

"Why, Hiram, what do yo'uns mean?"

"Yo'all knows 'bout that air 'lectric company a comin' in an' a takin' over folkses' farms so as ter build a dam. They has already drove Ed Roberts an' Sam Bates ter sell, an' they's a dickerin' with Tobe Alton right now. Tobe an' me has both made our brags that we'll not ever give up the land that our gran'pappies give us, but iffn they aims ter flood us over nohow I don't know what good fightin' kin do."

"That air 'lectric company won't take yer farm, honey. Why, hit's the best farm this side o' Reed's Ridge. An' 'sides, yo'all don't even know iffn they is a plannin' ter flood where yourn is."

"My land's in the valley, hain't hit? Hit's bound ter be in the path o' the water. An' that's why I needs yo'uns ter he'p me right now, Rosie. Tergether we kin git twict as much outen the land as I does by myself, an we kin make some

money an' even build up the place, so iffn I'se drove ter sell, I
kin git a good price fer hit."

Even Hiram could not realize that the plans of the electric
company were imminent and it seemed like such a faraway
thing to Rosie that she refused to think about it seriously.
How could Hiram even think that his farm would be flooded
over? Everyone knew that this electric company was only
talking about building a power dam. And even if they did
mean business, they wouldn't flood over all the good soil in
the hills. There would still be land for Hiram and her to farm.
And maybe he could even buy some machinery and those
electric things she'd heard folks in Hartstown talk about. She
could not understand why he was worried.

Give Me Thy Vineyard

Give Me Thy Vineyard

Chapter 2

*B*UT HIRAM was far from being the only one who was concerned about the activities of the United Electric Company. People up and down Reed's Ridge sensed that the building of a power dam in the valley was going to change the way of living which they had known for generations, and they wondered if the change would be good.

On that same afternoon in which Hiram and Rosie were discussing their future, several anxious men were gathered in Big Dave Gurney's general store in Clear Springs. Big Dave, Rosie's uncle, owned the only store on the ridge which supplied the hill people, and his establishment had become the social center of the region, where bits of neighborhood news were dispensed across the counter with the groceries. Seated on boxes and barrels on this particular day were Tobe Alton, Hiram's nearest neighbor and best friend; Aaron Hooks, a scrawny little moonshiner who also owned a farm in the valley; Sam Bates, whose property the electric company had forcibly bought two weeks before; and Young Tim McGonagle, Hiram's early boon companion on their drunken rides through the hills.

Tobe was bitterly telling his friends how he had fought the electric company officials all morning, but with no success.

"They might as well o' had my hands tied plumb behind my back," he said, "fer all I cud do. Them two slick-lookin' city fellers had their plans all made an' there jist warn't no use in argyfyin' with em'. They said iffn I didn't agree ter the price they set ter pay me, they'd have the land 'praised, jist like they done Ed Roberts' an' Sam's here, an' then iffn I still didn't want ter take what they offered me, hit would jist be too bad, cause they had got a contract with the state. I'd have ter take hit er leave hit, they said."

"How much did they offer yo'uns, Tobe?" Young Tim asked.

"Six hun'erd an' fifty dollars fer a hun'erd acres. That fer one o' the best farms in the valley. Me an' the boys has been a workin' hit up since my pappy give hit ter me. That air land might o' been worth six hun'erd an' fifty dollars 60 year ago, but hit shore is worth right smart more'n that now."

"Yo'd best take hit afore they 'praises hit, Tobe," said gentle Sam Bates quietly. "Me an' Ed Roberts got six dollars a acre fer our places, an' yo'uns knows that the worth o' our farms is as different as a saint an' a sinner. Ed know'd my land war a heap sight better'n his'n, an' he shore war surprised when I tole him how much the 'praiser give me. Then we figgered out that the company had set a figger an the 'praiser war a goin' by hit.

"Jist don't seem right folks nowdays kin do us like the Bible tells ole King Ahab an' his woman Jezebel done Naboth. He shore wouldn't sell his place an' I 'low the ole king war willin' ter pay any price ter git hit. Naboth shore felt like he ort ter keep hit seein's how his paw left hit to him when he died. Then ole Jezebel hired him kilt an' tuck hit nohow. This here 'lectric company works 'bout the same way. Some of us just 'bout as soon be kilt as ter have ter let 'em have the land our pappies worked a lifetime ter make a livin' ter leave their young'uns."

The miller, John Gurney, had come in while Sam was talking and had seated himself on a box near the counter. John was slow-moving and slow-thinking, but his heart was so big that his neighbors often wondered how it fit into his long thin frame. Everyone's troubles were John Gurney's, and although he was not as shrewd or as efficient as his brother Dave, people liked to talk to him because he felt with them so selflessly.

He had listened while Sam was talking, and his brow furrowed into deep lines as he aggravated himself over the injustice which he sensed was being done.

"Hain't there nothin' we'uns kin do?" he anxiously asked his brother, whom everyone inadvertently acknowledged as the best counselor on Reed's Ridge.

Dave's booming voice resounded through the store.

"I'se been a lookin' inter things with Squire Morgan," he said, "but like Tobe says, our hands is tied. The Squire, onct being a judge, like yo'uns knows, said we ort ter git some lawyer fellers on our side, so last week him an' two o' the other boys went down ter Hartstown. They was gone three days, an' do yo'uns know what they found out?"

The men looked at him.

"They found out that the 'lectric company has bought up ever' lawyer fer 50 miles 'round. They'se even got the shuriff a workin' fer 'em!"

Little Aaron Hooks shook his head sadly. "Reckon yo'uns an' me'll have ter go in fer moonshinin' full time, Tobe," he quavered resignedly. "They shore hain't no more pay in farmin'."

John Gurney stroked his black beard meditatively. Then again he looked at his brother and asked, "Dave, member 'bout eight year ago, when our kin, Luke Clayton an' his woman, war a passin' through here on their way ter Calfornie?"

The big man nodded.

"Wal, then I reckon yo'uns 'member that they come from Tennessee an' they war a tellin' us how the gov'mint war a buildin' a power dam up there. But kin yo 'member 'em a sayin' anythin' 'bout the folks a fighten' that air dam like

9

folks is here? I shore cain't."

Dave leaned against the counter and reached into his pocket for a crumpled bag of peppermints before rumbling, "No, John, I shore don't 'member nothin' like that, 'cause Luke never said hit. He didn't have no reason ter. The way I heerd tell 'bout that air dam war that the gov'mint paid them folks what their land war worth, an' sometimes even more, iffn the families war turrible big er needy. An' I heerd too, jist a little while ago that they war a fixin' ter give them folks cheap 'lectricity. But they shore hain't been nothin' like that a comin' out o' this here 'lectric comp'ny."

"Maybe they'll give us cheap 'lectricity, too," Young Tim volunteered. "We'uns hain't never had none o' that stuff roun' here. Shore would like ter try some."

"Don't fool yerself, Young Tim," Dave growled. "They'se a buildin' that air dam ter bring power ter the folks down ter Marshallville an' maybe even as fur as Springfield an' roun' there. Them folks is rich an' kin pay plenty fer 'lectricity. The comp'ny hain't goin' ter set low rates jist fer us hill folks. We'uns is jist plumb out o' luck, I'se afeard."

Just then the screen door banged open and Hiram Jackson walked into the store. The men were glad to see the young mountaineer, for despite his hair-trigger temper, he was well-liked on the ridge. Now his older friends looked at him with that patronizing tolerance of married men toward a bachelor soon to enter their clan, and made ready to tease him a little.

But though he had just left Rosie, Hiram's mind was temporarily full of something else.

"Fellers, yo'll never reckon what I jist heered!" he said excitedly. "Ran inter Clark Harmon up the trail a piece an' he tole me that the 'lectric company done paid his pa three hun'erd dollars fer thet worthless piece o' swamp land he owns in the valley. If that's what they is a payin'–"

The soft voice of Sam Bates stopped him.

Give Me Thy Vineyard

"Wait a minute, Hiram. Don't git yer hopes up. Shore that's what they'se a payin'. Lige Harmon had 50 acres down there. They paid him six dollars a acre, like they'se a payin' ever'body. Iffn Lige had got that land 'praised right, he would o' got a lot less money, but I'se willin' ter bet that when he heered 'three hun'erd dollars' he grabbed it so quick the comp'ny man didn't have no chance ter change his mind."

Hiram was bewildered. "Yo'all means ever'body's gittin' the same price?" he asked, his voice tightening.

"Tha's right," answered Tobe.

"But what 'bout yo'uns, Tobe? Yo'all shorely didn't sell yer land fer no six dollars a acre."

"I hain't sold yet, but after heerin' what the boys has been a sayin', I reckon I'd better, 'cause they is givin' me a few cents more 'thout 'praisin' hit."

Hiram's eyes turned to glistening ice as he stared at the men in the store.

"I'll kill anybody what tries ter make me give up that land o' mine fer six dollars a acre!" he blustered. "An' I hain't a foolin', neither. I'd as soon be flooded out o' the valley as ter sell that farm fer less'n two thousan' dollars."

Give Me Thy Vineyard

Give Me Thy Vineyard

Chapter 3

*I*N THE DAYS that followed, Hiram rode about the ridge blustering and bragging what he would do to the 'lectric company before he would sell his gran'pappy's land. His elation over his engagement to Rosie subsided and she was hurt that their plans for establishing a home had taken a secondary place in his thoughts.

Their friends thought the engagement was sufficient reason for a celebration so a party was arranged for the following Thursday night. As far as Rosie was concerned the party was a failure, because Hiram appeared distracted and miserable and made no effort to disguise his feelings. He scarcely responded to the congratulations of his friends.

But Hiram had a right to be despondent. The day before, representatives of the electric company had come to buy his farm. After looking over the productive, well-kept soil and the sturdy cabin and barn, they offered him $1,000 for the whole place. Hiram had refused. Then the men had told him that this was the best price anyone in the valley had received, and if he was stubborn they would have to initiate condemnation proceedings. He understood only the meaning of "condemnation" and lost his temper. Violently he ordered the two men off his property and told them he would shoot them if they came back again. But early the next morning one of them did come back, accompanied by the sheriff and a court order which said that Hiram was to appear at a hearing the following Wednesday.

Rosie tried earnestly to understand these developments as Hiram explained them to her later, but he hardly understood them himself. He was too angry to think clearly. All he could see was that he was being forced off his farm – that he would have to give it up for half its real value. He seethed with hate. If only he could do something to stop this. What right did the company have, anyway, to rob a man of his land just because they wanted to cover it with water? It was wrong, all wrong ...

"I hain't even shore I ort ter ask yo'all ter marry me now, Rosie. I cain't offer yo'uns nothin' no more," he said painfully. "I jist never expected that air company would work so fast. I reckoned we'd have six months – maybe even a year – ter work things out."

Now Rosie was on solid ground. Being warm and comforting was something she understood and she did it from the bottom of her heart.

"Yo'all hush that kind o' talk, honey," she began in her pleasingly resonant voice. "I ain't in love with yo'uns fer yore farm. I'd marry yo' iffn yo'uns didn't have nothin', an' tomorrer, too, iffn Pa warn't dead set agin' hit. But yo'uns is a gittin' sump'n, Hiram. They is a goin' ter give yo' a thousan' dollars. Yo'all said so yoreself. An' 'sides, yo' has got the mare an' them three cows an' the pigs an' the little flock o' chickens. Yo'uns kin start all over agin jist fine, an' I'll he'p yo'. Now jist stop lookin' like yo'uns war sorry we is engaged!"

Hiram's eyes softened.

"Yo'all shore kin make a man feel easier, Rosie," he said, "but yo'alls left a lot out. They ain't 'nother piece o' land fer 40 mile roun' as good as gran'pap's, an' I wants ter stay near the ridge an' I knows yo'uns does too. An' speakin' o' gran'pap, he air hardly cold in his grave yet. Hit's plumb sinful ter sell the land he worked so hard a buildin' up all these years. Hit'll jist kill me ter do hit, Rosie."

Give Me Thy Vineyard

"Well, other folks has been a sellin' their land, Hiram, an' they shore don't want ter part with hit no more'n yo'uns do. Yo' all jist got ter take what comes, honey. Ask God ter he'p us an' everythin'll come out all right." Rosie knew Hiram did not possess her kind of faith, but she felt in such a time as this that he too would feel the need of God's help and guidance. She had long cherished the hope that someday Hiram would accept the Saviour and they could raise a family in a truly Christian home. Oh, how she wished she could bring him to faith. But it was not going to be as easy as making him stop drinking. She was certain of that.

"Hmph, God!" he sniffed. "A feller'd be kind o' yaller ter do like I'se been a doin' an' then howl fer God to he'p him jist 'cause he's in trouble. I'se jist like that feller the preacher war tellin' 'bout a Sunday night over ter Stony Point. That old king wanted his grape patch an' 'cause it had been his pappy's he 'lowed ter keep hit. Then the old king and his woman had him kilt an' tuck hit nohow."

Rosie knew Hiram's grandfather had brought him up without religion. Old Abijah Pemberton, like many another who possessed a simple faith common to mountain people, felt that a disgrace that had come upon them was a punishment sent from God. He had quit the church the day his daughter came back from studying nursing in St. Louis, with the shamed announcement that she was going to have a baby.

Though wood's colts, as illegitimate children are called in the Ozarks, are not uncommon in the area, Abijah was too proud of his family name to take such a thing lightly. Neighbors whispered that he did everything in his power to try to get the man responsible for Lucy Pemberton's condition to marry her, but without success. But no one really knew any of the details. Rosie had often wondered who the man was and why he couldn't marry Hiram's mother, but the secret had died with Lucy Pemberton as she gave birth to her blonde son, and if Abijah knew the baby's

15

father, he never said anything about it to anyone.

After that there was no more church attendance in the Pemberton household. The dour old man did not even want to give the child a name from the Bible, but the name "Hiram" was on his daughter's lips as she died, and Abijah's ailing wife, Martha, insisted that the baby have that name.

Abijah Pemberton had then given him the middle name "Jackson" after the beloved Confederate general under whom he had fought, and had added his own surname. But as the boy began to grow up, his blonde hair, fair skin and big, muscular frame were in such contrast to the small, dark Pembertons who lived all over the hills, that the hill folk commented, "He shore ain't no Pemberton," and from his adolescence he was known as Hiram Jackson.

Rosie remembered the stories folks had told her about the fuss the old man had made when his daughter died. He did not want to give her a Christian funeral, but all the neighbors had come to him and begged and pleaded and finally threatened to quit neighboring with him if he didn't allow her to be buried according to the church custom. It was no wonder that Hiram was so irreligious for although many times he had seen his forbidding grandfather take down the family Bible from the fireplace mantel, and read silently from it, he had never spoken of any of its contents and no audible prayer had ever passed his lips. Rosie hoped that perhaps now, however, in his time of trouble about the farm, Hiram might be led to see his need for help outside the human realm.

She told him she would go to the courthouse in Hartstown with him next Wednesday and be right beside him during the hearing.

But as far as helping him was concerned, it would hardly have made any difference to Hiram whether she was there, or not. He understood only the bare essentials of the legal proceedings himself and Rosie certainly was no aid. When the hearing was over he had to try and explain to her that what they had just heard meant that appraisers would come out to his farm and set a price on the value of the land, at which he would have to sell.

The next week the men came out, looked the land over, and told Hiram that the company would pay him $6 an acre, or $960 for the whole quarter section.

The young farmer was stunned.

"But jist a minute!" he gasped, "that's even less money than them company fellers offered me in the first place. Yo'all knows that this here farm's worth twict that, an' more!"

"That's what everybody 'round here's been telling us about their land," one of the appraisers said in a bored tone. "Nine hundred and sixty dollars is all you're going to get. Take it or leave it."

Hiram felt as if all the breath had been knocked out of him. Once, when he was a little boy, he had fallen off his horse and lost his breath for a minute from the impact. That same sickening, dizzy, gasping feeling hit him now, and he could hardly talk.

"Git out," he muttered finally, towering over the two appraisers, "git out afore I throws yo'all inter the river. I ain't a takin' hit an' ain't a leavin' hit. I'se a stickin' here an nothin yo'uns say's is a goin' ter make me move!"

But even as he talked, Hiram knew he was beaten and he was almost overcome with despair.

The next day, when the adjuster from the electric company arrived, again accompanied by the county sheriff, Hiram was very quiet.

The sheriff was much relieved at the young man's tractability.

"Guess I won't have ter use this here ouster on yo'all, Hiram," he said in his hoarse voice. "This here ouster was gived ter me by the jedge, so's I could force yo'uns ter git offn yer land. But I reckon yo'uns decided ter be smart, arter all."

Cold sparks flew from Hiram's eyes and again his

hair-trigger temper blazed. So they were going to force him off his land if he didn't come peacefully? They were treating him as if he were a cow or a pig. He'd show them. He was making things too easy for them. Let them squirm a little, too.

And so when the adjuster held out the check for $960, Hiram said, "Nope, I'se sorry, but I jist cain't take that air piece o' paper."

The adjuster stared at him blankly.

"What did you say, young man?"

Hiram repeated, "I ain't a goin' ter take that air piece o' paper. Gran'pappy allus learned me ter take hard money, an' I 'low iffn yo'uns kin take this here place from me, then yo'alls got ter pay me gold."

The adjuster's eyes narrowed. Did this dumb hillbilly really know he was in his lawful right, demanding legal tender? Or was he just trying to be difficult? The adjuster shrugged his shoulders. *Oh, well,* he thought, *another day.* He'd just give the boy his gold tomorrow and be done with it. Pulling the sheriff, stupid with misunderstanding, along with him, he politely told Hiram that he would be back in the morning with payment in gold, and he expected that the deal would be closed in gentlemanly fashion.

The next day, with the sheriff riding beside him, the adjuster again made his way on his unfamiliar and uncomfortable horse along the thickly wooded trail to the valley. He tried to get relief with the thought that soon this business would be over and he would be back in his comfortable home in St. Louis.

But suddenly a rifle shot exploded from behind him, and he tumbled to the ground. The sheriff took one terrified look at the blood pouring from his companion's body and bolted down the trail. Someone was shooting from ambush and he had no desire to be the second target.

An hour later, bolstered by a four-man posse, he returned

to the spot where the shooting had occurred. The adjuster was lying where he had fallen, and no one could be deader. But the gold which he had been carrying in a chamois bag was gone.

The sheriff sighed. He hated responsibility.

"I reckon Hiram Jackson shorely done hit," he said to his men. "He was powerful mad at this yere feller yesterday, even iffn he pertended ter be a holding hisse'f in. I knowed his temper would be a gittin' him inter trouble. Reckon I best go git a warrant an' 'rest him."

Give Me Thy Vineyard

Give Me Thy Vineyard

Chapter 4

*H*IRAM LOOKED worried as he opened his door to the sheriff and the four-man posse.

"Hiram Jackson," the officer announced grindingly, "we'uns has come ter arrest yo'uns fur the murder o' the adjuster fer the 'lectric company."

"I don't know what murder yo'uns air a talkin' 'bout," Hiram muttered, looking at his feet.

The men eyed each other significantly. He was lying. Maybe he was going to give them a gunfight. Their hands tightened on their rifles.

"Hiram, yo'uns ain't never been a good liar. Now is yo'all comin' along peaceful-like er does we'uns have ter tie yo' up?"

"I didn't do hit," Hiram said, looking in every direction into the muzzle of a gun, and sat down heavily.

"Yo'all better prove hit mighty quick, son."

Hiram gazed hopelessly around the room. "I jist didn't do hit, that's all."

The sheriff followed his gaze, and his eyes lit on Hiram's old cap and ball rifle which was pegged over the door.

"Dick," he ordered one of his men, "go look at that gun an' tell me what yo'uns thinks."

Dick Flynn, a grizzled old mountaineer with a reputation for shooting turkeys out of season, examined Hiram's gun carefully.

"The barrel hain't warm, but these here powder marks shore is purty fresh."

Hiram's voice was drawn thin. "I war a shootin' squirrels yist'day atternoon."

"But yo'uns don't know nothin' 'bout no murder terday, huh?"

Hiram looked up at him and opened his mouth, as if to say something, but closed it quickly.

"Wal?" pressed the sheriff.

"No," muttered Hiram. "I don't know nothin'."

They took Hiram to the county seat in Hartstown and put him in jail.

Though there were no telephones, the word about the adjuster's murder and Hiram's imprisonment covered Reed's Ridge in a few hours. Everybody was talking about it and few questioned his guilt. All agreed that Hiram had done the right thing. If only they had the courage to fight the electric company – they'd blow them right out of the hills.

But Rosie Gurney was almost beside herself. She simply could not believe that Hiram, her Hiram, had shot an unarmed man in the back.

"I won't believe he done hit till he tells me so hisse'f," she said to her father as she saddled her black stallion, Fred, for a trip to Hartstown. Her father shook his head. He liked Hiram and he knew he was a decent boy. But he had a dangerous temper, and there was no telling what he would do when he lost it.

Hiram was sitting on the iron cot in his smelly little cell when Rosie was brought in by the sheriff. With a sigh of relief, he took Rosie in his arms, to hold her close. Suddenly she became the most important thing in his life. How comforting to know she still believed in him.

Without her faith in his innocence everything would have been utterly hopeless.

For a time neither of them spoke. Each felt the need of the

comforting nearness of the other. Rosie felt safe in the physical strength of this man she loved. His hard muscles pinioned her in a vise-like grip that hurt with a welcome, delightful pain. He loved her. Nothing in the world was big enough to destroy all that. Not even the electric company. But it was the strength of Rosie's fine womanly character from which Hiram drew comfort. He was in deep trouble. His spirit was wounded. His heart was bruised and bleeding. Only Rosie's gentle caresses and abiding faith had the qualities to heal his injuries.

Withdrawing from his close embrace, Rosie looked intently into his drawn, stern face.

"Hiram, darlin'," she murmured, "say yo'all ain't done no killin'. Please say hit," she whispered.

"'Course I hain't kilt nobody, Rosie."

She was surprised at the firm calmness of his voice and looked hard into his eyes. He was telling the truth. She knew it.

"But I cain't prove that I ain't done hit," he said lamely.

"'Course yo'uns kin, Hiram. Jist tell 'em what yo'all war a doin' when that air compiny feller war bein' kilt."

"I cain't tell 'em."

They had been whispering to avoid being overheard by the sheriff who was standing on the other side of the bars. But Rosie forgot to whisper as she asked in a frightened tone, "Why?"

The sheriff leaned closer as Hiram breathed, "'Cause hit'll jist git me in worse'n I is already. I'll tell iffn I has ter but maybe they'll find out who really done the killin' afore I needs ter say nothin'. Now, sshh!"

He took her hand and pulled her down beside him on the cot. The look in his blue eyes begged her to understand. But she didn't understand. He was keeping something from her. What was it? Why couldn't he tell *her* the whole truth? She was his girl. She was going to be his wife.

"Tell me, Hiram," she whispered fiercely. "Tell me what

yo'all war a doin' so's I kin have faith in yo'uns."

Hiram shook his head and jerked hls chin at the sheriff.

"Hit's a long story and he's a listenin' too hard, Rosie. But I'll tell yo' when I kin, honest I will."

Then the sheriff re-entered the cell and took Rosie away. But he told her that she could come to the coroner's inquest the next day.

The hill people were convinced that Hiram could not possibly be convicted on the evidence the law had against him. The men who had heard him vow he would kill whoever forced him off his land had kept their mouths shut, so all the coroner knew definitely was that the bullet in the dead man's body matched the kind Hiram used in his gun. But every man in the hills who owned that particular kind of old-fashioned rifle – and there were few who didn't – used the same kind of bullets.

The next afternoon, as Rosie sat tight against Hiram in the rough courtroom and heard the meaningless legal gabble going on around her, she was filled with anxiety. What was in Hiram's mind? Did he know who really had committed the murder? If so, why was he protecting the murderer? She prayed for God to give him strength and wisdom.

A sudden commotion in the corridor interrupted her thoughts, and, with everyone else in the room, she turned around and watched in surprise as Ray and Clark Harmon forced themselves into view.

The girl disliked these dark, hulking men, and it had always been difficult for her to be polite to them. Clark had been trying to court her for about two years, even after she became Hiram's steady girl. She could hardly bear to be near them. Clark, with his sneaky, narrow eyes and his breath always smelling of whiskey, made her feel unclean. He had proposed to her three times, but everyone knew he would not be faithful to anyone he might marry.

But what were the Harmon brothers doing here now,

raising a fuss at the inquest? She watched as they forced their way past the officers and toward the coroner.

"We'uns got somethin' 'portant ter tell, yore honor, 'bout the killin'," Ray said to the coroner in his soft, sly voice which had always jolted Rosie because it was in such contrast to his bear-like appearance.

"What is it?"

"We war a makin' the turn in the trail yist'day mornin' an' we seen Hiram a runnin' away from the company feller's body an' inter the woods. He war a packin' his squirrel rifle."

"What?"

Rosie saw Hiram's fist clinch and he was breathing hard. She looked at him, but he was staring at Ray Harmon, his eyes blazing in hot anger.

Ray repeated what he had just said, and Clark backed him up. They said they would swear to the truth of their statement.

"But why didn't you go immediately to the sheriff and tell what you had seen?"

Both brothers looked at Hiram and then looked away.

"Wal," Clark drawled, "Hiram's been our friend since we war young'uns. We'uns jist hated ter tell on him. But then we reckoned hit wouldn't be right iffn we'uns didn't."

Hiram's face whitened. He stood up at the coroner's order.

"You heard what these men have just said, Hiram Jackson. Do you deny it?"

"They ain't lyin'," he said in a flat voice. "I run away from the feller's body."

Rosie hardly heard the gasp which filled the room. Her heart seemed to be pounding against her brain. Was this what Hiram had been afraid to admit? Then he was saying:

"I was a cuttin' through the woods on my way ter the store yist'day mornin'. I didn't know what time that air a'juster war a comin', so I reckoned iffn I warn't home he could wait a spell fer me. But when I got ter the trail I seen a man layin' in the dirt with blood all roun' him. His face war turned up, an' I could see hit war the a'juster feller. I was skeered stiff and I didn't know what ter do. I looked aroun', but they warn't nobody 'bout. I reckoned then that whoever kilt him might be hidin' someplace an' a fixin' ter shoot me, too, iffn I didn't git out o' there. So I turned roun' an' run back inter the woods the way I come. I didn't want ter have nothin' ter do with that air killin'. Hit warn't none o' my business."

Rosie and the other hill people who knew Hiram well knew that the young mountaineer was telling the truth. Lying was one thing he had never been able to do convincingly.

But the law did not believe him and in a few minutes the coroner's jury retired to the jury room to consider the evidence. The half hour that elapsed before the coroner read their verdict seemed an eternity to Hiram and Rosie. They sat side by side, paralyzed with fear, as the coroner read:

"We find Theodore Fisher came to his death from a shot fired by Hiram Jackson."

The prosecuting attorney immediately filed a criminal information against Hiram charging him with murder in the first degree.

Rosie was horrified as they took Hiram away. She hardly knew what she was doing as she moved dazedly out of the courtroom. Then she heard a rough voice at her side, and realized Clark Harmon was near her.

"Oh, yo' – yo' low-down varmint," she hissed, "don't yo'un come inter my sight!"

"'Tain't my fault Hiram's a killer, Rosie," he drawled.

"Yo'all could o' kept yer big mouth shet! No one else in the hills would o' done what yo'uns done! An' he ain't no killer nohow! Yo'uns lied."

Then a new thought flashed into her mind and she backed away from Clark Harmon, her eyes widening into black pits of terrible knowledge. "Yo'uns done hit! Yo' an' Ray! I knows hit shore as I is a standin' here. Yo'uns kilt that air man an' yo'uns robbed him, an' yo' blamed hit on Hiram!"

Give Me Thy Vineyard

Ray had joined his brother, and several other people, hearing Rosie's accusing voice, crowded around them. Both brothers looked at each other and Ray smiled uncomfortably.

"Yo'alls excited, Rosie. Yo' jist ain't a thinkin'. What would we'uns do somethin' like that fer?"

"Plenty o' reasons. Ever'body on the ridge knows that yo' Harmons'd do anythin' fer money. We'uns knows how yo'all cheated Buck Reeves outen part o' his land an' how yo' didn't pay the Widder Gray the money yo'all promised her fer them hogs she sold yo'uns, an' – an' lots o' stuff. An' 'sides –" her eyes narrowed – "yo'uns has been jealous o' Hiram ever since I come ter be his gal. Hit ain't no secret how Clark said he war goin' ter git me away from Hiram, an' yo'uns – Ray – yo'uns kept a comin' by our cabin till Pa had ter throw yer out!"

"Yo're crazy, Rosie Gurney!" Clark declared, losing his temper. "Knowin' Hiram's a killer has gone plumb ter yore haid. Come on, Ray, we'uns don't have ter listen ter no more fool jabberin'."

The Harmon brothers pushed their way through the muttering crowd of hill people and jumped on their horses to ride away.

Give Me Thy Vineyard

Give Me Thy Vineyard

Chapter 5

HIRAM'S TRIAL was a quick one. He was defended by old Squire Morgan who had quit his law practice five years before, and was no match for the state's attorney and his chief witnesses, the Harmons, who swore they had seen Hiram leaving the scene of the crime.

When it was over, the jury found Hiram guilty. The judge sentenced him to life imprisonment, as the jury had recommended mercy, which barred the judge from condemning him to hang. But when Hiram remembered what he had heard of the steel and stone State Prison, with the sun barely squeezing its way through the bars, and no air, and only a few feet of space to move around in, he wished the jury had not done him this favor.

During the trial Hiram had been asked repeatedly where he had hidden the gold, and repeatedly he had insisted that he had never seen the gold. At last the state's attorney gave up, figuring that a year or so in prison would probably loosen the young hillman's tongue.

Everyone on Reed's Ridge had crowded into the Hartstown courtroom for the trial. When the sentence was passed, ominous glances burning with hatred were cast at the jury, the judge, the state's attorney and the representatives of the electric company. So much feeling was evident that the judge, fearful of open warfare, ordered the court cleared and Hiram was placed in jail. He was to be transferred to the penitentiary on Tuesday. However, on the Sunday previous, just as dark was covering the hills, two men rode up to the jail and told the sheriff that Tobe Alton and Charlie Raiford and their boys were feuding.

"Where they at?" the man of law inquired uneasily. This looked as if it might be real trouble. He recalled that both men had stills, the location of which had so far escaped him. He knew they hated each other because Tobe was always trying to undersell his competitor.

"About five miles down the holler in the hickory grove on the back forty of the old Jim Cox place," his informants shouted as they galloped away toward the place.

Leaving a man to keep an eye on his prisoner, the sheriff called his chief deputy and they rode down the trail together. As they came within hearing distance of the shooting he scowled darkly. He was not eager to interfere in this feud. He might even get shot. But he had to do something. Everyone who had voted for him would hear about this and expect him to do his duty. Tobe and Charlie and their sons were all good shots. In fact, young Steve Alton was one of the best shots on the ridge. The sheriff shivered as he motioned his deputy toward the hickory grove. *Why couldn't these fools do their feuding in some other county?* he thought as he drew nearer to the place of combat.

During a lull in the shooting he was heard to roar through the tall trees:

"Now, yo' fellers stop this here shootin' er I'll have ter put you'all in jail!"

As if in reply, a cloud of bullets whizzed over his head and he hit the ground with a grunt. *What kin I do with 'em?* he thought bitterly. He wasn't going to get himself killed. But he had to stop them. Each time he tried to rise, lead peppered the trees around him. He peered at his deputy. The man was hiding behind a bush trying to shoot in the direction from which he thought the bullets were coming. "Good boy," the sheriff said to himself.

Crawling on his belly to a deep ravine nearby, he thought it best to make his way back to the village to organize a posse. He knew some men whom he felt sure would enjoy such a fight. When he reached the ravine and rolled into its secure depths, he rose to his feet and ran swiftly away from the shooting although he knew it wasn't the nearest route to his horse.

He comforted himself that it wasn't fear that prompted his actions. A man in public office, he rationalized, just shouldn't take too many chances with his life. The people depended on him to protect them and he needed to be careful.

He expected to find the men who had told him about the feud on the trail, but it was deserted. Not a soul was to be found. It flitted through the sheriff's mind that this was a queer instance. He might have pursued this thought to pertinent reasoning if a great quietness had not arrested his attention at this moment. The shooting had ceased.

He removed his hat and with a red bandanna mopped his sweating brow, heaving a great sigh of relief.

His deputy approached from the direction of the shooting, inquiring of the sheriff where he had been, and that noble officer grinned expansively.

"Wal, I knowed yo'all war a holdin' 'em off down there, so I cum up here to git my men to go inter that air bunch and show 'em they cain't feud in this here county. I guess they seed me a comin' an' jist knowed they warn't no use a resistin' the law no longer."

The deputy acknowledged these congratulatory excuses with disgusted silence.

"I reckon we jist better let this here thing drop," the sheriff continued. "They warn't no harm done, an' they won't go at it agin, 'cause I reckon by now they knows I means business."

"Yeh, I reckon we better let it drop," the deputy agreed, sensing this wasn't any real feud. Something was going on and he didn't know what it was. Furthermore, he didn't care. As Sheriff Clemson said, no harm was done, apparently. And he and the sheriff had done a good job with Hiram Jackson. In a couple of days they would turn him over to the state authorities. It would relieve them of a lot of responsibility. He hadn't liked the attitude of the folks from Reed's Ridge on the day of Hiram's sentence.

However, when he and Sheriff Clemson turned this desperate criminal over to the prison keepers they would be in a favorable position with the voters in general over the county and he would be assured of the next election. "Yep," he congratulated himself, "they jist warn't much doubt about who'd be next sheriff of Johnstone County."

Nearing the jailhouse, the sheriff and his deputy found a nervous and excited guard.

"Don't look so skeered," the sheriff said, dismounting. "Jist a bunch o' fools a shootin' at t'other. I quieted 'em quick. No harm done atall."

"No harm done!" the jailkeeper cried, wild-eyed and stammering, as he led them to an empty cell, so lately vacated by Hiram Jackson.

While the two men stood speechless, gaping into the empty cell, the embarrassed deputy who had been left to guard Hiram confessed that he had gone out, too – just a little way down the trail – to see what was happening, and while he was gone, Hiram Jackson had escaped through the hole in the window where two steel bars had been filed out.

Give Me Thy Vineyard

Give Me Thy Vineyard

Give Me Thy Vineyard

Chapter 6

CHARLIE RAIFORD'S cabin was four miles from the next habitation and a good place for Hiram to hide.

When he got there, following closely behind Bob Raiford, Charlie's 13-year-old son who had helped him file his way out of his cell, Rosie was waiting for him.

She began to cry as he took her in his arms, and Hiram felt his own throat tighten with emotion. He kissed her with new tenderness.

Charlie's wife, Bessie, bustled around the cabin shooing youngsters out of the way, preparing supper and trying to keep her eyes off Hiram and Rosie, all at the same time. There would be a lot of people here tonight, she thought, and she wanted everyone to have enough to eat. This was a big night. She'd never been mixed up in such excitement in her life.

But hardly had she begun to put the plates on the long table when good-natured shouts outside told her that her men were home.

Big, hairy Charlie Raiford and his first and second sons, nearly as big and hairy as himself, stampeded into the cabin, followed by Tobe Alton and his boys, Steve and Jack. When they saw Hiram there was so much shouting and handshaking, laughing and patting of backs, that Bessie Raiford, her bony little girl, Minnie, and Rosie Gurney retreated to the other room. The menfolks had taken over and they felt stifled and out of place.

Hiram still could hardly comprehend his freedom. When the noise subsided a little, he scratched his head and asked, "But, Tobe, I reckoned that yo'all and Charlie here war bounden enemies. How come yo'uns got tergether like this ter git me out?"

The two giant mountaineers looked at each other and roared with glee. Even taciturn Steve Alton, whose expression was a perpetual grimace, smiled and snickered and happily pummeled Bob Raiford on the head.

"We reckoned the shuriff'd think so, too, Hiram, an' he shore did," Tobe explained. "The folks has been a workin' this here idea o' gettin' yo'uns out since yore trial. We all reckoned hit war 'bout time Charlie an' me stopped a tryin' ter put each other out o' business and got tergether. We kin make a lot more money thataway. An' 'sides, we'd ruther fight that air 'lectric company than each other. So we all fixed this here thing up. An' here yo'uns air, Hiram boy, all free an' ever'thin'!" For the second time, he clapped Hiram mightily between the shoulder blades.

"Hit shore war easier than we reckoned," Charlie added. "We knowed the shootin' would git the shuriff an' one o' the deputies outen the jailhouse, but we war a fixin' ter tie up t'other one. We had the McGonagle boys an' Aaron Hooks a sneakin' 'round ter the side with ropes, when all of a sudden they seen that air deputy walk right out o' the door hisse'f! Then all Bob had ter do was pass yo'uns that air file, right peaceful-like," he explained in a tone of regret.

While they ate, the men guessed that when the sheriff got suspicious of the "feud" – and by now he must have – he and his deputies and perhaps some of the company men, would go to question Tobe first because his cabin was nearest to Hartstown. But Tobe would not be home. Then, the mountaineers calculated, they would go to Charlie's cabin. They should arrive in, roughly, four hours. But Hiram and

Give Me Thy Vineyard

Rosie would be gone and the Raifords would know nothing about either them or a feud.

Hiram decided to hide out in the hills until it was safe to come back. He was sure the real murderer would be found soon. And even if it took a little longer than he hoped, he could still manage very well. He knew the hills like few others. Two weeks from tonight he could meet Tobe near the blasted oak up on Gobbler's Knob. By then he would probably know exactly what he was going to do.

He was so nervous that he could not finish eating. Despite the assurances of his friends that the sheriff could not possibly arrive for hours, he kept turning around to look at the door. Finally he stood up.

"I'se sorry, folks, but I jist cain't stay no more. I'se as jumpy as a fox."

Hurriedly thanking Tobe and Charlie for their help, he started across the room. But Charlie stopped him.

"I reckon yo'all'll be a needin' this more'n me, Hiram," he said handing him his newest rifle, and while the outlaw tried to refuse it, Bessie pushed a big sack of food into his other hand. In the end, he had to take both.

Rosie walked with him across the clearing. Hiram hoped she wouldn't cry or raise a fuss. And there was a gleam of pride in his eye when she murmured quietly, "Be right keerful, darlin'."

"Don't worry."

"I won't," she lied bravely. "But I'll be a prayin', Hiram," she whispered. And they parted.

Give Me Thy Vineyard

Give Me Thy Vineyard

Chapter 7

WHEN TOBE met Hiram on dark, heavily wooded Gobbler's Knob, the night was dark and foggy. The moon – like Hiram – was hiding most of the time. There were few breaks in the heavy, dark clouds. The wind, blowing intermittently, softly moaned through the cedars. The very night reminded one of the foreboding fear in the hearts of the two men. The older man wished with all his heart that he could have some cheerful news for his younger companion.

Instead he had to say, "That air shuriff be'n a tryin' ter git up a posse ter fin' yo'uns, Hiram. He ain't had much luck yet, 'cause most o' the boys has suddenly 'cided that they war real sick ter the stomach er sump'n, an' they jist couldn't come out. But they cain't keep that air stuff up forever. Thet ole fool is shore arter yo'uns, so yo'd better stick close ter where yo're a hidin' out. Say, where is yo'all a hidin' out nohow?"

Hiram frowned as he said, "I ain't a goin' ter tell yo'uns, Tobe. I'se made up my mind I warn't a goin' ter tell nobody. Ye knows I trusts ye, more'n anybody else 'ceptin' maybe Rosie, but – well," he hesitated, "yo'uns knows how yo'uns gits when yo' air hog drunk. It ain't that yo' means ter do nothin' wrong, but yo'uns jist fergits what–"

Tobe felt the blood rush to his head and he knew his face flushed crimson. Then he blanched white and felt weak and trembling. Beads of cold perspiration popped out on his forehead. If Hiram could have seen Tobe's agitation, he would have regretted his remarks. Grateful for the curtain of darkness, Tobe answered weakly:

"Shore, shore. I knows how yo'all feels, Hiram. Fergit hit. Yo'uns war jist speakin' 'bout Rosie. That gal is a goin' crazy a thinkin' 'bout yo'all. She cried an' ever'thing a tryin' ter git me ter fetch her with me ternight. I war afeared the shuriff'd have someone a follerin' her, 'cause he don't trust her one bit since that day yo'uns got out. I'se shore he thinks she knows where yo're at. But yo'd best see her purty soon."

Hiram's mouth twisted. "I wants ter see her orful bad, Tobe. But how kin I now iffn they's all a gunnin' fer me? They ain't no sense in takin' chances lest I really has ter. We'uns'll jist have ter wait a little while longer."

Tobe nodded.

Hiram was silent as he gazed through the darkness out over the undulating hills, where he was as much at home by night as by day. The sounds of the lonely night that struck fear in many a human spoke to his understanding soul a language he could understand – a language that warned him of impending danger or assured him no enemy was near. Finally he asked:

"Tobe, do yo'all think I ort ter take out fer Oklahomie er Californie, er maybe Ol' Mexico?"

"Nope, don't reckon so, Hiram. That's jist what th' comp'ny is hopin' yo'all'll do. They cain't ketch yo'uns here in the hills an' they knows hit. But iffn yo'uns lights out, they'll ketch yo'all shore."

Suddenly he was stricken silent. "Hiram," he said quietly, "I plumb fergot ter tell yo'uns. They'se got reward notices posted up fer yo'. They's offerin' five hun'erd dollars fer yo'uns, dead er alive."

Hiram stiffened – "dead or alive." The picture of the discs of plain white paper with the small black circle inside that big Dave always fashioned with such preciseness for the annual shooting match rose in his mind. He felt himself to be the black circle with everyone aiming at him. The feeling struck him dumb, not so much with fear as with futility. Why couldn't he have hanged? He sighed heavily, as he dropped his head, covering his face with his great hands.

Tobe was right. He didn't dare leave the hills. But would he have to stay in that cave he had found forever? Five hundred dollars reward was a lot of money. He could think of at least five people, not even counting the Harmons, that would probably turn him in for that much.

Tobe was saying, "'Course, most o' the folks on the ridge is yore friends. They wouldn't turn yo'uns in fer no 'mount o' money. But like I said afore, yo'd best be mighty keerful. Jist cain't tell 'bout certain folks when they's money ter be made."

Then the big mountaineer gave Hiram his full cartridge belt and an old Colt revolver.

"Me an' the woman figgered yo'uns war shootin' enough ter eat," he said, "so she didn't reddy up nothin' 'ceptin' this here bread." He pulled it out from under his shirt, and Hiram smiled wryly in the dark as he thought of eating bread that smelled of Tobe Alton.

"Don't yo'all worry none 'bout me, Tobe," he said in a sure voice. "These here back hills has allus been jist like home ter me. I ain't skeered o' nothin' out here. I'll git 'long jist fine. An' say, tell Rosie I'se all right, will yo'uns? An' that – I loves her?" His voice was low.

"Shore will."

The two men shook hands and agreed to meet again in the same place two weeks later. Then Tobe started off through the woods. Hiram waited a few minutes and headed in a different direction.

Give Me Thy Vineyard

Give Me Thy Vineyard

Chapter 8

ABOUT THREE MILES southwest of Gobbler's Knob, which stood a lone Goliath, dwarfing the neighboring hills, Hiram had his hideout. It was in a wild, narrow canyon, undisturbed and unbroken by the feet of men or cattle. The bottom of the canyon was covered with sumac, buckeye, blackberry and grapevines. Heavily wooded limestone cliffs on both sides gave it a dark and forbidding appearance. No one would ever think that the cliff on the left side housed a deep room-like cave which was now Hiram Jackson's home.

Hiram had found this cave 10 years before.

When he was a little boy he and all the other boys in the region liked to explore the wild back hills and hollows for caves. The Ozarks are full of them, some so small that a child can hardly crawl in, others so tremendous that mile after dangerous mile of red, orange, yellow and blue stalactites and stalagmites with strange frightening shapes can be passed without ever coming to an end.

Hiram, being of a more solitary nature than his friends, liked to explore the hills alone. One day he decided to enter this particular shadowy, desolate canyon and see what he could find. After climbing aimlessly for several hours in the underbrush, he came upon a tunnel, screened from the outside by a network of bushes and vines. In excitement and half-fear, he crawled up the tunnel for about thirty feet and found at the end a large cave. But it was pitch dark inside and Hiram was afraid to venture too far. The rocky floor might suddenly end in a thousand-foot drop, as many caves did.

Not telling anybody about his discovery, he came back the next day with a lantern. He found that the cave was like a big circular room with two narrow passageways leading out of the back of it. Cautiously he walked up one of the passageways to find the source of what sounded like running water. Sure enough, a tiny, swift underground stream ran from one side of the rocky passage to disappear in the other. He knelt down and tasted the water. It was cool and sweet.

Hiram decided that this would be his cave. No one else would know about it. Here he would come and explore on his own, for both narrow passageways went for miles into the ground in opposite directions. Maybe he would even find some Indian treasure. The Indians had been here, for there were arrowheads and little bones all over the large room and along the passageways. The hair on the back of Hiram's 11-year-old neck rose and he shivered as he thought of meeting the ghost of some Indian brave, or even worse, a live Indian, deep in the belly of the earth. For Hiram and his young friends were convinced that the Indians had not all gone south and west, but that some of them still lived in cities miles under the ground, where air came through mysterious hidden shafts in the gigantic cliffs, and strange lights gleamed all the time.

Now that Hiram was an outlaw he was thankful he had kept quiet about the cave. It was a perfect hideout. During his adventurous boyhood he had piled old gunny sacks and torn blankets on the floor for the time when he would dare spend a night there alone. He had also piled cedar wood in a corner and built fires, the smoke of which had followed the mysterious air current which flowed up one passageway and down the other. Now he curled up in those old gunny sacks and was warm and comfortable at night, and the fires he made cooked the squirrels and rabbits which he shot for his meals.

Since becoming a fugitive he had made a habit of rolling a big rock over to the cave entrance when he was inside. But as the rock was not quite large enough to fit snugly into the passage, he stuffed the spaces with short poles, each sharpened to a point. He then carefully draped an old blanket over the opening. Thus if anyone discovered the tunnel entrance, no light from his fire inside the cave would show to betray his hiding place.

The loneliness of this life might have told on other men, but Hiram was used to it. In fact, he genuinely liked it. When he was younger, he recognized that he liked to be alone more than the other boys, and it made him feel a little different. He had always enjoyed walking by himself through the dark virgin woods, feeling the jealous brambles and weeds pull at his feet, and the soft leaves and grass give way under him, and the bushes part at his tug, perhaps their first feel of the hand of man. It made him feel important – like a pioneer.

He loved the moist, heavy smell of the woods, especially during the night, and the huge stars which seemed sometimes to be so close and so alive that he was sure that they were showing off just for him.

But frequently he was a little ashamed of these thoughts and he felt himself unmanly for thinking them. He knew none of his friends thought about nature like that, for he had guardedly questioned them. As a result, when he was with the other boys, he wrestled more brutally, played harder, climbed higher and shouted louder than all of them to show them – and prove to himself – that he was the strongest, most fearless boy on the ridge.

But when he was alone he liked to take off his clothes and swim in the cold, swift water of the mountain streams, or to relax in the tall, resilient grass, and sink his face into the wild blue violets, the speckled sweet williams and the crackling lady's slippers, smelling their warm, rich, powerful, earthy smell, and feeling, as he lay there almost buried by them, that they were a part of him.

When he fell in love with Rosie and they walked through the woods together, he told her how he felt about the growing things around them. At first he was afraid she would laugh at him. He knew Rosie was very religious and somehow he thought she wouldn't understand how he felt about nature and its relationship to God.

He explained to her that he held two conflicting concepts of God. When he sat in the meeting house, and heard the preacher talk of God in a loud, scolding voice, he pictured Him as a stern old man, not unlike his grandfather, with a crown on His head, dressed in white robes and sitting on a throne, as he had once seen a king in an illustration in his second-grade reader. Folks said he ruled over the kingdom of heaven with His Son, whom Hiram saw as a black-bearded, sad-eyed Prince, something like John Gurney.

According to this mental picture, Hiram saw them sitting in judgment over all wrongdoers, meting out punishment in a stern and uncompromising manner.

Then he told Rosie when he walked through the woods closely observing the birds and flowers and wild growing things of the forest, he thought of God as a kind, gentle person who knew the reason for all things. Even as he plowed his fields and planted seeds he felt that the hope that entered his heart for a crop was really a faith in something so great and powerful that man could never understand it.

Instead of laughing at him, Rosie was delighted to hear him tell her of these deep feelings. Hiram was wayward and stubborn and she worried a great deal about his relationship with his Maker. Her heart took courage as she learned how earnestly Hiram did think of God. She told him that the reason he felt near to God as he studied nature was because God was the Creator of all things.

"I kin see how He war Creator o' the things o' the forest an' field," Hiram would argue, "but when hit comes ter man, I cain't see hit atall. He's the orneriest animal that walks the earth."

Rosie explained patiently that things of nature lived in their simple nativity just as God had made them, but that He had given man a mind to rule over the animals of the air and sea and land, and that man had become stubborn and carnal, defying the will of God. Then Hiram would tell her to hush; that he'd heard plenty of preachers say things like that and he never knew what they were talking about.

Rosie would hush. The hard life of mountain women teaches them patience and never to antagonize their menfolk. Nevertheless, hope soared high in her heart for she knew Hiram approached man's noblest concept of God when he walked with nature. She also knew that if she prayed earnestly enough that someday Hiram would also feel his need for Christ and His power to save a lost soul. For the time being she was content.

Hiram did not fear God. Neither did he love Him. He knew only a vague awareness of His presence.

And now as he lay alone in his cave, absently watching the black, dancing, ghost-like shadows which the fire threw on the cave walls, he thought about God and wondered if God had anything to do with him. Rosie had said God was good and just, but that He punished people for their sins. Had he, Hiram, sinned then, he wondered, and had God punished him by making him get convicted for a crime he didn't commit? But he hadn't sinned, as far as he knew. Of course, he admitted, he didn't know exactly what sin was. According to Rosie, many things you did were sins.

But then there were the circumstances of his birth. His grandmother had explained it while she lived as a young girl's misfortune, but old Abijah had never let him forget that his mother was a sinner and that God had punished all of them, never to be forgiven for her transgression.

All of these confused thoughts were too much for Hiram. As he reasoned it, here is what happened. The Harmon boys had killed the adjuster and then blamed it on him, because they knew he had good reason to kill the man. Why did they do it? Probably because they wanted Rosie and the gold. It was as easy as that.

Hiram never bothered with the deeper "why" of things. He just knew that they happened, that they were before him and that he had to live his life according to the things that happened.

Now he had to figure out a way to prove the Harmons' guilt. He wanted to lay for them and kill them in cold blood for what they had done to him, but first he wanted them to confess. The problem was: How could he make them do it? He hoped they would confess without any effort on his part. He knew they were cowards at heart. They must be frightened to death of his revenge right now. He smiled grimly as he thought of Ray and Clark fearfully riding along the narrow forest trails, terrified at passing each tree lest Hiram was hiding there.

And then he began to think of Rosie and his bitterness gave way to a pleasant warmth. He guessed that he had always loved her, but he never realized how much he needed and wanted her until that first time she came to see him in jail, the day he had been arrested for the murder. He remembered the softness of her as he held her close. And she hadn't cried. He was proud of her for that. He remembered also her habit of aloofness; the easy way she had of withdrawing from his embrace, quickly diverting her interest to one of the many subjects that seemed always to occupy her active mind. Hiram had deep respect for her. She was strong and determined like the sturdy oaks about him. He liked her for that. Rosie was good. He was proud of her.

Now as he lay in the cave thinking of Rosie, he chafed against the things which were keeping her from him. He had secretly convinced himself that he could talk her into getting married long before the two-year deadline set by her father, but now this murder had thrown everything upside down. It might be six months before he could show himself on the ridge as a free man. He'd have to arrange to meet Rosie somehow before then. When he met Tobe again they'd have to figure out some way for him to see the girl.

Give Me Thy Vineyard

Give Me Thy Vineyard

Chapter 9

WHEN HIRAM AND TOBE met the second time on Gobbler's Knob, the big moonshiner had good news for his friend. The hill people, enjoined by Dave Gurney, had persuaded the sheriff that if he wanted to keep his job, he had better stop looking so hard for Hiram. Most of the notices with Hiram's description on them, offering $500 for his capture, had been torn from the trees along the main trails. And the company was so busy with the dam that the detectives who were supposed to come with bloodhounds to comb the hills for Hiram had never arrived.

"But when kin I come down, Tobe?" Hiram asked anxiously. "This ain't no kind o' life fer me ter be a livin'."

Tobe frowned as he answered, "Hit shore air a heap sight better'n livin' in the state pen, an' don't yo'uns fergit hit, Hiram."

The outlaw felt that Tobe was thinking him ungrateful. He was quick to say, "I ain't fergittin' hit fer a minute, Tobe. I knows where I'd be iffn hit weren't fer yo'all an' Charlie. An' iffn I warn't in love an' thinkin' 'bout Rosie all the time, I reckon I'd like ter live somethin' like this fer the rest o' my life. I kin do whatever I wants, go huntin' an' walkin' 'roun' as much as I wants. Only – well, yo'uns knows, Tobe – I jist ain't free, not really free, I mean. When I'se out a huntin' I keeps turnin' 'roun' ever' time I hears a noise fer fear somebody's out a huntin' me, an' I cain't go down ter Clear

Springs er talk ter none o' the folks. But like I said, all that wouldn't really mean nothin' iffn Rosie–"

"Shore, Hiram," Tobe interrupted softly. "I unnerstans, but hit seems ter me like this air a goin' ter blow over. With the shuriff not a lookin' fer yo'uns much no more an' the company not seemin' ter keer one way er 'tother, yo'all kin come down outen these here hills in a couple o' months."

"I shore do hope so!" His eyes lit up. "Yo'all knows, Tobe, like I started in a tellin' yo'uns, iffn I could bring Rosie up here with me, I wouldn't keer iffn I didn't see no one else fer the rest o' my life. But I don't reckon she'd keer fer this kind o' livin'."

"No, I don't reckon so, Hiram. Women likes a real home an' other women roun' so's they kin show off their young'uns an' talk 'bout how bad their husbands is a treatin' 'em."

Hiram smiled and thought of Tobe's taciturn wife, who never said more than a few words to anybody about anything.

He said, "Tobe, I'se been tryin' ter figger out a way ter meet Rosie. I'se jist gotter see her purty soon. But I knows her pa won't let her out at night by herse'f and I don't dare meet her durin' the day."

Tobe scratched his head. "Wal," he began meditatively, "I reckon yo'uns kin meet her durin' the day 'thout too much danger now that the shuriff ain't on yore trail no more. Why don't yo'uns meet her at the hickory grove outside o' Hartstown, er someplace way offn any trail that yo'll both know 'bout?" He smiled in the dark. "Yo'uns shore ain't been a sparkin' Rosie fer three years 'thout knowin' how ter let her know where ter meet yo'uns."

Hiram smiled, too, and remembered a lonely sycamore clump about three miles south of the strange rock formation called the Devil's Table. That would be a fine place for him and Rosie to meet, he said, and Tobe agreed.

A week later Rosie was in his arms and she was crying and

laughing all at the same time, and asking him all kinds of questions.

Holding her off at arm's length, he noticed Rosie was pale and a little tired-looking. She confessed that she hadn't slept much in the past month. But she was so happy to be with him now that the tired film which clouded her eyes seemed to be breaking up in the glints of joy that flashed from behind it.

When at last they sat down on a stump to talk, Hiram felt wonderfully flooded with relief and peace, and he realized again, this time a little sadly, how much he needed Rosie.

She said, "I fetched a basket o' stuff along fer yo'uns, darlin'. When I rode off with hit, the folks in Uncle Dave's store thought I war a goin' on a picnic. Hit's over there by Fred." She jerked her chin at the black stallion who stood nibbling leaves a few yards away. "Uncle Dave put some eggs an' coffee an' a couple o' sacks o' beans in there fer yo'uns. They's some shells fer yer gun, an' I baked yo'all a cake. An' here –" she reached into the pockets of her jeans – "I fetched yo'uns a Bible, too."

Hiram seemed pleased. "I cain't read hit very good, Rosie," he said, "but maybe hit'll he'p keep me minded o' God. 'Pears like I thinks o' Him heap more'n I used ter."

Then he frowned and asked doubtfully, "Rosie, does yo'uns mean Dave knowed yo'uns war a comin' out here ter see me?"

Her low voice pleaded, "But, honey, yo's gotter trust somebody. Now wait a minute" – she broke in as he started to protest – "I has talked this whole thing over with Uncle Dave, Hiram. Yo'all know he's got more sense than anybody else on the ridge. Folks'll do anythin' he tells 'em, an' rightly, too. An' he said he thought hit would be a good idee fer yo'uns ter come down ter his store reglar – say on Saturday nights – when he's open real late and get supplies yerse'f. Yo'uns knows yo' kin trust him, Hiram. Most ever'body on the ridge is on yore side, nohow, but Uncle Dave would do jist anythin' fer yo'uns an' fer me."

Hiram waited a full minute as this rush of sentences sank in and found their proper places in his brain.

"Well, Rosie," he said slowly, "yo'all knows I cain't be sure o' no one, 'ceptin' yo'uns, o' course. But I reckon I kin trust Dave purty much, an' I shore likes ter think iffn most o' the folks from the ridge sees me they won't tell on me. But this business o' goin' ter the store reg'lar-like – well, I don' know. I shore would like ter come down onct in a while, fer hit's plumb dangerous fer Tobe a comin' ter bring me stuff, what with his still an' all. But I couldn't take supplies from Dave fer nothin', Rosie."

She smiled happily as she always did when she could break down his stubborn will. Things were working out as she had hoped. "Uncle Dave an' me, we'uns figgered yo'd say that, Hiram. So he said iffn yo'd fetch him some yaller percoon ever' time yo'all come ter see him, he'd trade yo'uns bread an' other stuff fer hit. Uncle Dave's a buyin' ginsen, ginger an' bloodroot, too."

Hiram thought it over. It seemed all right. He knew where there were many patches of the strong-smelling yellow and red roots which the hill people dried and used for medicine. And digging for the roots would keep him busy.

"Yep," he admitted at last, "reckon hit air a purty good idea, Rosie. I'se glad Dave thought o' hit. Tell Dave to bill my stuff fer sale. The cows, my mare, hogs, chickens an' tools ort ter fetch right smart. That I want Dave ter keep fer me. Yo' an' John git my stuff outen the cabin an' take it to yore place. Take good keer gran'pappy's fiddle. Next time yo all comes, fetch hit."

"Shore will. I'se been workin' out somethin' else fer yo'all Hiram. Yo'uns 'member Cliff an' Annie Montgomery's big dog?"

Hiram nodded, picturing the huge Montgomery dog who was part collie and part something else – probably wolf.

"Well," Rosie continued eagerly, "she's a fixin' ter have herse'f a litter o' pups any day now, an' I thought I'd fetch yo'uns one as soon as they gits borned. Hit would be good fer yo'uns ter fetch somethin' up, Hiram, an' 'sides, yo'all needs a good dog ter watch out fer yo'uns as long as yo' has ter hide out like this."

This suggestion won Hiram's immediate and delighted approval.

And when at last he reluctantly let Rosie go home, he felt proud and thrilled that a girl like her was in love with him. But his mouth suddenly twisted as he remembered what he was, and that Rosie could come to him only when she dared. Many other men would be proud and thrilled to have Rosie's love. This being away from each other was bad. Maybe she would get tired of it and stop loving him. Such tormenting reasoning almost obliterated the joy she had brought him.

Rosie rode slowly along the darkening narrow trails toward Gurney's Mill. She was shaken with devotion and pity for Hiram. She had no idea he entertained such feelings of jealousy and couldn't have understood if she had known. She was as incapable of infidelity to Hiram as to God and she felt so sure Hiram knew this that she never even gave thought to it.

Iffn only I could do sump'n, she thought repeatedly, worrying about the hunted, nervous look in Hiram's blue eyes and trying to adjust herself to the month-old stubble on his always clean-shaven face.

Then she murmured, "God, dear God, in Yore great wisdom, he'p us ter git Hiram out o' this here mess he's in an' show us Yore mercy!"

A few minutes later Rosie turned sharply to the right and directed Fred up a tiny, heavily foliaged path that was a shortcut to the main trail. It was so narrow that the horse could just only pass between the trees and Rosie was stricken with consternation when she heard another rider coming toward her. The other horse was almost in a gallop, and it was so dark that Rosie was afraid he might not see her. Quickly she tried to get Fred to squeeze himself through the thick underbrush along the side of the trail. But just then the other rider pounded into view. They recognized each other at once. It was Clark Harmon. He reined up his horse so abruptly that the animal was almost thrown off balance.

Fury tore through Rosie at the sight of the big, rough-bearded man. She wanted to scream at him, hit him with all her might and spit in his face. Instead, however, controlling herself with an effort, she tried to force Fred through the bushes to bypass Clark without speaking to him.

She wasn't successful. Clark directed his own horse in front of Fred and would not let him move.

"Git out o' my way, Clark Harmon," she said in a taut voice. She prayed that he wasn't drunk. Both Harmon brothers were like wild beasts when they had too much liquor in them.

But his voice was soft and pleading as he said, "No, Rosie, I ain't goin' ter let yo'all git by till yo'uns hears what I has ter say."

She sat up stiffly and waited. What else could she do with his big strawberry roan blocking her path?

"Look, Rosie Gurney," he began. "This ain't where I reckoned I war a goin' ter talk ter yo'uns but hit's as good a place as any, long as yore here." He leaned toward her. "I'se in love of yo'uns, Rosie, an' I wants yo'uns more'n I ever thought I could want any gal. Now wait. Don't say nothin. I know yore a lovin' Hiram. But he's a outlaw now. Nobody even knows where he's at. Yo'all might never see him agin. An' yo' ain't the kind o' gal that kin keep a lovin' a boy what ain't 'round ter give her no love. Yo'uns gotter keep a bein' loved, Rosie. An' I cain't think o' nothin' else but yo'uns. Let me come a sparking yo', honey. Give me a chanct."

Rosie wanted to say something that would make him fall

dead. A hundred ideas choked her mind but she could only sit there staring at him, boiling with wrath. How could he dare talk to her like this, in his soft whining voice? And after what he had done to Hiram, too. How disgusting he was! Oh, how she hated him!

And hate made her black eyes blaze so fiercely that they seemed to crackle. Clark's breath quickened with excitement as he watched her.

He laughed aloud and teased her. "Rosie, yore shore purtier'n a pitcher settin' there mad all over," he said. "But yo'uns ain't allers a goin' ter hate me. Now that Hiram's gone, I–"

"Shet yore dirty mouth, Clark Harmon!" She found her tongue at last. "An' git out o' my way afore I starts screamin'! We'uns is right near the main trail an' I reckon somebody'll hear me an' come fer yo'uns a shootin'!" She got Fred back on the trail, but again the strawberry roan was in front of her.

"I ain't afeard o' nobody, Rosie, an' they ain't nothin' I ever wanted that I ain't got, one way er 'tother. An' yo'all 'member what I said. Yo'll start in thinkin' 'bout me, Rosie, when yo'alls alone an' achin' ter be loved an'–"

"I'll spit right in yer face iffn yo'uns talks ter me any more, Clark Harmon! Yo' ain't got no right ter talk ter me like that!"

Clark laughed and again his voice eased into that irritating soft pleading which was almost worse than his nastiness.

"Hit don't make me no mind iffn yo' hates me now, Rosie, 'cause my pappy said hate war right close ter love. I kin wait. Nohow, Rosie, why does yo'all think Ray an' me done what we done? We'uns–" He stopped abruptly, realizing he had said too much.

Rosie's brain was momentarily paralyzed as she caught the implication of Clark's ill-spoken words. Her muscles tensed, and her breathing was laborious as she hissed in a scarcely audible voice: "Why, yo'–yo'–yo' low-down coward. Yo're lower'n any snake that ever crawled. God Hisse'f must shorely hate yo'uns. Yo'uns war a lyin' all a time 'bout seein' Hiram."

"I never said we war a lyin'. Shore we seen him a runnin' away."

Rosie's words were whiplashes as she snapped. "I jist pity yo'all an' yore no 'count brother, Clark Harmon. Hiram'll git yo' shore one o' these days. Yo'uns kin bet anythin' yo' own that he's a gunnin' fer yo'uns right this here minute."

"I ain't afeared o' Hiram – er nobody," Clark blustered, "an' I'll be a seein' yo'uns, Rosie, plumb soon." He rode off suddenly, and Rosie was sure he was afraid. And right she was – he was uneasy. As he raced his horse along the black, narrow trails, he wondered where Hiram Jackson was hiding. Things didn't seem to be going as he and his brother had planned. Everyone on the ridge hated them, and Dave Gurney wouldn't sell them supplies anymore. Clark began to ponder Ray's complaint yesterday: "No gal is worth all this here trouble."

It wasn't that their neighbors had ever loved them before. Ray knew that his family had always been heartily disliked on the ridge, but it had never bothered him. He was suspicious of people anyway. His father had often said, "Boys, folks is always tryin' ter git sump'n offen ye. So hit's up ter ye ter git sump'n offen 'em first."

But now they all looked at the Harmons with murder in their eyes, and Ray feared they might even start shooting one of these days. And Hiram was surely gunning for them. How they hoped the electric company men would catch him or kill him soon!

Give Me Thy Vineyard

Give Me Thy Vineyard

Give Me Thy Vineyard

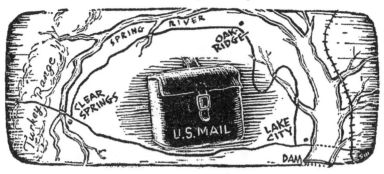

Chapter 10

*A*ND SO TIME passed away. Forty-eight months. Four years. The dam, built of solid concrete reinforced with steel, was firmly anchored in the bedrock of the deep gorge. This obstructive device, conceived in the minds of capitalists and politicians and born of the labor of man's hands, effectively harnessed the waters of Spring River. Moving with terrible power and precision to do the bidding of these captains of industry, the water flowed in prepared channels, turning the turbines that caught and stored the electrical energy which sold at high rates. The fat profits were to be reinvested in further electric-producing units until a controlling monopoly would be formed.

The United Electric Company had rolled through the valley like a giant snowball gone mad. As the hill folk moved, hundreds of laborers poured in to begin their work of desecration and destruction. The great oaks, sugar maples and stately sycamores, that for centuries had stood as guardian sentinels of the valley, came first, felled by the cruel ax of progress, without sentiment and without regret. Guided by a line which the engineers had designated as the water level of the lake which was to come, the workers made their act of destruction complete as they heaped and burned the plum thickets that in early spring were white masses of fragrant blossoms, and the plots of dewberries, blackberries and huckleberries where for generations the hill folk had gathered

Give Me Thy Vineyard

Nature's wild harvest in season. The little orchards of the valley farmers were laid waste, and cabins, barns and rail fences torn down and burned. When the laborers were finished, the valley looked as if war and blight had passed through it and everything was dead. The beautiful productive valley was now denuded – desolate – bare.

Then after four years of earth-shaking explosions and strange mechanical noises, the power dam was completed and turbines placed in position. The floodgates were closed and the waters of Spring River that had followed the same tortuous course for ages mercifully hid from view the depressing spectacle of man's wreckage. The impounded waters of the river, spreading out over the scorched land, compassionately covered the blackened wound and reached out to the untouched borders of wooded hills closed in at last to present once more a scene of tranquil beauty.

The newspapers had called the capitalists who built the dam, men of vision and courage. *Who before*, read the editorials, *had dared believe these rocky immovable hills could be made to produce anything of great remunerative value?*

But the newspapers had not considered the good people who had owned the productive farms, located in the valley of Spring River, before they had lost them through the condemnation proceedings instigated by these same captains of industry and finance. These farms had come to them from their fathers who had carved them from the wilderness before the Civil War. The owners who had been forced by skillful manipulation of the law to surrender their heritage were only normally resentful. With characteristic courage and determination, the former valley farmers took the stingy exchange the United Electric Company gave them for their property and built homes on the stony ridge. There they began again what their ancestors had begun on far more promising territory before the Civil War.

The wildlife of the woods also had fled before the

onslaught of the laborers to the haven of high ground. There the fox, the deer, the turkeys, squirrels and songbirds found new homes, common refugees among the people who had lived with and loved them before.

To Rosie Gurney the four years passed with slow torture, like a dark nightmare, lit only by a gleam of hope which her optimistic nature kept alive. She was a person who dreams a terrible dream, but who keeps saying although still asleep, "Don't worry; it's all a dream. You're going to wake up soon."

But she did not wake up. And now there seemed to be hardly a chance any more that the Harmons would confess. Did this mean that Hiram would have to be an outlaw forever? True, the company officials seemed to have forgotten about him, and there was a long period – around election time – when the sheriff pretended he had never even heard of Hiram Jackson. But the reward still stood, and as long as he was wanted, Hiram could not come down from the hills. There was always a chance that somebody would turn him in.

The situation was almost beyond Rosie's ability to handle. It was against her eager, full-blooded nature to postpone her desires and to live in uncertainty and fear. Like most people who dwell far from the complexities of civilization, Rosie was elemental and understood best the things closest to life itself. To be Hiram's wife and to establish their home on a farm which she and Hiram would work together – this was what Rosie Gurney wanted out of her earthly existence, and she was baffled and hurt because the years were going by and she was not getting even a part of it.

More and more she turned to God, begging Him to reveal to her how she had sinned – for she was sure she had sinned somehow to deserve such punishment – and at the same time imploring Him to help Hiram. She tried to live an exemplary life. Where she had always been reasonably well-behaved and kind, now there was nothing she would not do to prove to the Lord that she was walking in His way.

Soon after her 18th birthday Rosie took over the job of delivering the mail for Reed's Ridge.

When the old mail carrier, Gade Starrett, died, Big Dave Gurney, the postmaster, began to search among the young men who hung around his store for a successor. But his niece pleaded with him to give her the job. Didn't she know the 25-mile mail route as well as anyone? she argued, for hadn't she and her stallion, Fred, frequently accompanied old Gade on his trips? What if she was a girl? There wasn't any law against girls carrying the mail, was there? (Rosie was doubtful when she asked Dave this, but he didn't seem to know of any such law and she perspired with relief when he rumbled "No" to her question.) And besides, wasn't she as healthy as any man in the hills and as strong as a lot of them? And she didn't drink and Dave could always depend on her. Her petitions finally wore her uncle down and she got the job.

He felt she would be better off to keep busy so as not to think so often of Hiram. But the chief reason – of which Big Dave was innocent – she wanted to carry the mail was because there were some good, lonely spots along the heavily wooded mail route where she could meet Hiram without anyone seeing them.

The four years of the building of the dam had limped by for Hiram, too, and made him bitter and sad. But where Rosie turned to religion for comfort, Hiram began to hate the outside forces, whatever they were, that were keeping him from a normal life, and he frequently lost his temper when Rosie talked about God and having faith. To Hiram the only real things now were the trees and the rocky earth, the limestone cliffs and the animals. He no longer trusted any people. Even Rosie became an object of doubt and misery for him. Whenever he saw her he would look long into her eyes to see if she still loved him, and he would ask over and over again if she was sure she did, and if she wasn't just saying it because she felt sorry for him. Without Rosie's love he would have become a savage.

The dog, Bullet, which Rosie had brought him when he first began to hide out, became his closest companion, almost his other self. He shared Hiram's distrust of people, and was fiercely wary even of Rosie and Tobe Alton and Charlie and some of the other good friends whom Hiram met occasionally. Both he and Hiram became acutely sensitive to sound, and both learned to slink unnoticed through miles of forest, often close to unsuspecting people, without crackling a leaf or a twig. When Hiram was in exposed parts of the hills digging roots, the big brown dog found a high place to lie, where he could see, hear and smell for hundreds of yards, and warn his master instantly of anything out of the ordinary.

Several times Hiram saw the Harmon brothers passing through the woods, and his finger yearned to squeeze the trigger of his rifle. But long hours of thinking had convinced him that shooting the Harmons would not solve anything. It might even prevent the truth from ever being discovered. So he gritted his teeth and spared them.

As the years went by and the sheriff gradually relaxed his vigilance, Hiram came out more often in the daylight. When Rosie became mail carrier, they arranged to meet a couple of times a month in isolated spots on hidden trails off the mail route. But though these moments with Rosie were good and he knew he could not get along without them, they were not satisfying. They both knew it was fraught with danger and neither of them was ever wholly at ease. They longed for the time when they could complete their plans for marriage.

With the passage of time, Hiram and Big Dave Gurney developed a satisfactory working agreement. On Saturday nights after the hill people had done their heavy weekly trading and gone home, Hiram would wait on the rock formation known as the Devil's Table which overlooked

Give Me Thy Vineyard

Clear Springs. At a signal from Dave, Hiram would know it was reasonably safe to come down, and following a trackless route which he himself had devised, he would reach the store in about an hour, trade his roots for supplies, pick up the note which Rosie usually left for him, and head back quickly into the woods. But there were times when Dave did not signal, and then Hiram would return early to his cave, disappointed and yet oddly relieved. Going down to the store took a lot out of him.

Give Me Thy Vineyard

Give Me Thy Vineyard

Chapter 11

T HE EVENING SHADOWS were playing a game of tag
with the sunbeams as Hiram, on a late Saturday afternoon, stealthily approached his lookout. His movements,
guarded and slow, were like those of a fox faring forth from
his den. Bullet preceded him a few paces down the path.

Give Me Thy Vineyard

He was deeply tanned from constant exposure to wind and sun. His face which once was relaxed into a sort of half-contemptuous sneer, prompted by the arrogance of his youth, plus a boastful confused mental attitude, now bore the marks of great suffering – tense, firm muscles, deep furrowed lines, and a set square jaw.

He was dressed in the conventional Ozark fashion: shirt unbuttoned at the throat, sleeves rolled well up along his muscular arms, blue denim trousers and staunch Western-style boots. His hat was a wide-brimmed, low-crowned black felt, the brim rolled on either side to come to a point over his forehead. The thumb of his right hand was inserted between his belt and his body, just back of the holster that housed a heavy Colt's revolver.

Suddenly the young mountaineer wheeled, gun in hand, as a rustling sound, like someone walking behind him, arrested his attention. Darting a glance here and there, trying to locate his unseen enemy, he stood poised ready for action. Bullet, too, stood frozen in his tracks ready to pounce upon animal or human who showed himself to be an enemy to his master.

When a large gray squirrel flashed across his path, halting at the base of a large oak tree as surprised and alarmed as the fugitive himself, Hiram relaxed.

"Pore thing!" he murmured. "Scairt, too, hain't yo'? Cain't even go a acorn huntin' 'thout watchin' fer somebody a layin' fer ter kill yo'uns. Reckon yo'all an' me's in the same boat," he continued bitterly, "'ceptin' I kin kill, too, an' yo'uns cain't. Run along now and git yore supper, fer I shore hain't aimin' ter bother yo' none. I knows jist how hit feels a bein' hunted all a time."

Turning, he continued his way to his lookout. His naturally keen eyes and ever listening ears, expertly trained now by four years of vigilance, missed no movement nor sound about him.

Give Me Thy Vineyard

He chose the Devil's Table for his observation point because it commanded the best general view of the ridge. Where the rest of the mountainside had been worn by erosion, this single chunk of blackened granite jutted far out over the valley. Its top was covered with scrub pine and a few large oaks, creating the illusion of continuance with the mountain. But because it sheered off so abruptly, many unwary men had stepped over its edge, falling to the valley hundreds of yards below. From these violent deaths the formation had merited its name and its dangerous, frightening connotation.

But Hiram, fearing nothing but people and his own weaknesses, knew only that the Devil's Table was the best lookout in the hills. From there he could see the new lake and the ferry crossing at the recently built town called Lake City – a town begun nearly three years before the lake was created. Directly across from him was rocky, forbidding Hammond Range, out of which Turkey Creek flowed down the mountainside to join Spring River, just above the ferry. To his right was the dam, looking like a small, square gray rock in the fading daylight. To his left was the hamlet of Clear Springs, the oldest settlement on Reed's Ridge, and his destination.

On this evening, Hiram reached his vantage point as the sun traveled westward within an hour of its downing. Shinnying up the trunk of an old tree, he removed a long black spyglass from the hollow of a discarded woodpecker's nest. Dropping to the ground, he unfolded the glass to observe the scene below him. The hills west of the river had flung their shadows in a zigzag pattern far across the ridge, which looked like a giant lawn landscaped by time and the elements.

Every trail was filled with hill folk homeward bound from their weekly pilgrimage to Big Dave's general merchandise store – the social and political center of the community. Here they exchanged neighborhood gossip, as they bartered poultry, eggs, butter, medicinal roots and animal pelts for the "storeboughten" goods they needed. Now, as they returned home, a slow-moving caravan of pedestrians, horseback riders and horse-drawn wagons, they presented to the young man who was covertly watching them a pattern bug-like in appearance.

As he looked at the scene with his naked eyes, the trek reminded Hiram of ants crawling up the side of a hill. These folk were like ants in many ways he thought – diligent, determined and resourceful.

Most of the wagons had long since parted with their spring seats and now wide boards across the tops near the front accommodated the fathers and mothers of families. Their bodies swayed and jolted as the wheels of the wagons, without shock-absorbing springs, bumped over rocks and ruts. Behind them, on a bed of straw in the beds of the wagons, broods of youngsters bounced about. They ranged in size from tiny toddlers to early-matured replicas of their parents. To complete the assortment, nearly every mother young enough held a nursing child in her arms. "Lap young'uns" they were called.

The sun went down and the last lone rider disappeared from Hiram's sight. That was Tim McGonagle. He remembered how the two of them had always ridden home together, lagging an hour behind the other folk of the ridge. It helped them assert their independence. Proved to the old and young alike that they had grown up. Men they were! The bottles of whiskey on their hips gave emphasis to the declaration. They arrived home just in time to do their share of the chores, eat a hurried supper and dash off to a party miles away.

It all seemed very childish to Hiram now, who in the last four years had really become a man. Young McGonagle, too, had settled down somewhat. He had never found a companion as daring and bold as Hiram, and so had gotten into the habit of riding alone. He was courting Sally Bates seriously and they were soon to be married.

Give Me Thy Vineyard

In a little while lights from kerosene lamps began to twinkle through windows from widely scattered homes all over the hills below him. Hiram knew the folk who lived down there. They were his friends and a nostalgic loneliness and longing engulfed his heart as he stood watching the clear smoke from wood-burning supper fires ascend lazily toward heaven like incense offered to a beneficent God for the stored bounty within those secure walls.

Hiram folded the spyglass to its shortest length and replaced it in the oak. Then he stood relaxed, waiting and listening. Familiar sounds from the distance reached his ears. Cows were bawling to their offspring that supper was ready to be served; pigs squealed at their troughs; ducks and geese bewailed the late Saturday feeding; and high above all was heard the loud *potrack–pot–rack* of the guinea fowls. No sooner had the noises of the farmyards been quieted, when the whippoorwills, bullfrogs and crickets began tuning their voices with the wailing, violin-like sound of the locusts for their nocturnal symphony.

Then, just as the moon rose over the crest, from far away in the distance came the long, plaintive wail of a fox horn – three blasts, then silence, three blasts repeated. Dave's signal.

"Thank the Lord," Hiram said, not irreverently. "Now we'uns kin go, Bullet. That air war Dave."

Rapidly recrossing the Devil's Table, the man and dog plunged down the wooded slope toward Clear Springs.

A little over an hour later the oak door at the back of Big Dave's store creaked open as the latch string was pulled from outside. Big Dave sat in his chair with his eyes closed. His broad face hung loose in complete relaxation. It had been a good day, as Saturdays invariably were, and his profits gratifying. A sense of well-being had taken over his soul.

"Dave, where air yo'uns?" a husky voice whispered.

The startled merchant's head jerked up, but when he discovered whose voice it was, he laboriously raised his great bulk from the chair and moved forward.

"Oh, hit's yo'all, Hiram. Yo'uns scairt me. I must o' been nappin'. How air yo'?"

"Reckon I'se all right."

"Come on in an' fasten the door behin' yo'. I'll bolt the front one. Hit's past closin' time, nohow." Big Dave crossed the room, slid a strong crossbar into the notch cut in the door facing, and turned the heavy key in the lock. Then blowing out the large hanging lamp that suspended from the ceiling, he moved to a position near the nervous Hiram who stood lurking in the dark shadows.

"Got news fer yo'all, my boy," he rumbled. "Shuriff war here last Monday 'lectioneerin' fer his deputy. 'Pears like he's afeard he won't git the nomination. I told him iffn he's aimin' ter git votes here 'bouts, he best fergit ter look fer yo'uns altergether. I 'lowed iffn he'd quit lookin' why then when 'lection time rolls 'roun' we'uns all'd vote fer him. An' he'll be a needin' them air votes, Hiram."

"Reckon yo'alls right, but I shore air aimin' ter watch all a time nohow," Hiram replied in a tense voice. What if the sheriff wasn't on his trail? He'd still have to hide. This was not news. It was an old story.

"I'se weighed up yer last poke o' roots. They come ter eight dollars an' forty cents. Shore had some nice yaller percoon in that batch, my boy," said Dave cheerily.

"Thanks."

Quickly the young hillman gave an order for beans, bacon, crackers, coffee and dried peaches – foods he could easily prepare over a campfire.

The merchant placed the purchase in a tow sack. Then he picked up a stub pencil from the counter and, by the light from the candle, painstakingly added the amount of the sale.

"She comes ter a dollar an' six bits, Hiram."

"Figger hit out o' my roots an' make a ticket fer the rest, like yo'uns always does, an' put hit with the other I'se got comin'!"

Give Me Thy Vineyard

Big Dave scratched his head and chewed the end of his pencil. "Les see," he mused, waddling to a file of bills that hung from a big nail back of the counter. Placing them on the counter near the candle, he thumbed through them one by one, while Hiram impatiently chewed his lower lip and fingered his revolver. Why was Dave so slow?

"Well, sir," he drawled at last, "she's ninety-six dollars an' two bits. With the six dollars and sixty-five cents that yo've got a comin' terday, hit makes one hun'erd an' two dollars an' ninety cents. Yo'uns has over a hun'erd dollars, Hiram, 'sides the money yer stuff fetched."

"Rosie leave me a letter?" Hiram asked, thinking if Dave talked any more he'd lose his temper.

"Shore did. I'll git hit."

Hurriedly Hiram took the envelope and murmured, "Here's a note fer her frum me, Dave."

Then, picking up the sack of groceries, he cautiously opened the back door, and gave a low whistle. When Bullet did not answer with a warning bark, Hiram knew the way was clear.

"So long, Dave," he said.

The storekeeper responded, but Hiram hardly heard him as he stepped out into the night and rejoined Bullet who stood hidden by the bushes outside. In a minute they were back under the cover of the black friendly forest where they could relax.

From far up the river they heard the somber *who-who-whoo! Who-whoo!* of the owl. And from some high ridge, the call of a wolf, sounding in the crisp clear air like the unison cry of an entire pack, mingled with the voices of hounds hot on the chase of a fox.

Big Dave made his way slowly to his cabin, seated himself in his heavy rocker, removed his shoes, and enjoyed his daily extravagance of 5 cents' worth of peppermint candy in silent contentment. His was the satisfaction of one who has been useful to a friend. He felt important for he knew Reed's Ridge needed him and it was nice to be wanted. Thus he sat for an hour. At last he arose, picked up his shoes and entered the cabin, leaving the Ozark night to solve its own problems.

Give Me Thy Vineyard

Give Me Thy Vineyard

Give Me Thy Vineyard

Chapter 12

O N THE FOLLOWING Thursday morning, Rosie left a little earlier than usual on her 25-mile ride through the hills. Dawn was just reddening the sky and the morning mist swirled around her in thick clouds. Rosie had to stay crouched in the saddle to avoid being struck by low-hanging branches which she could hardly see.

Hiram's note last Saturday had asked her to meet him today in the sycamore clump just south of Oakridge if she thought it was safe. She knew it was safe enough and that Hiram was overcautious. She reckoned she couldn't blame him though. The life he had had to live the past four years had been enough to keep a man from trusting folk.

She was anxious to see Hiram. It had been nearly a month since their last meeting. There had been such a fuss over the opening of the dam and so many strangers crowding in and out of the valley that Rosie had not taken a step beyond her usual route. But the hubbub had quickly subsided and things were back to normal again.

Rosie was aglow with excitement at the prospects of seeing her lover once more. As she rode along she conjured up mental pictures of what their meeting would be like. Hiram would be securely hidden by the thick growth of trees and underbrush. He would have reached there before daylight and probably would remain until the darkness made it safe for him to return to his hideout.

Give Me Thy Vineyard

Rosie had packed a lunch with some extra goodies for him to take back to his cave with him. The cookies she had made herself. Brown sugar cookies, they were, with walnut meats and raisins in them. She had also baked the salt rising bread that imprisoned thick slices of cold boiled ham (no one could cure ham like John Gurney) in nutritious, delectable sandwiches.

She wondered how Hiram would look. She hoped some of the hunted look would be gone from his eyes. To her knowledge he had not come down from the mountain for several weeks. She was fearful of what the imprisonment had done to his temper and his thinking.

If only he could read better. Then the Bible she had given him would be a help in his lonely hours. But Abijah Pemberton had never given proper attention to Hiram's schooling. His grandmother had made feeble attempts to train him properly and keep him in school, but she was too ill to be very successful. At the time of her death, Hiram had completed his third year and he never attended regularly after that. By the time he was 11 he had stopped going altogether. Consequently he could only read the simplest sentences and wrote so poorly only Rosie had the patience to decipher it.

Thinking of his fair, handsome face, Rosie suddenly remembered the time she had, nearly four years ago, trying to get Hiram to shave his beard. She grimaced. Long months in the cave had given him a thick, blonde, bushy growth of which he had become quite proud. But she had thought it looked like a badly kept brush heap and made him appear years older. Finally she talked him into shaving it, and made her Uncle Dave keep him supplied with shaving soap. She had carried the razor, strop, shaving mug and mirror to him herself, along with towels, note paper and pencils.

That was before she persuaded Hiram to let her go with him to his cave one time. She knew it had been a foolish thing to do and that she had exposed both herself and Hiram to needless danger. Hiram had asked her repeatedly to bring his grandfather's old fiddle to him and she had agreed to do it only when he promised to show her where he was hiding out.

That was two years after his conviction and since it hadn't caused any additional trouble she was glad she had gone. But she had never dared repeat the adventure.

Hiram had proudly showed her the comforts of his lonely habitat. It was as cozy as any man's cabin she had ever seen. There was a calendar propped up against a box, and the shaving supplies which she herself had furnished him. There was a tin cup, plate, spoons, skillet and coffeepot. Matches sealed tight in a fruit jar were protected from dampness. The floor was swept clean with the stub of a broom. Hiram pointed to his improvised bed, not far from the fire that smoldered in the center of the room, a pile of clean clothes and a good-sized box of groceries near the little spring where it would keep cool.

It was indeed like a home and Rosie knew she should be happy that Hiram was at least comfortable. But some way she wasn't quite; woman-like, she wanted Hiram to want her in every way that a man ever needs a woman and here she found him sort of contented and comfortable with his own housekeeping and way of living. A tight, hard feeling possessed her as she thought perhaps he didn't really need her after all.

In all her life Rosie had never known what it was to be jealous. Now she was suddenly angry, and afraid of something she couldn't name. Hiram, too, frightened her here in this small, gloomy place. He loomed too big, and too strong, and when he looked at her, his blue eyes had seemed to flicker like an animal's in the firelight. She was glad when they were outside again in the sun.

With all these thoughts racing through her mind, Rosie

was entering Lake City before she realized how far she had traveled. The town was just waking up to the ruddy day. Quickly she deposited her bag of mail in the little store which also housed the post office, and cleared out.

Lake City was one place she didn't like and she knew why. It was built around the dam which she hated with all her heart. Most of its residents were connected with the dam. The men with whom she came in contact there were chiefly from St. Louis and Kansas City and thought hill girls were easy pickings. They used to whistle and call to Rosie as she rode through, and she kept telling herself that someday she was going to turn around and tell them just what she thought of them. She was sure they were laughing at her and insulting her. She had no idea what a fascinating figure she was to them, for the four years had not altered Rosie's beauty. As gracefully as ever, she rode by every morning, dressed in a brightly colored cotton shirt, unbuttoned at the throat, bibbed overalls that allowed for greater freedom of movement for this outdoor work, and rebellious curls protruding from under her knit cap. She wore on her feet firm, sturdy boots.

The workers' interest was genuinely piqued by her healthy good looks and her high-spirited personality.

But today she wasn't even thinking about them as she rode past the huge concrete structure and started back into the hills. Her mind was on one thing – meeting Hiram. She was wishing now, as she had many times before, that she and the outlaw could visit together at Gurney's Mill. But it was impossible. The mill and the house were almost always full of people. Her father held open house 24 hours a day, and folks took advantage of it. A visit there was seldom just a call. It usually lasted overnight, or even a couple of days, for there was a comfortable attic in the large cabin. Too many people liked her good-natured father, Rosie reflected, but she had to admit that her baking had something to do with the company, too.

She also would have liked to meet Hiram at Dave's store when he came down on Saturday nights. But he had never suggested it. She knew he felt unsafe so near town and always tried to get out as soon as possible. And besides, Rosie might be seen coming there after closing time and the sheriff might suddenly feel that he had to get busy. No, it wasn't a very good idea.

Rosie sighed as Fred topped a little knoll and turned sharply toward a low shallow place where they could ford the creek. But as he was wading into the clear stream, he stopped abruptly with a soft nicker and jerked the reins.

"Why shore, yo'all kin have a drink, darlin'," Rosie said. But as the horse seemed ready to spend the day standing and drinking water, she chided, "Now, Fred, hurry up. I'se surprised at yo'uns. Ort ter know we'se got things ter do. We'se a packin' the medicine fer Gran'pappy Benson an' we'se got some stuff fer Dave Emory way offn the trail. An' 'sides, we'uns gits ter see Hiram later, iffn they's time. So come on!"

But the spoiled Fred was in no hurry. Several minutes passed before he raised his head, gave it a self-satisfied shake that sent a shower of spray from his wet muzzle, and splashed leisurely across the stream. It was with difficulty that Rosie got him into a trot as they turned up the rocky bluff toward Dryknob Range.

They followed the down current of the stream for several miles along the bluff. Finally they turned into a narrow trail that led through a gap and traveled up a sharp incline to emerge later on a bare ridge a mile above the stream.

Rosie noticed with pleasure that the mist had nearly disappeared. She pulled her horse to a halt. "Has yo'uns fergot we allers stops here fer a minute, Fred? Somehow, I'se jist got ter stop an' look ever' day. Shore purty, hain't hit? So quiet an' peaceful-like. Allers makes me think o' heaven."

Give Me Thy Vineyard

The bald crest of the ridge was nearly circular in form. As far as could be seen in any direction was a timbered landscape broken with little green valleys and bare brown cliffs. Far to the north was the dim outline of the newly formed lake, its water resembling a wide silver ribbon stretched through the valley.

The horse stood motionless while its rider drank in the virgin beauty of the hills. Quietly the girl bowed her head and softly prayed: "Dear God, hit seems so clost ter heaven up here, Yo'uns shorely kin hear me a askin' Yo' ter keep watch o'er Hiram. An' keep me faithful an' trustin' an' he'p us prove he never done hit."

An hour later Rosie reined up at Ray Benson's mailbox, where he stood waiting for her.

"Mornin', Rosie. Reckon as how yo'alls got Pa's medicine?"

"Shore has. Here 'tis. How's Gran'pappy a feelin' this mornin'?"

"Right porely. His misery's so bad he cain't sleep ner rest none. But I 'low this here medicine'll ease hit, an' then he'll sleep an' git better agin."

"Shore hope so, Ray. I'se real sorry fer Gran'pappy, an' I'd be right proud ter do anythin' I could ter he'p him. Iffn yo'uns ain't a havin' plenty o' company ter set up nights, I'll come."

"Thanks, Rosie, but they's more offered ter come than we'uns needs an' they's jist a takin' turns."

"Well, tell Gran'pappy that I'se a comin' down ter see him next trip nohow," Rosie said as she started up toward Oakridge, the highest inhabited place on Reed's Ridge.

Reaching her destination, she tied her horse to the well-worn hitching rack, at the place left for the mail carrier's horse, in front of the general store post office.

Untying two mailbags, Rosie pulled them from Fred's back and half-dragged, half-carried them into the building.

Twenty-odd men, women and children were awaiting the

arrival of the mail. The men were seated on two rude benches near the stove, whittling and talking. Mountaineer fashion, they made no move to open the door for Rosie or to assist her with her load.

"Yer on time terday, Rosie," the postmaster greeted her. "So late last night when yo'uns left out fer Clear Springs, we'uns 'lowed dark had shore overtuk yo' an' somethin' had ketched yo'."

"Reckon iffn sump'n had ketched me, they'd a let me loose soon's daylight come," Rosie bantered.

The men laughed. She was a general favorite.

"Don't know 'bout that, Rosie," the usually bashful Squire Morgan declared with nervous courage. "Iffn I war a young feller like I onc't war an' ever ketched yo'all, I shore wouldn't turn yo'all loose." He roared at his own joke.

"Thought thirty days was all yo'uns could hold a body, Squire, less'n hit war the Widder Gray," Rosie shot back.

The men slapped their thighs in high glee, for Squire Morgan had been famous for imposing 30-day sentences in his court, and his nightly trips to the Widow Gray's for 14 years also were well-known.

The old man's face flamed, and thoroughly silenced, he returned to his whittling.

Then Rosie was going down the steep grade from Oakridge and making a sharp detour along the almost invisible path at the end of which was Dave Emory's new stone house. This trip didn't take long and she was soon back on the trail, heading for Granny Smith's ancient mailbox, fashioned from a cylinder of hollow log tied with hickory bark to a low fork of a white oak tree.

Granny Smith was Rosie's closest woman friend in the hills. The old lady was a distant relative who had been in the Gurney cabin when Rosie was born and her mother had died, and who had kept an eye on the girl as long as she was able. Other women on the ridge had felt obligated to John Gurney to help out with raising his girl and there was scarcely a home in the community where Rosie hadn't spent a few days being fitted with new dresses and things.

John was perpetually grateful. "I don't know how I'd ever a raised her iffn it hadn't a bin fer the wimmin folk hereabout," he often said. But of all of them Granny Smith was Rosie's favorite. It was to her, whom she knew she could trust, that she told her secrets.

The old lady had come to the hills 50 years before with her third husband. Folks said she had been forced to leave Kentucky because of the wild way she had carried on there. She was supposed to have been strikingly beautiful, although her now wrinkled, slack-jawed face seemed to mock such a possibility. However, she had always lived a quiet and completely respectable life on the ridge and the Ozark folk accepted her for what she was. Rosie never could see that she was any different from other women she knew except she made more liberal allowances for folks' wrongdoings.

As Rosie reached the mailbox, she caught sight of Granny Smith laboriously hobbling down the long slope from her cabin. The girl dismounted and sat down on a stump.

"Rosie," the old woman called, "will yo'uns back this here letter fer me? My writin' ain't so good no more an' hit's 'bout all I kin do ter write Willie ever' week."

"Shore, Granny, be glad ter. An' I'se got sump'n fer yo'all from Kaintuck. Looieville, hit looks like." She squinted at the postmark.

"Oh, hit's from my kin. Don't know when I'll ever be a answerin' 'em."

Taking a pencil from the handy pocket of her overall bib, Rosie printed Willie's name and address on the front of the envelope and affixed a stamp in the corner.

"How's Willie a makin' hit?" she asked, recalling to memory Granny's tall, spare son who had left the hills for Kansas 10 years ago.

Give Me Thy Vineyard

"He's still a workin' an' sends me what he kin spare ever' week. Hit shore keeps me a goin'. I cain't garden none, ner can, ner dry no more. Gettin' old ain't no fun, Rosie. But I fetched yo'uns some blackberry cobbler, honey. Here 'tis."

Granny extended a small heavy blue china bowl, covered with a white cloth. "Spoon's inside. Thought yo'uns might be hongry, a ridin' so fur. An' I knows how much yo' allus liked hit."

Rosie did not want to take it. She knew the old woman had hardly enough to eat herself. But hurt pride was worse than hunger to people like Granny Smith. With a smile she said "Thanks heaps, Granny. Shore war nice o' yo'all. Mmmm. Hit's real good. Wisht I could make flaky crust like this." She gave Fred a bite of the crust.

Granny Smith chuckled. "Rosie, I reckon as how when yo' an' Hiram marries an' has young'uns they'll all be fat and purty iffn yo'all takes as good keer of 'em as yo' does o' that black Fred o' yore'n."

Rosie sighed. "Don't reckon I'll ever have no young'uns, Granny, Hiram a havin' ter hide from the law like he is."

"Why shore yo' will, honey. Hain't fergot, has yo'all, what the Good Book says 'bout the Lord a workin' in queer ways ter fetch 'bout His wonders? Why, I kin 'member when my first husbin–"

"Yes, I know Granny. Yo'uns had two husbans ter die an' married a third un afore yo'all had Willie," broke in Rosie irritably, "but that don't do me an' Hiram no good. Looks like me an' him jist ain't ever goin' ter git married atall. Hit's bin months since that air murder an' we'uns jist thought they'd find out who done hit long afore this. But I'se got ter be a goin'. Got lots o' places ter stop terday. Goodbye till I sees yo'all again."

Granny Smith watched Rosie mount her horse and ride away. Then as she made her slow, painful way to the house, she wondered about her and Hiram. She knew Rosie was a good sensible girl and hoped with all her heart that she was as strong as the faith she possessed.

Rosie had not gone quite a mile when she brought Fred to a standstill in the trail. She listened intently and looked about in every direction. In the sky a few white-cap clouds floated lazily by. Down the ridge, squirrels quarreled noisily. But not another human being was within miles. She sat motionless for a brief moment, then cupped her hands to her mouth. She gave the *Who-who-whoo* of the owl. The call echoed and re-echoed. Then from far down the slope came the answering call, *Who-who-whoo-whoo-oo-oo!*

"Come on! He's a waitin'," Rosie cried, as she dug her heels into the flanks of the startled horse. Taking a sharp turn off the trail through the underbrush, she directed Fred over bushes and fallen logs and through thick forest until she reached the sycamore clump where Hiram was waiting.

"Oh, Hiram! Hit's so good ter see yo'uns!" she sobbed, as her arms reached around his neck.

"Been a countin' the time all day a waitin' fer yo'uns, honey," he answered, holding her close, and kissing her upturned mouth.

At last they sat down in the grass and Rosie began unpacking the picnic lunch.

"Honey, yo'all looks so nice," she murmured, handing a sandwich to Hiram. "How yo' been?"

"Feelin' purty good, now that yo're here," he said, watching the glow of her eyes light up her face.

"Uncle Dave said he told yo'uns some good news 'bout the shuriff, but I didn't understand what hit war."

"'Tain't really nothin'. The shuriff sorta promised not ter try an ketch me iffn ever'body here 'bouts'd vote fer his deputy. 'Course, we'all knows he's aimin' ter git the deputy job next year hisse'f."

(In explanation to the reader, at the time of this story a sheriff could not succeed himself to office in Missouri.

Give Me Thy Vineyard

Therefore, it was a political custom for the sheriff and his chief deputy to alternate years campaigning for the office.)

"I keep a prayin' that hit'll come out who really done that killin', Hiram. But hit's goin' on four years an'—"

"Stop hit! Don't say yo're a beginnin' ter wonder er nothin' like that. I couldn't stand hit!"

She looked at him in surprise. "Why, Hiram. I never even dreamed o' sayin' nothin' like that. I ain't beginnin' ter wonder ary bit. But yo'all has gotter stop bein' so jumpy, honey. Youns needs ter have faith an'—"

"Don't start in on me agin, Rosie."

"I ain't startin' nothin'. But iffn yo'all believed in sump'n yo wouldn't be madden' up like this all a time."

"I believe in yo'uns, Rosie."

"Hush, Hiram. Hit's agin the Lord the way yo'all talk."

"The Lord shore cain't keep me from lovin' yo'"

"Oh, Hiram, don't yo'uns see? Believin' in God is lovin', too, only in a different way. Hit's somethin' yo' feel, deep inside. Hit ain't somethin' yo' think out in yore haid. Iffn yo does think 'bout hit too much then yo' jist don't git nowhere. But when yo'uns believes, an' knows yo' believes, hit makes yo strong cause yo're shore Someone's watchin' o'er yo'."

"I don't need no one ter watch o'er me. I jist need yo'all." He pulled her close to him. "Rosie," he began, "I wants yo'uns so bad I cain't hardly live. Come an' go with me and let's light out fer Californy er some place. Those Harmons'll shorely git ketched someday an' then we'uns kin come back an' start up farmin' here agin."

Rosie sat up in shocked amazement. "Why, Hiram Jackson Pemberton," she exploded, "that's the craziest talk I ever heard in my whole life."

The pained look on his face stopped her. "I'se sorry, honey," she apologized, her tone soft. "I guess we'se both a gittin' jumpy. Hit'd shore be nice if we'uns could run away an' be tergether all a time, but Hiram, yo'all knows we'uns wouldn't git out o' this here county afore them fellers at the dam would be a ketchin' us."

"I reckon yo're right, gal," Hiram answered lamely. "I jist gits ter thinkin' sometimes an' plumb lose my head."

Give Me Thy Vineyard

Give Me Thy Vineyard

Give Me Thy Vineyard

Chapter 13

A STRANGER walked along the narrow, heavily weeded trail to Stony Point. He was tall and thin, with brown hair, piercing blue eyes, and glasses. His suit, tie, low-cut Oxfords and the stiff way he carried himself marked him as a city man. And like a city man walking in the Ozarks he was thinking:

What a country! It's like a roller coaster. As soon as you fight your way to the top of one hill, you start sliding down the next one. Wish I'd taken a horse!

Heavily he sat down on a huge rock beside the trail and looked about him.

I wish I knew if I were going in the right direction, he mused, as he watched a gray squirrel frisk about, his bead-like eyes shining brightly. He came daringly near the stranger, as though he would invite him for a game of hide-and-seek.

Pangs of hunger began to disturb the foot-traveler's rest and a look at his watch as well as a gnawing sensation in his stomach told him of the nearness of the luncheon hour. But where he was to lunch, or upon what, he did not know. Perhaps it was a longing interest in the edibility of squirrel meat that directed his attention to the antics of the little animal of the woods, rather than the little fellow's whimsical mood of play.

At any rate, the stranger made up his mind that he would probably have to postpone the pleasure of eating until the end of his journey, which he hoped would be before the sun set. He hadn't seen a house for more than two hours so the prospects for stopping at a roadside home for luncheon seemed very remote. The trail grew dimmer and the woods more dense at the crest of every hill.

He rose from the boulder where he sat and stepped upon some twigs underfoot as he did so. The snapping of the dry wood made a loud sound and sent the little squirrel scampering up the trunk of the tree, his bold spirit of adventure completely deflated by unspeakable fright.

The stranger laughed aloud at the little squirrel and stretched his arms high above his head to relieve his tired muscles. He cast a glance about for a likely spot to build a bed of leaves where he could take a nap, thinking it might be a fair substitute for the lunch he would miss.

Just then he heard someone coming through the woods to the left of him, whistling a merry tune. He turned to face a narrow path leading out of the woods that up to this moment he had not noticed. A small boy carrying a large bucket pushed aside a clump of bushes and stepped out into the road. He was closely followed by a large dog of uncertain pedigree but which showed evidence of being able to claim some collie and some shepherd parentage.

The boy was startled into silence at the sight of the man beside the road, but quickly recovered.

"Howdy, mister," he said with a slight nod of the head.

"How do you do, son." The stranger glanced at the boy's overalls and flop-brimmed straw hat with holes cut in the crown. "I was resting here," he added. "I've been walking from Hartstown on my way to Stony Point. Do you know how far that is from here?"

"Nope, don't know how fur hit is," the boy answered. "But I'se been there. Went one day with my paw. Rover an' me is a goin' down here ter the spring ter fetch some water. Yo' better come 'long an' go back ter the house with us. Yo'uns hain't had yore dinner, has yo'?"

"No, but I don't think I'd better go to your house for dinner. Your mother won't be expecting company."

"Oh, Ma, she won't keer," the boy declared. "Pa kin tell yo'uns where Stony Point is. Yo'uns mus' be orful hongry."

"Well, yes, I am," the traveler admitted. "I'll go along with you, but I don't want to be any trouble. Won't you let me carry your bucket?"

"Naw!" the boy refused. "'Tain't heavy. Hit's jist a little step down ter the spring. Where yo'all from?" he inquired loquaciously, as the teacher stepped into the path to follow him down to the spring. Rover was leading the procession now.

"I'm from the north part of the state. I'm a schoolteacher looking for a job. The county superintendent sent me to see the school board at Stony Point."

The boy stopped short in the path and turned to face the teacher. "Why, they don't pay nuthin' over there," he said tensely. The teacher was puzzled by the note of suspicion in the boy's tone and manner. "What yo'uns wants ter go a teachin' over there fer?"

The man sighed. "I'll tell you what, son," he said patiently. "Let's go to the spring and get the water now. Then when we get to your house, I'll tell your father and mother all about myself, and you at the same time."

The boy nodded without answering and continued on down to the spring. The man tried to restore his friendliness but without success. He filled the bucket and maintained a moody silence as they walked up the narrow trail to his home.

As they came within sight of the weather-beaten log house, several hounds of various colors, but all lank and hungry-looking, alerted the family to the approach of a stranger.

A tall, powerfully built, unshaved man about 40 years old stood in the door and watched the man, boy and dog as they neared the house. He was flanked on all sides by as many children of varying ages and sizes as could crowd their shaggy heads into the door jamb around their father's huge bulk. Those who couldn't find room at the door satisfied their curiosity by peering out through the narrow kitchen window.

The stranger pondered in his mind what to say as they steadily came within speaking range of the house. He scarcely knew how to introduce himself to this giant of the hills, who displayed neither friendliness nor hostility as the trio came nearer.

The boy, however, was not abashed and he said to his father in clear tones, "Pa, this here is a feller what says he is a goin' ter Stony Point ter teach school. He said he war hongry so I brung him up fer dinner."

"Come in," the hillman said noncommittally. Then he turned in the door to let the teacher follow him into the house.

The stranger found himself in a crudely furnished two-room cabin. The room he stood in was littered with shoes, clothing boxes and old chairs. In the center was a long handmade table, flanked on both sides by benches of the same length. The workings of a fireplace and an old stove had thoroughly blackened the ceiling. He glanced into the adjoining room and saw a woman lying on one of the beds.

"Oh," he said, turning back. "I hope you will forgive me. I didn't know you had sickness."

"Aw, 'tain't nothin'," the hillman explained matter-of-factly. "Woman's just a punyin' with a young'un. Yo'uns shore air plenty welcome. Come on an' eat."

"You're sure I'm not intruding?" the teacher said politely to a small girl who was placing another plate and service on the long narrow table.

"Naw, don't pay her no mind," the girl replied, nodding toward her mother. She was so abstracted with this city man's "purty ways" she could scarcely open her mouth to speak.

"Set," the man of the house invited, indicating to the stranger a place beside a row of boys on one of the crudely built benches that was drawn up close to one side of the table.

The teacher by this time noticed that the bench on the opposite side of the table was also filled with growing boys. The father sat at one end of the feasting board and the little girl took her place at the end near the stove where she could easily replenish empty bowls and coffee cups.

As soon as the father was seated, each one bowed his head as the father intoned, "Lord, we'uns shore thank Yo'all fer this here food an' ask Yo' ter keep on a watchin' o'er us. Fergive us, Lord, when we'uns does what we hadn't orter."

The boys then began without further ceremony to reach for the huge bowls of beans, gravy and fried potatoes and filled their plates unstintingly. With the prospects of appeasing the hunger that tormented them, they had almost completely lost interest in the stranger.

The teacher's appetite almost equaled that of the boys, but he managed to conceal it better. The men at the table paused to look on curiously as he deferred his turn at each bowl of food to the little girl who seemed unable to keep up with the swift exchange of vessels going on about the table. Men of the hills always let the women look after themselves at meals as well as elsewhere – that is, after they have dutifully waited upon the men and small children.

Conversation was postponed until every plate was filled. However, no one waited (except the teacher) until his plate was full before he started eating. As soon as one variety of food was spooned onto the plate, the recipient began shoveling it into his mouth until a bowl of something else passed his way. Ordinarily the meals were eaten in silence, but today they had company so the father opened up the way for talk.

"Yo're a teacher, eh?" he queried. All eyes in the room were turned upon the guest at the question.

"Well, I haven't taught for several years, but I'm looking now for a teaching job. Your county supervisor directed me to Stony Point." He spoke guardedly.

"How come he sent yo'uns over there?" the host inquired, his voice crisp and hard. "They don't pay hardly nuthin'."

"I know," the teacher answered. "That is the reason he thought I might be hired. I am much more interested in securing a small place where I can live in the mountains than I am in drawing a big salary."

"Why?"

The teacher felt disconcerted and uncomfortable under this stern query. Fully aware of the roomful of hostile, curious eyes upon him, he told this story: "I used to teach school in northern Missouri. But six years ago my wife died. Our little boy was 5 then. His mother was never well after his birth. I gave up teaching and took the boy to live with my folks on their farm. But the boy never seemed to be healthy either and about two years ago he developed tuberculosis. I didn't know what it was for a long time, but when I finally found out, I was advised by the doctor to get him to a mild climate where the air is good. That's why I'm here."

"Why do you want to teach at Stony Point?"

"I don't care where I teach. It's the only place in the Ozarks that I know about where there might be an opening for me. I still don't know if they'll hire me. What do you think?"

"Don't rightly know," his host replied leisurely, as he rose from the table.

"Marthy, take some o' this here grub inter yore maw," he instructed his daughter as he turned to leave the room. The teacher noticed as he followed his host through the door that the bevy of boys had already disappeared.

"Don't rightly know iffn they'll hire yo'uns ter Stony Point er not," the hillman continued in the dooryard. "What did yo'uns say yer name war?"

"I didn't say, but it's Rogers. Grady Rogers."

When the mountaineer did not respond to this information, Rogers announced, "I must hurry on now. Thanks for the lunch. How far is it to Stony Point?"

"'Bout five mile. Jist follow the trail that turns offn the spring. Yo'll git there 'bout three o'clock. Cliff Montgomery's head o' the school board."

"That's what the county superintendent told me," Rogers replied as he started to walk away.

"Tell Cliff yo'uns et with me," his benefactor called after him.

Rogers stopped and turned back in the path. "In that case, I guess I'll have to ask your name," he laughed good-naturedly.

"Tell him it war Charlie Raiford," the hillman drawled, curving his large mouth into a half-smile.

Refreshed by the food and rest, although annoyed by the peculiar behavior of the Raifords, the teacher stepped swiftly down the path from the house and into the trail that led to his destination. As he approached Stony Point, the trail gradually widened and he found walking much easier. The sun was still high when he arrived at the home which another little boy told him was that of the chairman of the school board.

Cliff Montgomery lived in a solid-looking house made of the reddish tan rocks which abound in the Ozarks. Rogers was impressed as he walked up the long path through neat rows of tomato plants. Self-consciously, he tried to straighten his tie and smooth out his wrinkled suit. Then he jiggled the cowbell which hung near the door facing and in a moment a bald, stout, cheerful-looking man dressed in a khaki shirt and worn but clean corduroy trousers faced him.

"Are you Mr. Montgomery?"

"Shore am."

"I'm Grady Rogers. The county superintendent sent me to see you. I understand you need a teacher at Stony Point."

Montgomery smiled. "Yo'uns shore come ter the right time. Come in. We'uns air a havin' a board meetin' right now."

He brought Rogers into a neat bare room where two men in jeans and faded shirts sat at a table.

"Boys, this here's Mr. Rogers. Says he's a teacher."

Both men looked up with interest.

"Start talkin', feller," one of them said. "School starts in two weeks an' we'uns ain't got nary teacher yet."

Rogers told them about his former teaching experience, the death of his wife, and his sick boy – the reason for his desire to live and work in the Ozarks.

"Got yore teachin' papers?"

"Yes." He produced his certificates. The men studied them earnestly for a few minutes. As he looked on with curious interest, Grady Rogers wondered about these men of the hills. Why were they so strangely noncommittal? And if he were elected to teach their school, how could he be successful in a community where the folk were openly hostile for no other reason apparently than that he was a stranger? And why didn't they like strangers?

Finally, Cliff Montgomery said, "I guess we better talk this here thing over, boys. Mr. Rogers, yo'uns come back long 'bout suppertime an' we'uns'll let yo'all know."

"All right," Rogers agreed, wondering what he'd do in the meantime. He also wondered where he'd spend the night since he knew he couldn't return to Hartstown this day. But he didn't worry. He long ago had learned that it was best to live each hour as it came along. No need to borrow trouble. Every need would be cared for someway or other.

"Before I forget it, Mr. Montgomery," he began, "a neighbor of yours asked me to tell you that I ate dinner with him today. Charlie Raiford was his name."

Rogers looked quickly from Montgomery's face to the other two. They looked grim. He couldn't say, though, for sure that they were any grimmer than they had been all during his encounter with them. Yet the atmosphere definitely was charged with a certain tensity. What was the matter? If these men didn't like Raiford, why did he send Montgomery that message?

The teacher felt embarrassed. He thought he must go on talking but he couldn't think of anything to say. He was greatly relieved to hear Cliff Montgomery remark, "I 'spect Charlie'll be 'long here purty soon. Yo'uns kin come back later. They's a mighty purty walk down the trail from the back of the house," he suggested.

Grady Rogers smiled wryly. He'd had enough walking for one day, but at that he was glad to get away. Quickly retreating to the back of the house, the teacher discovered a narrow path that led to a wagon road in the woods, which he followed uphill and down until he reached the crest of a bald knob. There he stopped and gasped. What a view! North, east and west as far as he could see were hills and hollows of at least a dozen different shades of green, blending at last into a sky whose blue was so brilliantly bright that it hurt his eyes.

He gazed fascinated at the ever-changing pattern before him: the gray-green of the ridges, the blackish green of the thick woods below them, the broad patches of yellow-tasseled cornfields, the thread-like trails which looked brownish gray from where he stood and the distant hills of emerald, blue and purple-green. He compared these undulations with the flat country in his own part of the state and was pleased by his new surroundings. He took a deep breath of the warm, tingling air and felt exhilarated.

The majesty and silent grandeur of the scene spread out before him so affected the hopeful teacher, he closed his eyes, bowed his head and prayed to God who here seemed so real – so near.

"Dear God, please give Tommy this chance to get well and strong."

Give Me Thy Vineyard

Time seemed to stand still for Rogers as he stood gazing at the vast panorama spread out before him. A calmness took possession of his soul that he had never known before. It had been hammering at his brain all day but he hadn't had time to give thought to its significance. Now he realized that here was what he was seeking. A wonderful place to bring health to his boy and peace to his soul. He had no idea how long he had stood there and was startled into consciousness of his business at Cliff Montgomery's home when that person called his name.

"Mr. Rogers!"

He whirled to see Montgomery and the other two members of the board coming toward him.

"We got through quicker'n we calc'lated," Cliff announced happily, "and we'uns got good news fer yo'all. Yo're our new teacher."

Grady Rogers felt greatly relieved at this glad news and it was only then that he knew how badly he wanted this job.

"I don't know how to thank you, gentleman," he began. "I am sure I'll try to make you a good teacher."

"Oh, yo'uns'll do all right," one of the men spoke up. "We reckoned we best hire yo' seein's nary other man has asked fer hit. Hit don't make me no mind nohow, seein' as how my young'uns is a'ready fetched up."

Rogers thought this was a pretty careless attitude. A man should have a better community spirit than that. He decided not to say anything, however. He'd better go slow and feel his way with these folk until he understood them better.

"When will the term begin?" he inquired.

"We set fer hit ter begin the second Monday in July. Hit'll be out end o' February. We ginnerly has eight months."

"Oh, so soon!" the teacher exclaimed. "That gives me only two weeks to get moved here."

He thought of the long walk back to Hartstown. Now that he had the job he was anxious to get things arranged.

Give Me Thy Vineyard

"Do any of you know how I might get a ride back to Hartstown?" he asked of no one in particular.

Cliff Montgomery spoke up quickly and said, "Yo'uns best stay with me ternight and I'll take yo' ter Hartstown in the mornin'."

For the second time in the last half-hour Grady Rogers had a great feeling of relief. His problems seemed to be smoothing out in a wonderful way. He protested that he didn't want to be so much trouble, but Cliff Montgomery assured him that it "wouldn't disfurnish him nary a bit." They'd be glad to have him spend the night, and as for the trip to Hartstown, he needed to be going over there anyway.

So it was arranged. But instead of returning to the house with Montgomery, the teacher stayed on the cliff. He had some thinking to do. He explained to the hillman that he had never seen such beautiful scenery and he wanted to stay there for a while and rest. Montgomery was sympathetic. "Stay till the sun sets," he advised, "an' yo'll be a comin' back agin an' agin ter see hit all over. But don't fergit ter come down fer supper," he invited as he walked with his neighbors down the hill.

Give Me Thy Vineyard

Give Me Thy Vineyard

Chapter 14

YES, GRADY ROGERS had some thinking to do. He was grateful for the job that had been offered him. He knew the salary was inadequate, especially in comparison with salaries paid teachers in other sections. But he reasoned it would be enough that he and his little boy could get along on it. They would try to get a little patch of land where he could raise vegetables and maybe keep a cow and chickens. They would make out. The only important thing in his life was restoring his son to health.

But the teacher was puzzled by the attitude of the people he had met this day. They shied away from him as though he were leprous and yet they had employed him, a total stranger, to teach their school.

When he came to make application for the position, he had expected a few days to intervene before they would let him know for sure if he got the place or not. He thought they would want to verify his qualifications and correspond with his references. He would particularly have expected this procedure in view of the way they seemed to be so suspicious of him.

But what did they suspicion?

That was the thing Rogers couldn't figure out. It gave him a feeling of uneasiness and he was fast developing a doubtful timidity about accepting the position after all. But then pictures of Tommy's thin body and sunken, hollow eyes rose in his mind and he knew he must not allow fears and misgivings to keep him from grasping this opportunity to help his boy. The Lord was good to guide him to this place and he knew he must have no room in his mind or heart for anything but gratitude.

He rose and stood once more looking out over the beautiful stretch of scenery before him. He felt infinitesimally small here alone on this great cliff with such a display of the wondrous work of God before him. His roving eyes fell to the deep gorge that dropped immediately below him, going down, down, down to the water that flowed in its channel like a winding stream of silver. Lifting his head, he gazed at the rolling hills and valleys whose surfaces viewed from this great distance looked like they might be covered with cloths of green jade. Tiny cabins dotted the landscape of these valleys and the man who had so recently come into this strange land wondered about the people within those walls, and the kind of lives they lived.

Looking to the ridges that rose above the little green valleys, he saw vast stretches of wooded hills, their verdant foliage colored a darker green than the rest by the fog of blue mist that hung over them. Finally the teacher's vision came to rest upon the level of the faraway horizon where the mountains met the sky. And there in the misty blue rose little humps of black-green that seemed to Rogers to be beyond the horizon. *How far away they must be*, he mused. And what a magnificent view! It left a man breathless. It stripped him of all his self-powers. It struck him dumb! He couldn't even think. What thoughts of man would invade the significant solemnity of this glorious piece of creation?

A man like Rogers could feel only the power of God as though he stood in the actual presence of the Divine. A man like Rogers could only bow his head in prayers of gratitude and in submission to His will.

How long he stood there Rogers did not know. Neither did

he know his every movement was being watched by two pairs of curious eyes. True to Cliff Montgomery's prediction, Charlie Raiford had "dropped by" his neighbor's cabin while the school board meeting was in session. The men told him the stranger had gone for a walk and that they thought they would hire him for their teacher. They even let him examine the teacher's certifications.

Charlie didn't stay with his friends long but hurried on down to Tobe Alton's cabin. Together he and Tobe made their way up the trail behind Montgomery's house until they came within sight of the stranger standing alone on the great cliff. Then each of them hid himself behind a large oak and watched what went on. They saw Montgomery and the other school board members climb to the ledge and tell the teacher he was hired. They saw him bow his head in prayer before he turned from his observation point to follow the half-mile of narrow trail back to Montgomery's house.

Cliff Montgomery was sitting on the porch with his three young sons when Grady Rogers returned for supper. His wife, Annie, was in the kitchen putting the meal on the table.

"I figgered hit war 'bout time fer yo'uns ter be a gittin' hongry," the hillman greeted genially. "Supper's all ready. These here air three o' the young colts yo'll be a havin' in school," indicating his three boys. "Guess yo'll be a wantin' ter wash up a bit, so come on in the kitchen. Wash pan's in there."

He led his guest into a room furnished much like that of the Raifords, except things were clean and in neat order.

Mrs. Montgomery was busy at the stove and when she turned to set a dish of hot food on the table her husband introduced her to the stranger as "the woman." Grady acknowledged the introduction, washed and dried his hands and, with the family, sat at the table. While they sat with bowed heads, Mrs. Montgomery offered a fervent prayer of thanks.

"Now the table's narry an' the dishes set handy," Cliff Montgomery announced, as they raised their heads. "Jist retch in an' take out."

The teacher needed no second invitation and since no one else stood on ceremony, neither did he.

"So yo'uns has a sick boy," Montgomery began by way of opening conversation. "An' yo' 'low ter bring him here, eh?"

"Yes," Rogers answered. "The doctor advised me to get him to the mountains."

"Then yo'll be a needin' a snug cabin fer him."

"I was going to ask about that. Is there one available, not too far from the school?"

"Shore they is, jist west o' the schoolhouse 'bout a mile an' a quarter. Hit's kinda small, but hit's a right good place. Ginnerly the teacher jist boards 'round, but me an' the boys'll git yo'uns that air cabin. Don't reckon old man Green'll charge yo'all no rent. I'll he'p yo'uns move in."

"Thanks a lot. I hate to put you to any more bother."

"'Tain't no bother. I'm yore nighest neighbor."

"Oh, then the cabin isn't far from here."

"Jist a mile off'n the south trail."

Rogers grinned. A mile between houses was considered a pretty good stretch where he came from.

"Is there a church in the community?" he next inquired.

"No," his informer told him. "We'uns sometimes has meetin' ter the schoolhouse. I reckon yo'all comes from a place where folks goes ter church?"

"Well, not everybody," the teacher explained. "And I fear many of those who do attend go because they think it will help them in their business or because they wish to make an impression on someone and not for any love of God."

"My landies! Yo'all talks jist like a preacher," Annie Montgomery exploded into the conversation. "Be yo'uns one?"

"No, but religion means a great deal to me. I probably

would have gone to pieces long ago if it hadn't been for my faith in God."

"Why, Cliff, he talks so purty, I bet he could be a preacher iffn he wanted to," Annie Montgomery said across the table to her husband.

"How 'bout hit, Mr. Rogers?" Cliff inquired. "We'uns shore could use one in these here parts. Don't even have nobody ter hold layin'-away meetin' part o' the time."

Rogers ran his hand through his hair. "Well, I have never done any preaching," he said seriously. "But I do know something about the Scriptures. Maybe I could teach Bible classes or something."

Annie beamed. "Ain't this here jist fine? I'se shore glad they didn't hire no gal, 'cause now we'uns got a teacher an' a preacher all ter onct."

Rogers frowned, feeling weighted down with responsibility. He hadn't said he was a preacher.

"I don't know what kind of preacher I'll be, but I'll do the best I can for you both ways. You have been very kind to me."

"Yo'll do jist fine," Montgomery said encouragingly. "An' I shore hopes yore little boy gits well fast."

"Thank you," said Rogers. "Say, you said you thought Charlie Raiford would come by this afternoon. Did he come?"

"Yes, he come," Montgomery answered cryptically. He looked steadily at Grady, who returned his scrutinizing gaze.

Then the stranger blurted out, "Mr. Montgomery, the Raifords were very kind to me today. They gave me a good meal and seemed glad to do it, even when there was illness in their home. But all the time I was with them I had the feeling they didn't trust me. In fact, they seemed downright suspicious. Then when I came here, you and the other members of the school board evidently entertained the same regard for me. Yet you hired me at once. I don't understand."

Give Me Thy Vineyard

"Well, I reckon Charlie's got his reasons fer suspicionin' strangers, Mr. Rogers," Montgomery drawled at last. "Us, we don't objec' ter strangers iffn they're here ter work an' mind their own business. As fer why we hired you so quick, well, we needed a teacher right bad an' yo'uns looked like yo'uns could handle the job. They's somethin' 'bout a feller what's tellin' the truth, folks jist naturally know hit's the truth. Us fellers knowed yo'all warn't lyin'."

"What church does yo'all hold ter?" Annie Montgomery asked timidly, anxious to restore the subject of religion to the conversation.

"I seldom think of church as denominational. I am sure if we spent more time and effort in ministering to the needs of our fellow men and in teaching the love of Jesus, and the way of salvation, we would find it much more profitable than so much contention about unimportant differences."

"Shore right proud ter hear yo'uns talk thataway," replied Annie. "Most preachers what comes here, 'bout all they talks 'bout is what they believes in. They's allers a knockin' anybody what thinks different from what they does. Don't make me no difference what a body holds ter, jist so he preaches 'bout the things the good Lord done died fer."

"You are quite right," agreed the teacher readily. "If only more people could see it that way, the Church would do much more good in the world. It is hard to bring sinners into the Church when they see professed Christians constantly quarreling about the right and wrong way to become Christians," he continued wearily.

"I recall a readin' in the Good Book onct 'bout the Lord a prayin' fer us all ter be one. Don't 'pear like that prayer is a bein' answered very fast," Annie commented.

The teacher was amazed at her apparent knowledge of the Bible, for her surroundings bore evidence that her opportunities to gain an education had been very poor. With these thoughts in mind, he said to her admiringly, "You must have studied the Bible to be able to talk that way."

"Oh, I reads it ever'day an' prays, too," she returned simply. "I begun it 'way back when my young'uns war little. They warn't no Sunday school er meetin' a goin' on, an' I jist didn't want my young'uns a growin' up 'thout a knowin' nothin' o' the Lord an' His ways, so their paw an' me tuck ter readin' the Word to 'em. Now jist seems like things don't go right when I misses."

The admiration of the young man for this sincere hill-woman increased as they talked and he came to believe she would be one to whom he could turn when the lonely hours overtook him, for he knew that life here in such a strange land would not be easy.

"How'd yo'all like ter go a frog huntin'?" Cliff Montgomery wanted to know, as they rose with one accord to file from the table.

"I'd like it very much," his guest answered. "Were you planning–"

"Yep, me an' the boys goes most ever' night. Better git ready," he admonished the boys, who dashed off soon to reappear with lanterns, buckets and hooks.

No sooner had the men set off on the trail than Annie Montgomery hurried down the road that led to the Altons' cabin. She had news for Sarah Alton.

Give Me Thy Vineyard

Give Me Thy Vineyard

Chapter 15

TOBE ALTON ROSE to his full height of 6-feet-3. He had been hiding behind a large oak, near where the stranger stood. In a few seconds he was joined by another heavyset giant dressed in the same kind of tattered denims: Charlie Raiford.

"What yo'uns a thinkin', Charlie?" Tobe asked anxiously. "Reckon he air a teacher er be he a revenoor?"

"Wal, he tole the school board same's he tole me at dinner, Tobe, 'bout how he 'lowed he'd be a bringin' that air kid o' his'n here, sayin' as how the kid war a lunger. An' he shore has got his teachin' papers."

"But they's no way o' knowin' so we's jist got ter be keerful," Tobe said advisedly.

"Yo'uns air plumb right – soon's he left my house I sent Bob an' Pete ter warn Steve, an' I cut acrost here." He scratched his head. "But no revenoor ever went huntin' a job a larnin' young'uns. Somehow, Tobe, I believes he's all right. He seemed kinda honest-like an' they war tears in his eyes when he war a talkin' 'bout that lunger kid o' his'n; an' nohow, him a standin' there a prayin' so quiet-like, shorely he warn't a askin' God ter show him no stills!"

Plainly worried, Tobe sat down on a stump.

"Hope yo'all's right, Charlie, but we better hide that still – fu'ther up Spring Creek Holler." He hesitated and his eyes narrowed as a new thought entered his mind. "Say, Charlie, mebbe the 'lectric comp'ny has a finger in the pie somewheres. They's a startin' in agin a tryin' ter ketch Hiram. This here feller might be a tryin' ter git the job a larnin' the young'uns ter Stony Point so's ter find out where Hiram's hidin'!"

"Yo'all might be right, Tobe. I never did think o' that. Say, now I 'member how I heerd over to Hartstown that them air fellers 'low ter build 'nother dam. Iffn they does, they'll shore do anythin' ter git shet o' Hiram. If fer no other reason jist ter show out."

Tobe pulled his ear meditatively. "Yo' an' me ort ter see Hiram an' tell him ter be right keerful. He shore ort ter lay low fer a spell."

Both men lapsed into thought. Then Tobe declared, "'Course, we best not be a takin' no chances, like you says. Reckon we best move that still as soon as we gits done a cookin' off that air batch o' corn."

Silently the two mountaineers turned and walked down the trail leading to the lower level of Spring Creek. Here the wild path led on and on around the bordering bluffs until it came to a large opening under an overhanging ledge where a still was being operated by Tobe's son, Steve, a taciturn boy of 19.

"How's she a comin', Steve?" Tobe asked.

"Jist 'bout ready ter draw. T'other batch is a'ready drawed an' jugged. Hit's a coolin' down ter the spring," Steve replied.

"Feller come in terday a lookin' fer a school," his father said. "They done hired him to larn the young'uns over ter Stony Point."

The boy looked worried.

"Hain't fergot, has yo'uns, Paw, as how that air revenoor ketched Coon Stark? Coon, him a thinkin' he war a wantin' ter buy lumber?"

"No, Steve, I hain't. Don't worry none. This here still is a

114

goin' fu'ther up the holler jist as soon as we gits this here run jugged."

The three mountaineers began drawing the white corn liquor and running it into gallon jugs which were taken to the spring and placed in the cool, clear water. The drawing finished, they set to work to remove all signs of their labor. The still and coils were shouldered and carried three miles farther up the river where the country was practically unbroken. Here the valley of Spring Creek narrowed and the limestone bluff which rose hundreds of feet on both sides of it was cut in many places by ravines covered with virgin timber, and tangled undergrowth of hazelnuts, berry patches and swamp willow. No one lived nearer than six miles away. It was an ideal spot for moonshining, and the men looked carefully to see if anybody else in their trade had found it first. But it abounded with an untouched loneliness, and soon the men were satisfied.

After they had set the still in its new place, the three made their way down the trail with the quick, swinging stride of the natives of the country. Night had already settled thickly over the timbered ridges.

Following the trail which widened at last into a road, the mountaineers crossed a ford and stepped into the clearing that surrounded the cabin of Tobe Alton.

"Charlie, stay fer supper," Tobe invited, turning to his friend who nodded his head in acceptance.

Sarah Alton, Tobe's thin, tight-lipped wife, stood in the open door watching for her men's return. She was dressed in a faded gingham, high at the throat, with wrist-length sleeves and a full gathered skirt that met her sturdy black shoes laced above her ankles.

"Yo'all is shore late," she shouted irritably, "but I'll go coddle yo' up a bite o' supper nohow. The young'uns has a'ready et."

The men and Steve washed at the well as Sarah Alton quickly placed beans, turnips, coarse bread and fish on the crude table. She sat opposite her husband and began to talk to him with animation, a thing she hardly ever did. Tobe glanced at her in surprise.

Annie Montgomery had just left, after telling Sarah all about the new teacher. Now she eagerly told the news, not realizing that the men already had knowledge of the board's action. And she would never realize it, if they could help it.

"Right glad they hired that air feller over ter Stony Point," she opined. "Annie 'lowed he 'pears ter be a right good man, an' we shore do need someb'dy ter hold prayer meetin' agin." She looked at her husband meaningfully. "I hopes yo'uns'll give up runnin' that air still an' go ter meetin' reg'lar with me an' the young'uns. Crops this year ain't bad an' we kin git 'long 'thout what yo'uns gits from that air likker, an' yo'uns knows what the Good Book says 'bout not prosperin' none lest yo'all does the Lord's biddin'."

Her husband frowned and then laughed nervously.

"I'll take keer o' myse'f an' the Lord'll take keer o' Hisse'f," he muttered. Then eying his wife, he said in a bantering tone, "Sary, yo' shore done tuck a fancy to that air teacher, a tryin' ter convert two hard ol' sinners like me an' Charlie here."

"An' speakin' o' prosperin', Sary," Charlie added, "what 'bout that air teacher, a grabbin' a job at twenty-five dollars a month? Shore looks like he could stand a little prosperin' hisse'f."

Both mountaineers chuckled and looked at Steve for approval. But the boy silently wolfed his food without even glancing at them.

"Well, Charlie," Sarah began in a grim voice, "that teacher's had death an' sickness, an' he ain't got no woman ter garden an' can an' dry none fer him. That makes a sight o' difference."

"Have hit yore own way, Sary, but we'se a aimin' ter watch him till we'se sure he's all right."

Give Me Thy Vineyard

Give Me Thy Vineyard

Give Me Thy Vineyard

Chapter 16

ON A HOT AFTERNOON late in June, an engine, two freight cars and a coach came to a jerky, hissing stop at Ferry Landing on the east side of the recently built lake. This was the last stop of the ramshackle single-track railroad which every day wound its way in and out, in and out, from one hill to another from Jeffersonville to Ferry Landing. Out of the coach on this particular day emerged the teacher, Grady Rogers, carrying his son, an emaciated boy of 11 who looked about 6.

"This is the place, Tom. Isn't it beautiful?" Rogers said.

"Mmmm. Nice." The boy craned his thin neck to look at the lake and the hills.

Rogers brought him to a waiting wagon whose stout owner sat holding lightly the lines that guided a large mule team.

"I'm glad to see you, Mr. Montgomery. I was afraid you might not have gotten my letter. This is my son, Tom."

"Right proud ter meetcha, Tom. I reckon we'uns'll git better 'quainted soon, fer yore cabin ain't fur from our'n."

Montgomery smiled kindly at him, and the boy stuck out a thin hand for the mountaineer to shake. His father helped him to the seat beside Montgomery.

"I'll leave Sonny here," he said, "while I see if our things have come."

He walked over to the stationmaster who was staring at

them from the platform.

"I'm the new teacher at Stony Point, across the lake. Rogers is my name. You should have some freight for me."

"Pleased ter meetcha. Shore am. Wondered who yo'uns war when yo' got off the train. That yer little boy yo'uns war a carryin'? What's the matter o' him? Air he ailin'?"

"Yes, he has had a long siege. And he's very tired. Now, about my things – has any freight come for me?"

Reluctantly the agent turned to business.

"A bed an' mattress an' a little stove come from Sears Roebuck t'other day an' three boxes all tied up tight from Milton. The charges is all paid fer. War yo'uns a aimin' ter git 'em terday?"

"Yes. My friend will help us load them."

He called Cliff Montgomery, who drove the mules around to the loading platform, and the three men loaded the goods into the wagon.

"Iffn yo'uns air a aimin' ter set up housekeepin' yo' shore hain't got no more'n yo'll be a needin'," the station agent offered, eager to continue the conversation.

"No, I suspect not." Rogers was hot and tired and irritated. "We sold most of our things. There are only two of us. The boy needs fresh air and sunshine more than furniture."

"Wal, yo'uns shore brung him ter the right place. Hope he perks up real fast. Where's his–" But Rogers had already climbed into the wagon and Montgomery had started the mules. The station agent was left staring after them, the question still wet in his mouth.

The teacher took his son on his lap and looked at him anxiously. The boy was gazing about, absorbed in his new surroundings.

They crossed the lake on a rickety ferry which was pulled by cable and a pulley device from one side of the water to the other. The boy could not take his eyes from the contraption.

"Look, Daddy," he repeated again and again. "Look! What

a thing!"

Back on the trail he said with a show of vitality, "Daddy, help me stand up and see the lake."

He looked slowly around. "It sure is pretty. Away down there it looks like silver. And what a high hill, and the sky is so clear you can see everywhere."

He sat down abruptly. "Is it much farther, Dad? I'm hungry."

Taking the boy on his lap again, Rogers said, "It's still kind of far, Tom, but I think we'll be there before dark. The mules are strong and walk fast."

"I'm tired, too."

Cliff Montgomery looked hard at the child. "What yo'uns ort ter have, young feller, is lots o' cornbread, an' butter, an' beans, an' fat young squirrels. Lots o' them where yo'all's a goin' ter live. Yo' know," he added seriously, "someway it jist 'pears like young squirrels makes whoever eats 'em as spry as they is theyselves. I reckon 'twon't be long till yo'll be a runnin' 'round a climbin' trees jist like a young squirrel."

"I hope so," the boy answered in an old voice. He hesitated. "But sometimes I think maybe I won't ever be any better and I think Daddy thinks so, too, only he won't tell me." He glanced furtively at his father.

Both men winced, only Rogers did so inwardly. On his face he wore only a smile which he cast reassuringly upon his son's upturned face.

Cliff Montgomery thought of his own three healthy boys, as peppy as firecrackers, and he pitied Grady Rogers. In his heart Rogers prayed, "God, help me make him live. Let him be strong once more, dear God."

To Tom he said, "Of course you'll be better, son. And real soon now, too. We're going to have fun here. You'll see."

"That air's a wood hen." Montgomery broke his thoughts as he pointed to a hen-like bird (that resembled a giant red-headed woodpecker) digging industriously into the rotten trunk of a dead oak.

Rogers nodded and thought, *I've got to learn a lot of things like that and teach Tom. If I can get him interested in nature, maybe he'll take his mind off himself and stop brooding.*

"Down this here hill an' up 'nother an' soon yo'll be home," Montgomery said cheerily.

The teacher stretched his cramped muscles as well as he could and roused his son who had fallen asleep in his father's arms.

"Tom. Wake up. Come on. We're almost there, boy."

"Uh-huh. I'm up."

"There's the cabin!" the hillman announced. "There's yore new home, Tommy Rogers!"

Tom was wide awake now and looked around curiously. "Hey, this is nice!" he approved.

They found the sturdy little two-room cabin clean and neat inside. Cliff confessed that his wife and four of her friends had been working all afternoon. They had swept and scrubbed the floors and washed the windows.

The teacher was so delighted at this show of hospitality that he could only smile and shake his head.

"Why – why – I just don't know what to say," he stammered. "Mr. Montgomery – er, Cliff, if you don't mind. You are all so–"

"Then don't say nothin'. Let's git this here stuff out."

Montgomery always felt embarrassed in the presence of sentimentality.

As soon as they had set up the bed, Rogers put his son into it and covered him up, although the evening was warm. The exhausted boy fell asleep immediately. Then the two men brought in the other things.

"What do I owe you for the trip?" Rogers asked the mountaineer when they were finished.

Montgomery shuffled uncomfortably. He hated to take money from this poor, worried-looking teacher, but he sensed that Rogers would be insulted if he refused payment altogether.

"Oh, I reckon three dollars ort ter be 'nough," Montgomery insisted. "I war right proud ter he'p yo'all out. Yo'uns best save yore money ter take keer o' the little feller."

And as Rogers opened his worn wallet, feeling that too great a favor had been done him, but not knowing how to protest, the chairman of the school board added:

"Say, don't 'speck you would objeck ter somebody runnin' in now an' then when yo'alls a larnin' the young'uns, would yo'? Some o' the womenfolks could fix the little feller a bite ter eat an' kinda look atter him when they has some spare time."

This, too. Rogers was almost overwhelmed.

"That would be fine," he said, trying hard to keep his voice even. He looked into the hillman's good-natured, friendly face. "I guess I don't have to tell you that I was worried about his having to be alone all the time." He sighed. "I just can't seem to figure out a way to make a living and be with him, too, as a father should. He's afraid that he's going to die. That's awful for a child his age. Sometimes it almost drives me crazy when he talks about it. You heard him as we came."

Montgomery nodded uneasily and moved toward the door.

"Tom'll git well down here. Don't worry," he said, "an' I shore hopes yo'uns gits along all right an' likes hit on the ridge. Annie left some pies, an' milk, an' a loaf of fresh bread in the wall cupboard, so's ye could git supper easier."

"You've all been so kind. I shall never forget it," Rogers said, forcing the three dollars into Montgomery's reluctant hand.

The man smiled.

"Reckon mebbe we know yo'uns'll he'p us when we'uns needs yo'. Folks a gittin' married an' bein' laid away. Shore hain't right ter lay 'em away 'thout prayin' an' preachin'. Yo'all kin he'p out thataway."

Give Me Thy Vineyard

Give Me Thy Vineyard

Chapter 17

SCHOOL HAD BEEN RUNNING along at Stony Point for a month. The new teacher was well-liked. The children of the district were showing their interest by regular attendance. Tardiness and absentees did not exist. This was a sure sign that things were very interesting in the schoolroom, for the daily attendance of the children on the ridge had been more or less spasmodic. It was a remarkable instance to have all the children at school on the same day. Whether or not the children should go to school was decided by the parents each morning, the decision being governed by the child's willingness, the condition of his wardrobe or the supply of food on hand with which to pack a lunch for his noon meal.

Two Friday afternoons the parents and their friends had gone to the school in response to the clever invitations the children had proudly delivered to every family in Stony Point district.

One of the special afternoons the program included the regular lessons of the school. The next was a spelling bee and ciphering match, after which the mothers served pie and coffee. Unheard-of doin's for Stony Point. Some of the patrons approved heartily, but for the most part they were sure no good would come from a departure from the old ways. Not a few had come to the schoolhouse to register complaints to the teacher about his fool notions of "larnin' young'uns" but when they got there they became so interested in the children's ready response to the teacher's quiet, masterful imparting of knowledge that they forgot their prejudiced grievances.

"Why, I never seen no sich larnin'," one mother exclaimed on the way out of the schoolyard. "Them children didn't throw nary paper wads er stick pens in each other er whisper er act up mean atall like I allers seen 'em do in school."

"No," her companion replied. "That teacher, he jist kep' 'em busy a larnin' somethin' all a time an' they seemed proud ter be a doin' hit!"

For the teacher's part he had plunged with all his energy into the task of orientating himself in his new way of life. He rose at dawn, ate breakfast and made lunch for Tom, cleaned up the cabin and walked the mile and a quarter to school. The school day ended at 4, after which he went twice a week to Big Dave's store for supplies and then home. With as much care as he could he prepared supper, for he wanted Tom to have at least one big and unhurried meal a day. After the dishes were washed he spent the rest of the evening talking and reading aloud to the boy. And finally, when Tom was asleep, he prepared the next day's lessons and went to bed.

As time passed, he began to have regular visits from Cliff Montgomery and his wife, Annie, and Zeke and Ruthie Barnes, who lived about half a mile from the schoolhouse. Cliff and Annie made it a habit to come on Friday and Sunday nights, and both the teacher and his son looked forward to their jolly company.

But for a long while these four people were his only friends. The others on the ridge he could only call acquaintances. Many of them were reticent in his presence, or even pointedly avoided him. Gradually he found out that this was either because of their moonshining activities or because they suspected he might be an agent of the electric company. But nevertheless they sent their children to his school and they came in large numbers to the religious services which he held in the schoolhouse every other Sunday. He knew that his position as teacher and preacher had earned him their respect if not their complete trust. He came to be known to one and all as "Brother Rogers" and realized that his first name would probably never be used even by people his own age because of his standing in the community. He was their preacher. Nor did Grady Rogers resent the appointment.

As time went on he found he was becoming more and more pleased with the religious work he was doing. It satisfied an urge in his soul that had subconsciously sought expression for a long time.

He remembered how, during his boyhood, he had many times played at being preacher and had exhorted from improvised pulpits to all and sundry whom he could gather together for a congregation. His mother had believed he should choose the vocation of a minister and had tried in vain to persuade him.

But his mind had been filled with visions of huge fortunes to be made and he gave no heed to her advice. Now, when he discovered he had ability to speak easily to an audience, swaying his listeners to his way of thinking and sensing the deep satisfaction that arises from the power of such ability, he wondered if his mother had not been right.

Not only have I failed to listen to the words of Mother, but perhaps I've denied the voice of God, he often mused, reflectively. *How different my life might have been. Perhaps even Tommy.* But at this point his musings would become too painful to bear and he would rouse himself to some task that needed doing to take his mind off this great sorrow in his life.

Slowly, but surely, he learned the customs and habits of life on Reed's Ridge. He discovered, among other things, that Dave Gurney, the postmaster and owner of the general store, held a mighty power and influence over the neighbors who came to him for supplies and advice. He had a keen insight into the hearts and minds of men that gave him the ability to judge men well.

Rogers himself, possessing rather accurate knowledge of the behavior of man, learned also through observation and from general conversation at the store that the sheriff and his deputy chief were vain, stupid men who were justly considered with contempt.

The first time he saw Rosie Gurney was late one afternoon when he stopped at Dave's for supplies. She had just come in from carrying the mail and her face was flushed from the exertion of dragging the heavy mail pouch into the post office. She was dressed in her usual costume: plaid shirt, overalls and boots. Wisps of curly black hair blew about her animated face, framing a picture of loveliness and healthy flower-like beauty that caused Grady's pulse to quicken.

Big Dave proudly introduced her as his niece who fetched the mail and she acknowledged his "How do you do" with the customary handshake and "Pleased ter meetcha," accompanied by a smile from smoldering black eyes that met his gaze steadily.

So this was the Rosie Gurney he had been hearing about since coming to the ridge. Whatever had been Grady Roger's esteem of Hiram Jackson, the outlaw, judged solely from hearsay, he felt at this moment that he must have some very fine qualities to merit the loyalty of such a lovely creature.

And Rosie found Grady Rogers interesting, but in a different respect. She knew much more about him than he did about her, for the Ozark grapevine is a busy one; and she wondered, as she had many times before, just what his position was in relation to her and Hiram. Was he indeed a spy for the company, as so many suspected? He looked honest enough, and he really did have a sick little boy. And besides, she heard that he had done wonders with the children in school and that his preaching was very satisfying, even though it was done in an odd, quiet way. Rosie decided to go to meeting. She had kept away long enough because she was afraid of Grady Rogers. But now that she had met him, he did not seem to be at all dangerous. Why wouldn't she take advantage of the opportunity to get some good religious teaching which she had always wanted so much? And besides, wouldn't this give her a chance to get to know Brother Rogers better? Maybe she could find out why he had come to the ridge.

When Rosie entered the schoolhouse the following Sunday a little late because she had not been sure just what time meeting began, people turned around to gape at the newcomer. She found her place amid the other worshippers with the calm self-assurance she seemed always to possess. Her face almost matched the rich pink of the flowers that trimmed her white Sunday dress. Rogers was speaking earnestly and his flow of simple, effective words immediately claimed her full attention.

After meeting was over, Rosie went to shake hands with the speaker. "I liked yore quiet, easy way o' preachin'," she said. "Jist didn't 'pear like yo'uns war a preachin' atall. More like yo'uns war jist a talkin' ter us."

"You must remember, Rosie, I'm not really a preacher," Grady Rogers reminded her pleasantly.

"Yo're jist as good as any we'se ever had," she retorted. "Folks hereabouts shore likes ter come ter hear yo'uns."

"I'm glad for that. I like to feel I can be useful in serving the Lord."

Rosie nodded approvingly and smiled at Rogers. She was impressed with his learning and easy, direct manner. He must be a very fine man, she thought.

Then a man and a woman came to speak to Rogers. They were from the village of Oakridge, eight miles up the ridge, they told him, and they had gotten up at dawn to come to meeting. There was a meeting house in Oakridge, too, they said, which also had not been used for a long time. Wouldn't he be kind enough to preach at Oakridge on the Sundays when he wasn't preaching at Stony Point? He could hold services in the afternoon. That would give him all morning to get there; he certainly could do a lot of good up there, they assured him.

At first Rogers refused. Oakridge was too far away. It would mean that he would have to be away from Tom almost all day. But at this point, Annie Montgomery and several of her friends broke in and offered to take turns staying with Tom on the Sundays his father would go away. Rosie, too, volunteered. But still Rogers was hesitant. After all, he was with the boy so seldom. But the couple from Oakridge saw that the women were on their side and took heart. They told him of the many people around Oakridge who seldom heard the Word of God, and Annie Montgomery declared that if God had given him the gift of preaching, then it was his duty to use this gift. And someone else reminded him that though the offering of the congregation would be small, it would still mean a little extra money for him and his son. Reluctantly he gave in, at last, and agreed that next Sunday he would go to the Oakridge community. Rosie Gurney was elected to come and stay with Tom.

Rogers remembered that he had heard she was in love with the outlaw, Hiram Jackson. What was that story anyway? He'd have to find out. When Annie and Cliff came to visit him Friday night, he asked them to tell him about Rosie Gurney and Hiram. Annie told him everything she knew – how Rosie and Hiram had fallen in love when they were youngsters and had become engaged, and that they would have been married a long time ago if it hadn't been for the murder, the trial, and Hiram's escape to the hills.

"They is still waitin', pore young'uns," she finished, watching him carefully, "to prove that Hiram ain't the guilty one. But hit's four years now, an folks is beginnin' ter wonder iffn they is goin' ter wait forever. Rosie ain't so young no more. Let's see – I reckon she's a goin' on 21."

Give Me Thy Vineyard

"And Hiram," Grady asked, "is he innocent?"

"Wal, things looked mighty bad at the trial," Cliff Montgomery explained. "Everybody knows he's got an ornery temper, an' he'd done a heap o' braggin' 'bout what he'd do afore he'd let 'em take his gran'pappy's land. But I reckon he war innocent enuf, Brother Rogers."

Give Me Thy Vineyard

Give Me Thy Vineyard

Chapter 18

THE TEACHER WAS READY and waiting when Rosie arrived at the cabin on Sunday to care for Tommy. He met her at the door and introduced her to his son. Then, giving the room a final survey to see that everything the two would need for their comfort was provided, he departed.

Rosie and Tommy Rogers took to each other immediately. She loved the boy's shy friendliness and his sweet disposition, even during the times when the terrible cough came and racked his body and turned his face deadly white.

On his part, Tommy thought he had never seen anyone as lovely as Rosie Gurney. He cherished a picture that he had of his mother who was blonde and pale and, his father had often told him, extremely beautiful. But now that he had seen Rosie, Tom thought in his secret heart that even his mother could not possibly compare with her. But he would never tell this to his father, he decided, because it might make him feel bad.

Rosie amused Tommy by reading stories he selected from his books. She laughed heartily at the things that delighted him, and when he tired of stories she sang songs to him in a low, sweet voice. Often the singing lulled his tired little body to sleep and she would move restlessly about the cabin doing odd little bits of dusting and straightening until he awakened.

Usually after a nap, Tommy felt hungry and Rosie would fix a lunch for him. Tommy liked to lie on his pillow and watch her as she moved about the room.

When the meal was ready, she would bring it on a tray to his bed. She always made a plate for herself because she knew Tommy didn't enjoy his food unless she shared it with him.

"You say the blessing, Rosie," Tommy had suggested on their first afternoon together. "Daddy and I take turns, but when we have company, Daddy always lets them say it."

Rosie laughed. "Tommy, I think yo're just lazy," she joked. "But I'll say it if yo'll promise to eat ever'thin' I'se fixed fer yo'uns."

They smiled admiringly at each other and dropped their heads while Rosie breathed a short, fervent prayer. But the note of solemnity was abandoned with the first bite and Rosie used every ruse she could think of to make Tommy eat all of his food.

Rogers usually returned just before dark, and he could tell each time that Tommy was more reluctant to let Rosie go. He talked excitedly of the things they had done during his father's absence and Rosie gave glowing accounts of his good behavior. Actually she had to reprove him severely at times because he jumped about in his bed more than she felt was good for him. She soon discovered that a sure method of winning his cooperation was to threaten not to come back again.

"I'll be good, Rosie, honest I will," he would promise. "Please don't tell Daddy I've been naughty, 'cause he wants me to be quiet and he wouldn't leave me if he knew I had disobeyed him."

"Well, we won't tell him this time," Rosie promised on each occasion, as she smoothed the covers on his bed.

Then quietly the two would sit and watch the evening shadows gather. Oftentimes he would ask her questions about things that went on outside and she would gently answer him.

One evening he said, "Rosie, don't any boys like you? You are so pretty, looks like lots of boys would come to see you."

"Why, yes, Tommy," Rosie replied hesitatingly, "lots o' boys like me, I reckon."

"But doesn't any special one like you awfully well?" Tommy insisted.

Before she realized it, Rosie was telling Tommy of Hiram. The child was so delighted with the spirit of adventure in the story of Hiram's conviction and escape that he failed to note the significance of the situation in Rosie's life.

"Why, Rosie," he exclaimed, "that sounds just like a story out of a book! Does Hiram actually live in a cave all by himself?"

When she assured him that he did, Tommy begged her to tell him what the cave was like. She told him in detail about Hiram's hunted existence, finding a peculiar relief in being able to talk freely of the thing ever uppermost in her mind. She felt no qualms of fear, for what harm could come from relating the well-known story to a sick little boy?

"Rosie," the little fellow inquired brightly, "does Hiram ever leave his cave at all?"

"Yes, honey, he jist cain't stand bein' shut up all the time. He comes out at night sometimes. He knows these woods like most folks knows their back yards, an' he goes out daytimes, too, sometimes to certain places, but he has ter be mighty keerful that nobody sees him."

"Have him come to see me, Rosie. He is a real hero and I never did see a real live hero. Besides, him and me can sympathize with each other."

Tommy regretted his erratic English. He liked to please his father by being very careful about his grammar. But he continued excitedly, "I won't ever tell anybody if he comes here, Rosie. I know Daddy will let him come. I'll ask him. Shall I, Rosie?"

At this request an idea was born in Rosie's mind. Maybe Brother Rogers would let Hiram come to the cabin and maybe she could meet him there.

Grady Rogers had become a very busy man in the

community. When his ministry spread to Oakridge, people from other communities began requesting his help. A call was even extended from the new town of Lake City. His time was taken for every Sunday and a night or two of each week. He scarcely knew where his work as schoolteacher left off and that of minister of the Gospel began.

Rosie became a great help to him. If she had not volunteered to help take care of Tommy, the teacher could not have become the spiritual guide for the entire region. It was commonly agreed among the housewives of the neighborhood for Rosie to look after Tommy each Sunday when his father was away and they took turns staying with him nights during the week. His father conducted a Bible study for the youth on each Wednesday night at the Stony Point school and preached on Friday nights in an adjoining community.

Rosie saw very little of Grady Rogers. He usually left a few minutes after she reached the cabin and gently dismissed her as soon as he returned. But she heard much of his work in the community. She knew he was generous with his small income as well as his time and influence. He had failed to heed the advice of Cliff Montgomery that he save his money to take better care of his sick boy. When he saw a person in need, he often dug down into his own pocket to supply the necessity. Especially was he concerned about children's privations and the people on the ridge were amazed to see him provide this child with glasses or another with shoes or perhaps an elderly someone with medicine. He kept a supply of Bibles and saw to it that every home he contacted had one.

This type of Christianity appealed to Rosie. She was generous and tender herself, and she understood and appreciated Grady Rogers' deep spirituality. She had come to feel that she could trust a man who had such abiding faith in God.

The fear that the teacher might be an employee of the electric company gradually faded from her mind and when Tommy suggested Hiram might visit him in the cabin, she felt she was ready to give Grady Rogers her full confidence. She decided to tell him the whole story of herself and Hiram, which she felt he doubtless had heard many times since coming to the ridge.

When Grady Rogers returned home that evening he found Rosie and her young charge both very much excited. He had scarcely closed the door behind him when Tommy began:

"Oh, Daddy, Rosie has been telling me all about Hiram. Do you know about him, Daddy? It's a wonderful story and he wants to come here. Doesn't he, Rosie?"

He turned to Rosie, who nodded her head slightly, and bending over the bed, gently picked up his thin white hand. Straightening, she met Rogers' gaze with a steady smile. In his eyes she saw a friendly, sympathetic understanding that gave her courage.

Rogers was pleased. It had long distressed him to see the deep unspoken hurt in her eyes. He admired her dauntless courage and he felt that her uncompromising faith that God in His own way would make everything come out right was a challenge of the highest sort.

To his son he said kindly, "Don't you think it would be better if we let Rosie tell me what she wants, Tommy? Of course, if there is anything we can do to help them it will make us very glad."

Rosie began at this invitation and repeated to Grady Rogers the story she had told his son earlier in the evening. Rogers listened intently, smiling and nodding at encouraging intervals. When she had finished, he said:

"Rosie, I feel Hiram would be taking a lot of chances to come here very often, but if he is willing to run the risk, I am sure he is welcome."

Rogers was fully aware that by his consent he was assuming plenty of risk, too, for while he believed in Hiram's innocence, it had never been declared, and until he was exonerated, any shelter given him could be interpreted as harboring a criminal.

"Thanks so much, Brother Rogers," Rosie said gratefully. Yo'uns don't know what this here means ter us. I tole Hiram how yo'all war a good, kind man." She looked wistful. "Hiram an' me, we ain't been in a house tergether fer four years. Yo'uns jist cain't know how much yo'uns've done fer us, Brother Rogers."

Then she walked over to Tom's bed and sat down beside him. Her face was serious. The sensitive child knew that she was going to say something important to him, and he waited anxiously.

"Tommy, I knows yo'all likes me, but I wants ter hear yo'uns say so."

"Of course I do, Rosie, very, very much."

"Then yo'uns wouldn't want anything bad ter happen ter me, would yo'uns?"

"Why, Rosie!" He was hurt that she should even ask him a thing like that and the hurt showed in his face. She felt a pang of remorse, but pressed on.

"Well, then, Tommy, I'se puttin' my life in yore hands. Yo'all heerd what I jist tole yore pa. When Hiram comes ter see me here iffn yo'all says somethin' 'bout hit ter Mrs. Montgomery er some o' the other ladies who comes ter visit yo'uns, the wrong folks might find out 'bout hit, an' then they'll kill Hiram an' maybe me, too."

Tom was stricken with the thought of the awful responsibility she was giving him. Through his feverish imagination passed a picture of Rosie murdered right there in the cabin. His heart began to beat faster.

"Oh, I promise, Rosie, I'll never say a word to anybody."

"Not even Cliff an' Annie Montgomery?"

"Not anybody, Rosie," he repeated solemnly. "Not anybody at all."

Give Me Thy Vineyard

Give Me Thy Vineyard

Give Me Thy Vineyard

Chapter 19

THE HARVEST MOON was shining its brightest on the night of Oct. 17. It was the kind of night for which the young folk had been hoping, for the party at Harrisons'.

Bill Harrison and his wife owned one of the most productive farms on Reed's Ridge. They were a jolly, easygoing couple who had no children of their own. But they loved having young folk about them and usually arranged to have several big parties a year for their entertainment.

This year they had "give it out" for the 17th of October. Rosie Gurney had helped spread the news around as she came and went on her mail route. By the appointed date there was no one on the ridge who had not heard of the affair and had made plans to attend.

As the moon rose to mingle its silvery light with the crisp tang of frost in the air, the youth of Reed's Ridge rode singly, or in pairs, along the wooded trails to the party. The drum-like beat of their horses' hoofs played a rhythmic *clop-cloppety-clop* on the rocky soil. Singing voices, laughter and lusty calls echoed and re-echoed through the hills.

But Rosie and Fred made their way down the long ridge far behind the others. The mail had been very heavy that day. There was medicine to deliver to homes far removed from the regular route and it was already dark when Rosie handed over the mail pouch to Big Dave at the Clear Springs post office.

Yet neither horse nor rider seemed to be pressed for time.

Rosie was not even thinking about the party. Later in the evening she was going to meet Hiram and her mind was occupied with thoughts that were of concern only to them.

Rounding the last curve in the trail, Rosie saw a large bonfire adding a red glow to the moonlight. She skirted the laughing, busy crowd around the fire and tied Fred securely to a tree apart from the other horses.

Dreamily, Rosie walked down the long tree-lined path toward the open door of the cabin, when suddenly a young hillman stepped between her and the light that came from the door and stood blocking her way.

"What 'bout yo' an' me bein' pardners fur the next game, Rosie?" he asked, his thick voice and breath of alcohol hitting her in the face.

She recovered herself.

"No, thank you, Ray," she said archly. "I'se promised ter he'p in the kitchen – an' 'sides, I wouldn't be your pardner even iffn I hadn't o' promised."

"Reckon iffn I war a hidin' out fer killin' a man, yo'd be right proud ter go with me," Ray Harmon snarled without moving. He was very drunk.

"Yo' don't need ter ask why I won't be the pardner with the likes o' yo'uns. An' git out o' my way!"

Rosie tried to push past him, but his fingers dug into her shoulders and he twisted her toward him and kissed her with brute passion on the mouth. She fought to free herself, kicking and pummeling him, but he only drew her closer.

Kiss after kiss was forced on her before the assailant released her.

"Yo' dirty polecat," the girl spat at him. Then, gathering all her strength, she rushed him with a mighty force. The unexpectedness of the impact sent him hurtling over backward across a fallen log.

Before he could rise, a well-directed kick that landed in the pit of his stomach left him writhing in pain, as the girl whirled and ran into the house.

"Why, Rosie, yo're all out o' breath," Mrs. Harrison said as the girl flew wildly into the kitchen.

"Yes. I ran plumb into a polecat in the path."

Rosie couldn't tell Mrs. Harrison what had happened, because she'd tell Bill and then there would be trouble, which would get back to Hiram. The girl tried to make her breathing seem even and natural.

"My goodness, Rosie, I shore cain't smell no polecat on yo'," Mrs. Harrison declared, sniffing.

"Oh, hit warn't the kind that stinks yo'uns all up. I ain't afeard o' them kind. They won't bother yo' none iffn yo'all lets 'em alone, but these here two-legged kind, lettin' alone ain't 'nuff."

"Why, Rosie, who's been botherin' yo'? I'll go tell Bill."

"No, 'twarn't nothin' really." Rosie knew that she had said too much.

"Let me he'p yo', Mis' Harrison." She took a deep breath.

"Wal, yo'uns kin cut the pumpkin pie an' put the pieces on saucers," Mrs. Harrison said, still eyeing her curiously.

When there was no more she could do in the kitchen, Rosie went out again to watch the merrymaking. This time she ran down the thickly lined path as fast as she could go. When she reached the clearing, she noticed Ray Harmon laughing loudly at something his partner had just said. He was apparently enjoying himself. Rosie wished she could have kicked him harder.

"Come on, Rosie," some friends called. "We'se havin' heaps o' fun."

"No, jist think I'll look on ternight," she answered with a forced smile. "I'se tired an' don't feel much like playin'."

She sat down on the edge of a large pile of leaves with two young married couples and watched her friends.

The gay girls in their bright cotton prints and the boys in jeans and chambray shirts made a pretty picture to Rosie as with mixed emotions she sat looking at them.

After a few hours the players began to tire physically for Ozark party games are vigorous, but their spirits were still high and they continued to play, laughing and singing and clapping their hands.

Ten o'clock was the customary hour for refreshments to be served so the guests could get home by midnight. When the clock struck the hour, Mrs. Harrison called her husband, who had divided his time during the evening between livening up the games and sitting along the edge of the porch chatting with some neighbors who had come to spend the evening.

"Bill," she announced, "supper's all ready. Call the young'uns in."

"Hit's all on the table now. Jist go in an' he'p yorse'ves," the host shouted genially.

The merrymakers entered the kitchen single file and each took a piece of pie and a cup of coffee. Then some stood around the kitchen and others went into the next room and sat down, all taking part in the gay banter that went back and forth as they ate. But Rosie was not with the group. None of them knew she had left and no one inquired about her.

She had arranged with Hiram to meet him at the sycamore clump at 10 that night. However, after her encounter with Ray Harmon, she felt restless and uneasy, so when the party seemed to be at its merriest, she quietly eased away into the shadows, mounted Fred and rode out into the moonlight. If she had given any thought to it at all, she would have supposed her disappearance was unnoticed by anyone. Actually, several interested parties saw her go. One was Ray Harmon, whose feelings rankled in reflection that she had so completely whipped him. He probably would have followed her, but he was well aware that at least three other men were watching her as she rode away. Her father lurked in the shadow of the tree where Fred had stood and down the trail not more than a hundred yards apart two friends of

Give Me Thy Vineyard

Hiram saw her go.

John Gurney did not wish to frighten his daughter by constantly reminding her of dangers that might befall her as she rode alone at night, but unknown to her he was very near at hand in case of trouble most of the time. The two young men who guarded her did so for the sake of Hiram.

Rosie was thoughtful as she slowly made her way down the trail. She quite naturally wanted to tell her lover of the insult she had suffered from Ray Harmon. She debated it in her mind and decided not to tell him for she feared if he knew he would lose his temper and probably would track Harmon down and deliver the beating he so well deserved at too great risk of his own personal safety.

Because of her impatience, Rosie reached the sycamore clump a good while before Hiram appeared. When she got to the appointed place she looked carefully around, then gave a whistle of three clear notes. There was no answer and she felt worried. She waited silently for a few minutes and repeated the call, only perhaps a little lower than before. Again no answer and her fears increased.

Presently Fred, impatient at the turn of affairs (for Rosie always gave him an apple or a carrot when she slipped from the saddle to greet Hiram), gave a loud whinny that startled the night birds who flew away in protest.

Just then Rosie heard a movement from nearby bushes and heard Hiram whisper, "Is that yo'uns, Rosie? I heerd yore whistle but it sounded so husky-like I war afeared it war somebody else. Then I heerd Fred whinny an' I knowed it war yo'uns."

By this time Rosie, badly shaken by her fear for Hiram's safety and her own unpleasant experience earlier in the evening, had alighted from the saddle and sought the comfort of Hiram's arms.

"Oh, Rosie girl, hit's so good ter have yo'all come," he said as he held her close. "Sometimes I worries 'bout yo' a comin' out here nights alone ter see me. Hit's a heap o' comfort ter me, honey, but I'd never fergive myse'f iffn anythin' ever happened ter yo'uns."

"Hush, Hiram," she replied, not unkindly. "I'se not afeared o' nothin' so long as I'se on Fred. I'd shore feel sorry fer the skonk what'd try ter bother me long's I'm a ridin' him." She laughed, although she trembled as she spoke and Hiram noticed it.

"Reckon yore right," he agreed, relaxing as he spoke. "But yore a tremblin', gal. What's the matter? Did yo' git skeered?"

"Not fer myse'f," she answered softly, "only fer yo'uns, Hiram. Somehow I feels oneasy 'bout yo'all ternight. I don't like ter say hit, but I don't think I best meet yer like this agin fer awhile."

Hiram stiffened. "What's the matter, Rosie? Has somethin' happened?" he asked in a tight voice.

"No, Hiram, nothin' happened, but they's jist too much danger fer both o' us fer me ter be a ridin' up here ter meetcha nights like this. Now, honey, I'se got a good idear for us an' I wants yo'all ter listen quiet whiles I tells yo' 'bout hit."

Hiram sat down and drew her close beside him while she told him of her plan to meet him at Grady Rogers' cabin. Before she was half finished, Hiram began to squirm and shake his head. Rosie looked into his moonlit face and pleaded with him. It had not been hard for Rosie to get Grady Rogers' consent to allow Hiram to visit her in his cabin, but she knew she would have real difficulty in persuading Hiram that he would be safe there.

"I tells yo', Brother Rogers is a good, kind man, Hiram," she repeated. "Nobody ever has done as much good fer folks as he has since he come here. An' a body jist cain't talk ter him 'thout a knowin' he b'lieves in God an' is a tryin' his best ter serve Him. Cliff Montgomery an' Uncle Dave an' my paw says a feller kin trust him. An' I jist know yo'd trust him, too, if yo'uns ever'd get ter know him."

"Yeh, Dave tole me down ter the store t'other night that he b'lieved he war all right. But somehow I jist cain't make up my mind ter take the chanct. Not that I don't like the idear o' seein' yo'uns in a house agin. That'd shore be plumb nice. But–" He lapsed into deep thought. Rosie, too, was silent.

Suddenly Hiram lifted his voice and asked, "Say, what do Tobe think o' this here feller?"

"I jist don't know, honey," Rosie answered honestly. "Sarah an' most o' the young'uns comes ter meetin'. But Tobe an' Steve hain't never been nigh as fer as I knows. Sarah is quite took with his preachin'."

"I'll tell yo', Rosie," Hiram promised, "I'll talk this thing over with Tobe. Iffn he thinks hit air safe fer me ter go down there, then I'll do hit."

Rosie was so glad of this agreement that she forgot to feel hurt that Hiram considered Tobe Alton's judgment better than her own. She heartily disliked Tobe but could scarcely say why. He always seemed to have a hangdog, guilty look about him, but Rosie didn't know of any wrong he'd ever done except get disgustingly drunk and make moonshine liquor. And Hiram trusted him, so she held her peace.

"When'll yo'all be a seein' Tobe?" she asked.

"I knows where his still is," Hiram whispered. "I goes there an' talks ter him an' Steve sometimes. But I hain't never told nary one o' them where my cave is. Yo're the only one what knows that. Dave hisse'f don't even know."

"I guess I'll see Tobe afore long," he said, getting back to the subject. "Yo'all meet me here a week from terday an' I'll let yer know."

Rosie told him goodbye and rode away. She had to be content with this unsatisfactory arrangement. As least she felt she was making some progress. But, oh, how long were things going to be like this? Would the Harmons ever confess their guilt so that Hiram could come down and they could be married? What of the future? What if they never could prove Hiram was innocent? Would they grow to be an old man and an old woman never knowing anything of life or love except the hunted, anxious existence they now knew?

Hiram returned to his cave that night weary and discouraged. He didn't think he could stand this kind of living much longer. He wondered if it wouldn't be better to give himself up and look to the court for mercy. Maybe it would be easier for Rosie if he did go to the pen. It wasn't right to ask her to wait forever. If he went away where she couldn't see him, perhaps she would quit thinking about him after a while and would love someone else.

When he reached his hideout he felt hungry, so he set about to prepare some supper. But he could scarcely eat for the hard, tight knot that grew in his chest and rose to his throat to choke him as he tried to swallow.

Bullet shared his gloom but ate more heartily of his supper than Hiram did. They both were restless. Finally Hiram took his fiddle down from the rock-ledge shelf. He tuned it carefully and sat down facing the blazing fire, with his back against the cave wall. He drew his bow across the strings that produced harsh, angry tones in uneven tempo. He fitted the music to his mood and the instrument sang in loud, wailing strains of rebellion and fierce anger and unhappy discord. Hiram remembered his lot as a fugitive, hunted by his own kind. Bullet howled sympathetically.

Then Hiram thought of Rosie and the voice of the violin softened. The music gradually became a sweet, slow melody that sang of love and faith and happiness. Pulling the bow against the strings again, he improvised a combination of a lullaby and the sounds of a crying child.

Soothed as usual by the music he played, Hiram became once again rational in his thinking and judgment. He thought of the great outdoors that he and Rosie both loved so much and knew so well, and he knew neither of them would know any happiness with him in prison.

Drawing the bow softly across the strings, he imitated birdcalls. The trilling, liquid octaves of the mockingbird, the plaintive wail of the whippoorwill, the soft mourning sound of the dove, harmonizing with the singing of water rushing over a steep, rocky bed, sounded as real as life.

"This here one is fer yo'uns," he said to Bullet, who sat up and listened expectantly. He played the wild, exciting strains of music imitating the baying of hounds following the hot scent of a closely pursued fox. Bullet was an appreciative audience. He made his way to his master's side and nuzzled his nose against him, as though he knew his and Hiram's lives were symbolized in the fleeing fox, barely escaping the pursuit of the aggressive pack of determined hounds.

Hiram put his fiddle away, rolled into his bed and slept peacefully. The next day he visited Tobe and Steve at their place of business. He told them how Rosie wanted him to meet her at Grady Rogers' cabin when she was there with Tommy. He asked them what they thought.

Tobe gave considerable thought to the question before he answered. It always amused his friends the way he pulled his ear when he was engaged in deep thinking. Finally he said:

"Hiram, me an' Charlie has been a watchin' that air Brother Rogers ever since he come ter these here parts. Lots o' times I finds him standin' 'lone on a ridge er a cliff a thinkin' an' a prayin'. An' he shore does mind his own business. He hain't ever asked nobody 'bout any stills er 'bout where yo'uns might be a hidin'. He shore does a sight o' good fer folks, too. Sary an' the young'uns goes ter meetin' an' Sary's plumb tuck with him. I shore b'lieves he's all right, too. I 'lows ter go ter meetin' myse'f some o' these days."

"No, sir, Hiram," he continued, "iffn he tole Rosie he'd like ter he'p yo'uns, I'd say he means hit."

"An' 'nother thing: them fellers er the shuriff'd never think 'bout yo'all a bein' there. An' his cabin is a settin' where it'd be right hard ter slip up on yo'uns 'specially if yo'all set Bullet ter watch."

"Yes, Hiram," he concluded, "I'd say hit would be plumb safe."

Give Me Thy Vineyard

Give Me Thy Vineyard

Give Me Thy Vineyard

Chapter 20

*E*VEN THOUGH HIRAM had been persuaded by Rosie and Tobe Alton both that it was safe for him to go to Grady Rogers' cabin, he still felt worried and uneasy. It was plain dangerous. But it was also dangerous for them to meet out on the mail route as they had been doing, so he supposed one risk was really no greater than another.

He knew he could move about on the mountain most of the time in comparative safety for the folk who lived there were his loyal friends. Plenty of them might have believed him to be guilty, but even so they would protect him because they all felt it was a justifiable killing. But the Harmons were a constant danger. Hiram knew they had been afraid of him since their testimony at the trial and that their fear made them more threatening than ever. They would do anything they could to get him out of the way.

Of course, the really safe thing to do was to stay near his hideout. There was scarcely a chance that anyone would ever find him there. But he had promised Rosie he would meet her at the Rogers cabin. And anyway, he'd just as soon be dead as to imprison himself in a cave where he could never see or talk to anyone but Bullet.

On Saturday evening before he was to visit Rosie on Sunday, he went as usual to Big Dave's store. But he did not return that night to his cave. Instead he made his way through the heavily forested woods to a place he knew about

300 yards back of the Rogers cabin. There on a rocky ledge that ran far back under a great bluff he made a bed of leaves and slept through the night with the faithful Bullet keeping watch.

The next morning they ate some bread and cheese which he had carried from Big Dave's store for breakfast and waited until it was time for his visit with Rosie. The hours sped by quickly for man and dog, for they had grown accustomed to sitting in the woods waiting for time to pass away.

Shortly before noon they began to move cautiously toward the house. The man found a great tree with a crotched fork and climbed quickly into it. There he remained securely hidden by the limbs of heavy green foliage. From this place of safety he could see the small cabin and the bit of clearing around it. He waited there until he heard Rosie and Fred coming up the mountain trail from the direction of the schoolhouse. Bullet bristled and Hiram climbed down hastily to silence him. "Hit's all right, Bullet," he said quietly, "hit's jist Rosie and Fred. Don't worry none." Grady had gone directly to his appointment.

As horse and rider came into sight on the narrow path, Bullet recognized them and relaxed. Hiram moved to the edge of the clearing. Rosie guided her horse to a nearby tree and tied him. Then she stood still and listened before whistling three low familiar notes. Hiram came out of hiding and ran to her.

"Go on inter the cabin an' see iffn ever'thin's all right," he ordered.

"Oh, ever'thin's all right," she said, "but I'll go see."

Hiram hadn't been in a house since he left Charlie Raiford's cabin the night of his escape from the jail. Now when Rosie stood in the door and motioned for him to come he almost collapsed with fear and dread. What was the matter with him? He was weak in the knees and his legs felt no heavier than corks. He slowly edged forward and followed the girl inside. She quickly closed the door behind him and he felt trapped. He wasn't sure he even trusted Rosie here.

Hiram looked and felt out of place. Rosie, too, was self-conscious and couldn't think of anything to say. Poor little Tommy was overcome with excitement and bewilderment. He was a little frightened, too. He had tried to picture in his mind how Hiram would look, but was wholly unprepared for what he saw in this man who towered above them all, large, awkward and ill at ease.

But the child was the first to recover his composure. "I'm Tommy," he announced from his bed. "Has Rosie told you about me? She's told me lots about you."

Hiram smiled in spite of himself and sat down.

"She shore has tole me lots 'bout yo'all, Tommy. An' I'se right proud ter meetcha."

"I'll bet you are hungry and I know I am," Tommy said. "Rosie, are you going to fix us something to eat?"

Rosie laughed. Everyone seemed more at ease now. Maybe Hiram would get interested in Tommy's bright conversation and would forget to be so stiff.

"Why, shore, Tommy, I'se a goin' ter fix yo'uns up somethin' ter eat," she answered. "Yo'all jist go ahead an' talk ter Hiram whilst I gits hit ready."

But conversation came hard. Neither the man nor the boy could think of anything to say. They eyed each other curiously and each had pity in his heart for the other. Hiram thought how much more he had than this little fellow who was sick all of the time and Tommy felt sorry for Hiram because he didn't know the security of a home and love and companionship.

Finally, Tommy thought of Bullet and asked Hiram about him.

"He's jist outside, Tommy," Hiram explained. "Jist don't know what I'd do 'thout him. He's all the comp'ny I has most o' the time an' I'se teached him lots o' things. Mostly how ter be mean an' fight. He don't trust nobody lessen he knows I trusts 'em. I reckon I wouldn't feel safe no place atall iffn hit warn't fer Bullet."

Hiram was feeling easier. He remembered about his hat and removed it. He sat nervously twirling it in his hands when Rosie said dinner was ready.

She brought Tommy's meal to him at the bed and fixed him so he could eat comfortably. She and Hiram sat at the table where he buried his head in his plate and wolfed down his food without looking up.

"Is the food good, Hiram?" Rosie finally asked anxiously.

"Hit shore is, Rosie. Ever'thin's good. I'se shore glad ter be here. Only I cain't he'p feelin' strange an' jumpy."

"Yo'll git over hit, honey. Hit's been so long since yo've been in a house. I feels kinda funny, too."

She took Tommy's tray and set it on the table. Then the three of them visited. It was Tommy's custom on the afternoons when he and Rosie sat alone to read stories aloud from his books. The reader and listener alike derived much pleasure from this diversion.

But today Tommy wondered if he should suggest reading aloud. Perhaps Rosie would rather talk with Hiram. But there were long, awkward periods of silence when none of them seemed able to think of anything to say. Tommy supposed he was in the way and felt miserable.

Rosie, too, was unhappy when conversation faded into an uncomfortable state of paralysis. But Hiram seemed not to notice. He was darkly moody and entered into the conversation only when forced by direct questioning.

Finally, Rosie asked Tommy if he wouldn't like to read. She didn't have much interest in any story at the moment except the tragic one that complicated her own life, but perhaps it would help lift Hiram out of such a state of dejection.

The little boy needed no second bidding. He eagerly picked up his book of Bible stories from a bedside shelf and read successively several selections in his very best style. Soon Hiram raised his head and gave attention. His face grew animated with pleasure and he seemed to forget his surroundings as he listened. Nothing could have given Rosie and Tommy greater pleasure and the quick, stolen glances they had for each other were pregnant with mutual understanding and appreciation that they at last had made their visitor comfortable and happy. But the little boy with the quick mind and weak body grew weary and his thin little voice trailed off into nothingness. Rosie and Hiram watched him fall into a peaceful slumber and were glad at last to be alone.

Grady Rogers made a hasty trip to Oakridge that afternoon. He cut the services as short as he could and broke away as soon as the session came to a close without the usual hour of handshaking and chatting with the worshippers who gathered there. He suffered an uneasiness knowing that the outlaw was visiting his cabin during his absence. What had made him promise Rosie she could use his home for a tryst with Hiram? His agreement to the plan had been an impetuous one and he had wished many times since that he hadn't been so impulsive, but he lacked the courage to say so to Rosie. He had no desire to encounter the scorn she would hold for his timidity and apprehensions. He had declared himself to be her friend and being a friend to Rosie meant doing anything necessary to help that person in time of great need. There was no place in her heart for fears or trepidations. Rosie was just that kind of woman.

Rogers drew a deep sigh as he walked along thinking about her and Hiram and he hoped fervently that nothing would happen to cause him to regret having lent his help.

He wished he knew if Hiram were guilty or not. If he could establish conclusive evidence that Hiram was guilty maybe things would change. If it could be proved to Rosie and the people on Reed's Ridge that Hiram, and not the Harmons, was really guilty, then perhaps the fugitive would give himself up and Rosie would turn her attention to someone else.

Grady had been busy trying to find out all he could. Only yesterday he had made a trip to Hartstown with Cliff Montgomery. While in the county seat he called at the printing office of the county paper and asked if he might look through the files to review the news accounts of Hiram Jackson's trial and conviction.

Jim Logan was the editor of the paper. He was also the county representative in the state legislature and had been for many years. He received the teacher cordially.

"I've heard all about you, Mr. Rogers," he said when Rogers introduced himself. "You're doin' a heap of good for the people on Reed's Ridge."

"Thanks, Mr. Logan, but I didn't come here to talk about myself, sir. I came to talk about Hiram Jackson. I'd like very much to know if he is guilty or not. I'd like to know why my neighbors, who seem to be good law-abiding citizens, protect him."

The old editor sat silently looking out of the dusty window. Grady waited with patience. At last he turned and said, "Hiram Jackson is innocent, Brother Rogers. I feel sure of that. All of the evidence against him at the trial was circumstantial. If it had been appealed, Hiram no doubt would have come clear. But he didn't have the money or a good attorney to help him fight.

"The men back of the electric company that built the dam were a lot of greedy men. Their means and methods were foul. Several of their top men were indicted and tried and convicted of fraud. They are serving time in the state penitentiary right now.

"Right from the first they did the people wrong. Before they started clearing out the valley where the lake now is, they hired all of the local lawyers whom they never used. With no lawyers to represent them the people couldn't fight against the prices the appraisers set on their farms. They just had to take what they could get."

"I heard about that," Grady stated.

"Of course, the court appointed some of the appraisers, but lots of them were bribed by the company. Some of them were proved guilty in court.

"The worst thing they did was the spending of money to elect legislators who would lobby for laws to favor the company. I was in the legislature then and saw a lot that was going on. There was a story that was going the rounds about the lobbyists blackmailing a preacher representative. He was invited to their rooms and when he sat in a chair a beautiful young blonde threw herself in his lap while a photographer snapped a picture of the pre-arranged act. He was told, so the story goes, that he could vote for the utility rate legislation as he was directed or the picture with a compromising story would be released to the newspapers."

"Incredible!" murmured the shocked visitor. "Was anything ever done about it?"

"No. It's almost impossible to prove any such things. A reporter for one of the St. Louis papers told me the whole rotten deal. But the preacher dropped out and never did run for office again.

"It's the way the United Electric Company crooked them that makes the folks on the ridge protect Jackson, Brother Rogers. I know that boy is a wood's colt but he comes from good stock. The folks down there figure that no matter what he's done he hain't no worse than the power company.

"I heard Hiram's trial. All that stuck him was what the Harmon boys testified. Of course, you know by now their reputation is none too good. If I had been on that jury, I couldn't have found Hiram guilty."

He stood up and reached for his hat. "You're welcome to look through the files, Brother Rogers. I don't think you'll find anything about the case you haven't heard, though. The clerk in the next room will get you the papers you want."

Grady Rogers spent the next hour reading the 5-year-old papers. He found the editor was right. The reported accounts were identical with the stories about the trial that he had been hearing on the ridge ever since his arrival there.

By the time the teacher had reviewed all of these things through his mind, he had left the main road and was on the narrow trail that led to his cabin. The closer he got to his home, the more anxious he became, and walked faster. Rounding the last bend in the trail that was really no more than a path, he heard the deep, low growl of a dog. Bullet. Hiram was there. How would he get into the house past that savage beast? He moved forward cautiously.

But Hiram, too, had heard Bullet's warning. He jumped up and made for the door through which he had entered the cabin, but Rosie was before him and blocked his approach. "That way, Hiram," she directed, pointing to a door that opened on the back side of the cabin and gave entrance to the shelter of the thick woods not three feet away. "Hit's shore ter be Brother Rogers," she said. "Yo'uns call off Bullet an' stay out o' sight till I calls yo' ter come back in here."

Hiram opened the door and stepped out into the gathering shadows as he called Bullet to him. The two of them retreated into the woods.

Rosie opened the front door and went to meet Grady Rogers. "Hiram's here," she said. "Did yo'uns hear Bullet?"

"I heard him and was afraid to move," he said. "Where is he now?"

"Oh, Hiram's got him outside. Let's go in an' I'll light the lamp an' call him in."

Rosie was afraid if she didn't get to Hiram soon that he and Bullet would be out of calling distance. She knew Hiram dreaded meeting Grady Rogers. The few preachers he had encountered in his lifetime had always upbraided him for his godlessness, and he supposed Rogers would, too. It was bad enough to have Rosie scolding him so much and he felt if Rogers started in on him, he'd have to teach him to mind his own business.

Rosie was right. Hiram and Bullet would have been gone if they'd had half a chance. But they had hardly reached their place of safety when the back door of the cabin opened, casting forth a beam of light from the kerosene lamp which Rosie held in her hand, and she called to him to return to the cabin.

Hiram went because there was nothing else for him to do. Rosie introduced the two men. Rogers acknowledged the introduction and extended his hand. Hiram looked at the teacher steadily for a few seconds and slowly responded to the handshake. All of the assurances that he had had from Rosie and Tobe Alton and Dave fled from his memory. He felt trapped and afraid. Why had he let himself be persuaded to come here? He didn't trust this "furriner" and made no effort to conceal the fact.

Grady Rogers was disappointed and angry. What kind of yokel was this that would accept a man's hospitality and repay him with such insolence? And what could a girl like Rosie see in the brute in the first place?

Rosie looked on, helpless and hurt. She couldn't understand Hiram, but she knew he was acting ridiculous. She wished she had never asked him to come here. And she wished with all her heart that he would behave like a gentleman.

No telling what might have happened if Tommy hadn't taken a hand. The commotion of opening and closing doors had awakened him and he saw all that was going on.

Finally he spoke from his bed. "Hiram, I thought we were going to be good friends and that you could come here whenever you wanted to and see Rosie and me. But I guess you don't like my dad and if you don't like Daddy, I don't want you to like me either."

Hiram dropped his head. "I'se powerful sorry, Tommy," he

said. He started for the door, but Grady Rogers stopped him.

"Wait a minute, Hiram," he said. "You have behaved like a fool, but I believe you really are sorry. I want you to know that I had no motive in permitting you to come here except to help. Perhaps you don't know it, but by allowing you to come into my home I am taking as much risk as you are because the law could say I was aiding a criminal."

"I never thought o' that, Brother Rogers," Hiram said humbly.

"If I didn't have a strong conviction that you are an innocent and wronged man, I wouldn't do it, Hiram. But at that I can't help you if you don't trust me."

"I don't trust nobody," Hiram responded doggedly.

"Oh, yes, yo' does, Hiram," Rosie argued. "Yo'uns trusts Uncle Dave an' Tobe Alton."

"Ever'body trusts Dave," Hiram answered, "an' Tobe's my friend."

"I'm your friend, too, Hiram," Rogers declared. "I brought Tommy here from another part of the country to help him get well. Since I've come, God has seen fit to use me in His own way and I am humbly doing my best to serve Him. I try to justify every man's actions from his own point of view and I believe I understand why you feel toward me as you do. And I don't know that I blame you. If I were in your place I'd probably feel as you do."

For one of the few times in his life, Hiram knew shame and remorse. This teacher was kind and generous as Rosie said. He wasn't the kind of fellow you guessed about. You just knew from the way he talked that he was honest and fair. No wonder people on the ridge set such store by him.

"Brother Rogers, I'se plumb sorry," Rosie heard him saying. This was the second time he had apologized in the past few minutes and she knew it was hard for him. "Yo'uns has been powerful good ter Rosie an' me ter let me come here like this. I never done that killin', Brother Rogers, but I'se had ter pay. An' hits 'furriners' what made me pay."

"How 'bout them Harmons, Hiram? They hain't 'furriners,'" Rosie interposed.

Hiram scowled. "What yo'all mean, Rosie?"

"What Rosie means, Hiram," Rogers was quick to explain, "is that some of the folk who live here in this isolated mountain country where you have grown up are honest and fine, and some aren't. The same is true of the people that you call 'furriners.' That is a lesson you mountaineers need to learn."

"Wal, I'll pick yo' fer an' honest one, Brother Rogers," Hiram said genially. "An' now me an' Bullet's got ter go."

"Goodbye, Hiram," Tommy called from his bed. "Be sure to come to see us again."

"I shore will, Tommy. An' I'se shore much 'bliged ter yo'uns fer that air man-talk yo'all give me. I shore had hit a comin' ter me."

Give Me Thy Vineyard

Give Me Thy Vineyard

Chapter 21

*H*IRAM APPARENTLY was fully convinced that Grady Rogers was a man to be trusted for he came to the cabin again and again. And upon each visit he was much less shy. He had liked the sick boy from the first and spent much time between visits thinking about him. He thought he had never seen such a strange and wonderful child.

Tommy was just as much taken with Hiram. He didn't even try to conceal his admiration for this big, powerful man who could tell him such amazing things about the animals and birds who lived in the woods outside.

They soon became fast friends, laughing and talking in such mutual enjoyment that Rosie felt twinges of jealousy that Tommy got so much of Hiram's admiration.

But she didn't complain because, after all, this was the most satisfactory arrangement she and Hiram had ever had for seeing each other. It would have been nice if she could have had Hiram all to herself, but one just never could have everything. She was grateful just to be near Hiram, to hear his voice, to know he was all right.

She was especially glad to see Hiram able to relax and seem to enjoy himself. Tommy got the credit for this. His bright chatter amused Hiram who enjoyed answering the little fellow's questions about the "woods critters." Usually after Rosie finished washing the luncheon dishes and sat with the two of them, Tommy would read to them until he fell asleep. Then Hiram and Rosie would visit until Grady Rogers came back.

But Hiram was slow in growing used to Rogers. He lapsed into a sullen silence in the teacher's presence, an attitude which puzzled and hurt Rosie. But Rogers seemed to understand Hiram's reticence and paid little heed to it. He behaved quite normally for a man with his background and bitter experience and the teacher felt in time he could win this young man's confidence.

In the meantime he treated Hiram politely and tried to be friendly with him. There wasn't much the two men had to talk about. Rosie told Hiram all of the interesting happenings on the ridge and Tommy gave him the opportunity to tell what he could of his life in the woods, so about all the teacher could do was to evince a friendly interest in him generally and make him feel welcome in his visits to the cabin.

On one of Hiram's Sunday afternoon visits he told Tommy all about his fiddle and the child was delighted.

"Bring it down and play for me, Hiram," he begged. "I don't ever get to hear any music."

"I'll do hit, Tommy," Hiram promised impetuously. "I'll play fer yo'uns the next time I come. That is, iffn yo'll do somethin' fer me."

Tommy was thoughtful. What could he do for this grown-up man?

"You know I'll do anything I can for you, Hiram," he said quietly. "What do you want?"

He looked quizzically at Hiram and saw that he was embarrassed. Hiram gazed hard at Tommy for a minute and then blurted out: "Tom, I'd shore be right proud iffn yo'all could larn me ter read them air books likes yo'uns does. Will yo' do hit next time I comes?"

The boy laughed outright. "You should say teach, Hiram, not learn. I guess I'll have to give you some lessons in grammar, too. You see, it's this way. I'll be the teacher and I'll teach you to read. You'll be the pupil and you'll learn. See?"

Hiram didn't see but he grinned at the little boy and nodded his head. "How 'bout me a larnin' ter read?" he repeated.

"Oh, I'll teach you, Hiram. Next time you come. It will be fun. I'll be my dad and you can be one of his pupils."

Rosie moved over to Tommy's bed and drew the covers up about him. "Tommy, yo'uns had better rest now an' go ter sleep," she admonished. "Yo' know yore paw won't like hit iffn yo'all gits too tired."

After Tommy was sound asleep, Rosie told Hiram she didn't think he should have promised to play for Tommy. "Hit's too dangerous, Hiram. Promise me yo' won't do hit."

"No, I'se made my promise ter Tommy," Hiram said obdurately, "an' I'se a goin' ter keep hit. Yer know, Rosie, that little feller hain't got long ter live. He looks paler ever' time I comes."

"Wal, be right keerful, Hiram. I'se a goin' ter be worried 'bout this."

And so Tommy was delighted as well as surprised to have Hiram open the door and walk in shortly after noon on the following Friday.

"Why, Hiram," he cried, "I didn't expect you until Rosie came again."

"I got lonesome so I thought I'd fetch the fiddle an' play some fer yo'uns," Hiram explained.

"Oh, I'm glad. You play a while and then you can learn your reading."

For more than an hour the young hillman delighted the child with his lively tunes. Tommy thought the imitations of the birdcalls and fox chase were the best.

"I liked your music very much," he said at last, "but I guess we'd better have your reading lesson now."

"All right," Hiram agreed, laying his instrument aside. "What does I do?"

"Sit over here by me where you can see," Tommy instructed. "We'll start with *Black Beauty*. It's easy and I have already read part of it to you."

Hiram sat awkwardly in a chair by the side of the bed, pushing his big body as near as he could to that of the sick child propped up in bed.

"Now I'll read a page and show you how to pronounce the hard words. Then you see if you can read by yourself."

His pupil listened attentively. Then he took the book and read aloud. The words were laboriously droned out in a faltering, hesitating monotone. The pupil knew he was doing miserably and he was much embarrassed.

"Wait a minute, Hiram," Tom interrupted as the man tripped on the word "wonderful." "Let me read it to you again. Daddy makes me read like I was talking to someone. It sounds better."

Hiram listened carefully while his instructor read the selection over. Then he grasped the book in his own hands and read it again and again. Each time he finished, Tommy complimented him on his improvement and they were both happy.

The teacher and pupil were so engrossed with what they were doing that they forgot about the passing of time. Once Tommy interrupted the progress of instruction to ask Hiram about Rosie.

"Hiram," he said suddenly at a time when that individual was struggling with a difficult word, "Rosie says you and her are in love."

Tommy knew he was using the pronoun incorrectly, but he thought it was the best usage to employ when talking with this backwoodsman. The outlaw looked keenly at the little boy on the bed, but he was pleased. He liked to talk about Rosie and so seldom got a chance.

"We'uns shore air, Tommy," he smiled.

"And – well – you like having the one you're in love with

around you all the time, don't you?"

Hiram nodded.

The boy looked at him earnestly. "Do I have to wait until I grow up before I can fall in love?"

"Nope. Sometimes young'uns falls in love when they is real young-like, an' they jist grows up a lovin' each other," Hiram answered seriously.

Tommy became lost in thought. He wanted to ask a lot more questions but he didn't dare. Maybe Hiram wouldn't like it. He'd have to ask his father.

"Do you wish to read some more, Hiram?" he said at last. "Let's try another page now."

His pupil assented readily and time marched on. Then their afternoon of happy companionship came suddenly to an end when they heard Bullet's low growl. Hiram quickly pushed his fiddle under the bed and ducked out the back door and into the woods with Bullet.

Soon he saw Grady Rogers come into the clearing. But he wasn't alone. Cliff Montgomery's boys were with him. Hiram supposed they had come to visit with Tommy and he knew he couldn't go back to the cabin for his fiddle. He was glad he had hidden it, and now he hoped Tommy wouldn't say anything about his having been there. He and Bullet went back farther into the woods to wait for the darkness.

When Grady Rogers went into his cabin he noticed Tommy was almost feverish with excitement. He gave breathless answers to questions and seemed scarcely to notice the Montgomery boys. He fidgeted restlessly in his bed and kept glancing out of the window. His father was sure something unusual had been going on and he had better get to the bottom of it, so he asked the two boys to please go to the spring and get him a bucket of water. The spring was several hundred yards down over the cliff in front of the cabin.

The boys went willingly, accepting half a dozen cookies each to munch on the way. No sooner were they clear of the house than Tommy burst out, "Oh, Daddy, I didn't know how I was going to tell you, but Hiram's been here. He brought his fiddle and played for me. It's under the bed."

"Where is Hiram now, son?" Grady asked.

"He's in the woods with Bullet, Daddy. Didn't you hear him bark? Bullet, I mean."

"No, I didn't hear him, Tommy. I had no idea Hiram was here. But you were so excited I knew something had happened."

"The boys will soon be back now and you must try to be quiet or they'll guess your secret," the father continued.

"But what about Hiram, Daddy? And his fiddle? He won't want to leave his fiddle here."

"Hiram is safely hidden in the woods, Tommy, and he is smart enough to stay there. We'll keep his fiddle safely concealed under the bed. Hiram can get it the next time he comes. Now please try to be quiet."

Grady hoped he sounded calmer than he felt. Hiram was taking a lot of chances coming to his cabin so often. This was Friday evening and the Montgomerys were going to sit with Tommy while the teacher went to the New Branch school to preach. The boys had come home with him for supper and their parents would be along later. There would be no chance for Hiram to come back to the cabin for his fiddle this evening. The house would be filled with the Montgomery family until nearly midnight.

When the boys returned from the spring, Grady Rogers was busily preparing supper. His son had grown quite calm and talked animatedly with his visitors about happenings at school.

Apparently Hiram was forgotten but Rogers knew that Tommy's mind, like his own, was filled with thoughts of their friend who was hiding in their woods. The father was deeply touched by Hiram's act of bringing his fiddle to the cabin to play for Tommy. He couldn't figure this man out, perhaps a criminal even, who would risk so much to bring an hour of pleasure to one little sick child. His own Tommy. There surely must be much good in the man to have such a big, soft spot in his heart.

Give Me Thy Vineyard

Give Me Thy Vineyard

Chapter 22

G RADY ROGERS had heard much about the preparations that were being made for the annual shooting match that was to be held at Clear Springs. In accordance with a custom of long standing the hour was set for 2 o'clock the afternoon before Thanksgiving Day. The teacher decided he would like to watch the shooting, so he obtained permission from his school board to dismiss the pupils at noon.

As soon as the last child was gone from the schoolroom, he fastened the door and hurried home to fix a lunch for himself and Tommy.

The day had begun with a cold, misty rain, never abundant enough to drip, but keeping the air hanging heavy with moisture. However, long before noon the sun made its persistent way through the clouds and as Grady Rogers walked hurriedly along his narrow path through the woods its rays shone warm and comfortable upon him. It would be a fine afternoon for the turkey shoot and he looked forward to it with eagerness.

He hadn't meant to go but Rosie had persuaded him.

"They'll be some powerful good shootin' goin' on, Brother Rogers," she told him. "An' I shore hopes some o' the folks hereabouts beats them fellers, but I'se afeered they won't. Them fellers is hired ter watch the dam an' they mostly does nuthin' only sleep an' eat an' practice shootin'. They shore ort ter be good. They's been a makin' their brags 'bout how they's a goin' ter show us hillbillies up, ter this here shootin' match. I reckon Pa shore will take hit hard if they beats him, 'cause he's won ever' shootin' match as fur back as I kin 'member."

But now as the teacher was hurriedly putting a lunch on the table, he told Tommy he thought he would do better to stay at home.

"Oh, no, Daddy," Tommy objected, "I want you to go. Then you can tell me all about it when you get back."

So two hours later, Rogers walked into Big Dave's store and found it well-filled with people. Most of the men were holding long-barreled, muzzleloading rifles that were almost as tall as their owners. They were all watching Big Dave as he cut strips of white paper into 2-inch squares. Placing a penny in the center of each square, he drew a circle around it with a lead pencil. Then he turned a small uncorked bottle of ink upside down and stamped the inside of the circle with the black ink that clung to the cork. Those were the targets for the match.

In a corner apart from the rest of the group were four young men in blue uniforms. These were guards of the dam; powerfully built men whose dress only added to their height and stature. Stretched diagonally across each man's chest was a wide band upon which was appliqued the word "Guard" in large white letters. The emblazoned labeling of their purpose in the community was a fresh reminder to these hillfolk of what the United Electric Company had done to them and their hearts were filled with hatred and distrust that grew stronger as they observed that the guards each held a modern high-powered rifle wholly unlike the hillmen's guns.

Rogers could feel the tenseness which charged the air as Big Dave picked up the targets and went through the door calling loudly, "All right, boys, le's go!"

On each of 10 boards driven into the ground 4 feet apart a

174

target was carefully tacked. A straight line was measured parallel to the targets 40 yards away. Then several men carrying two crates of five turkeys each walked from the store to the crowded sidelines of the shooting ground. It was almost time.

Grunting from exertion, Big Dave brought out a chair, sat himself heavily into it and called:

"Ready now, boys! Ten o' yo'uns kin shoot fer two bits apiece. The one who hits nearest the center o' his target gits the turkey. Come on, fellers, hit's jist a quarter 'piece."

The guards bought the first four tickets, with Rosie's father, John Gurney, right behind them. Five other hillmen took the remaining chances.

The teacher stood watching the proceedings with interest.

"Aren't you shooting, Cliff?" he asked his friend who stood beside him.

"No, I ain't. I'd ruther watch terday." Cliff Montgomery lowered his voice as he continued, "This is a goin' ter be real good, Brother Rogers. Them boys has made one brag too many, so some of us has kinda fixed things a little. Me an' 'nother feller dug up a gallon jug we've had hid fer some time. Gov'mint stuff. We had Aaron Hooks come down early an' hide hit in the millrace. Then I kinda sidled up ter them fellers an' sold 'em several good snorts 'bout 10 o'clock. I reckon by now they shore ort ter be a little shaky so they won't be a doin' much good shootin'!"

He winked slyly at Rogers and the teacher decided to skip the lecture that was forming in the back of his mind.

The four guards shot first. The first one put a bullet in the square outside the black circle. The next two missed the target entirely. The last guard hit the edge of the black circle.

John Gurney carefully examined the percussion cap of his long rifle and polished the front sight with his thumb wet with saliva. Then he lay flat on his stomach with the barrel of the gun resting on a rock. Slowly he drew a bead on the target.

Give Me Thy Vineyard

When the rifle cracked, it was a moment before the spectators could see through the thick smoke of the black powder. Then they saw. His bullet had split the circle dead center.

The guards were stunned and looked it. But the hill people laughed and shouted.

"That's hit, John!"

"Good ole John!"

"That's pretty good," one of the guards admitted.

"Good!" roared the usually placid John. "Man, that's perfeck!"

"Yo' other fellers wants ter take yore chanct?" Big Dave called.

"No, reckon hit hain't no use. Cain't beat that."

Nine more turkeys were to be prizes earned in the same manner. The guards always shot first, followed by John, who made the match progress slowly due to his habit of leisurely measuring the gunpowder each time he reloaded. But he won seven more turkeys and the guards gave up.

"Wal, iffn yo'uns is a quittin', I will, too," he drawled. "Dave, pick me out a fat young gobbler from them eight. I'll give the others back. The rest o' yo'uns kin shoot fer em free."

The keen rivalry continued, but the teacher soon went home. He wanted to tell the news of the match to Tom. He had taken his rifle with him in case he got a chance to shoot a squirrel on the way back. Tommy liked them so much. He never seemed to get enough of them.

Now as Rogers returned home he found he was so anxious to reach Tommy to tell him the story of the exciting shooting match he had almost no interest in hunting. But Tommy would also be delighted with a squirrel, so Rogers took a few minutes to leave the narrow path that led to home to look for squirrels. His detour was rewarded, as he shot two of the frisky little animals.

When he neared his cabin, even before he came in sight of it, he heard the familiar deep growl of Bullet. The teacher stood quite still and soon Hiram came out of the woods.

Give Me Thy Vineyard

"Hiram, what are you doing here?"

"I come back ter git my fiddle," Hiram answered.

"But, man, aren't you taking an awful chance, coming here so often?"

"Not so much, Brother Rogers. I knowed ever'body'd be down ter the shootin' match. I been a playin' fer Tommy more'n a hour. When I first heered Bullet I tuck ter the woods till I war shore who it war. I'se shore glad hit war yo'uns," he grinned.

They walked side by side to the house and when they reached the narrow door, Rogers placed his hand on the latch and turned his back against the door to push it open. Hiram passed by him into the room.

"Oh, Daddy," Tommy called from his bed, "I'm glad you are home. Did Rosie's dad win the shooting match?"

"Yes," his father answered, closing the door, "and I shot some squirrels for our supper."

He threw the squirrels on the floor and crossed the room to build up the fire. Hiram reached down and picked up the dead animals. He examined their lead pelted bodies and shook his head. Tommy and his father watched him with interest.

"Yo'uns ort ter shoot 'em through the eyes, Brother Rogers," he said reproachfully.

"Through the eyes! Why, I was aiming at 30 yards. It would be pure accident to hit a squirrel in the eyes at that distance."

"Naw, 'twouldn't. That's the way I allers shoots 'em. Don't lose no meat thataway an' hit kills 'em quick."

The teacher looked chagrined, but Tommy's eyes and mouth hung open in wondrous admiration. Someday he was going to learn to shoot like that.

Hiram felt embarrassed before this man and his son whose feelings were so plainly a mixture of envy and admiration.

"Tell us 'bout the shootin' match," he said at last.

"Oh, yes," Rogers began. "I almost forgot." Then he told

most of the details of the events of the afternoon, purposely omitting the part whiskey played in winning the match. When he related how John Gurney won, time after time Tommy bounced up and down in bed and clapped his thin little hands.

"'Ray for Mr. Gurney!" he shouted happily.

A low growl from Bullet caused Hiram to jump up and bolt out through the back door. Tommy sat up expectantly and Grady watched out the window. A black horse appeared around the bend in the trail and he heaved a sigh of relief.

"It's only Rosie," he called to Hiram and the fugitive returned to the house.

"Come in, Rosie," Rogers invited, standing in the open doorway that faced the only trail to his home. "I've got a surprise for you."

"Oh, no, yo' hain't," the girl refuted. "Hiram's here, 'cause I heered Bullet way down the trail. Nob'dy kin slip up on him."

She entered the room a little breathless, with a small basket on her arm. "Hiram, how come yo'all air here?" she said directly. "Hit's mighty dangerous."

"Brother Rogers has a'ready scolded me fer takin' the chanct," he replied.

Then he explained about his fiddle and how he knew everyone would be at the shooting match.

Rosie looked doubtful and warned him to be more careful.

"I brought yo'uns some stuff fer Thanksgiving dinner," she said to Tommy. "Huckleberry pie, an' fish, an' butter, an' a loaf o' fresh bread." She set it all out on the table.

But neither the little boy nor Hiram saw any of it. They had fastened their eyes on the fresh beauty of Rosie's face, each one admiring and longing for her in his own way.

"Now that we're all here like this, why don't we fix supper and eat together?" Grady Rogers suggested. "That is, if you feel safe about it, Hiram."

Give Me Thy Vineyard

This met with happy approval. Hiram said, "I don't know anyplace where I feels safer. I reckon yo'all an' Rosie knows nobody's a goin' ter git close ter this here cabin long as Bullet's a watchin'."

They knew what he said was true. While Bullet knew now that Rosie and Rogers were Hiram's friends, he never let even these friends enter the cabin without a bristling protest. Rosie took over the preparation of the meal.

"I'll boil these here squirrels nice an' tender an' brown 'em in the oven with onions," she said as she looked around for the utensils she would need. "An' I'll fry some 'taters an' cook these here fish."

"Can't I do something to help, Rosie?" Grady Rogers asked, feeling awkward and helpless here in his own kitchen before this efficient young woman.

"No, Brother Rogers. Thanks jist the same. Fixin' vittles hain't fittin' work fer a man—"

"I've wondered about that, Rosie, lots of times," Rogers said quietly, watching her deft fingers at work.

So, while Hiram and Tommy laughed and joked about the things Rogers related concerning the shooting match, Rosie put the supper on the table.

It was a happy party and the three grown-ups ate with the zest of people who spend a lot of the time out-of-doors. The boy tried his best to keep up with the others. His face lit up as Rosie smiled at him across the table and Hiram reached over and patted him on the shoulder. Rogers had never seen Hiram in such a congenial mood.

"Good boy," he said, "clean up yer vittles like that all a time an' some o' these days I'll take yo'uns 'long ter see some o' them woods critters I been a tellin' yo'uns 'bout."

The table talk was lively. Every little bit Grady thought of another interesting item to tell about the shooting match.

Finally, he pushed back from the table. "I think Tommy should go back to bed now."

Give Me Thy Vineyard

While Rogers put his son to bed, Rosie cleared away the dishes. Tommy was very tired and almost at once fell into a restful sleep. When Rosie finished the last of her tasks, she sat in a low chair near Hiram and they continued to visit. It had been a good time for them all. They so enjoyed the opportunity to be able to cast off their respective worries even if only for a brief time, that each one dreaded for the day to end when they would have to face life's perplexing realities once more.

Hiram sought to prolong the good talk but the time had come for today's visit to end. Rosie didn't want to keep John Gurney worrying about her by staying out late and it was dark enough for Hiram to return safely to his cave. So they told the teacher goodbye and stepped out into the night, Rosie with her basket, and Hiram carrying his beloved fiddle.

Give Me Thy Vineyard

Give Me Thy Vineyard

Give Me Thy Vineyard

Chapter 23

WHEN GRADY ROGERS went to Oakridge to preach on Sunday after Thanksgiving, he heard some startling news. Squire Morgan had proposed to the Widder Gray. No one ever knew what had suddenly happened to this bashful man that made him finally pop the question after 15 years of courting.

"He jist up an' ast me," the Widder Gray told her friends demurely. "Said, 'Molly, hain't hit 'bout time we war hookin' up in double harness?'"

And that was all this usually talkative woman would say.

The Squire asked Grady Rogers to marry them.

"We'uns knows yo'uns won't make no big speeches," he said. "We'uns wants this here weddin' quiet and quick."

Grady Rogers was sympathetic. He was a timid man himself and could well understand why this man who had endured so much teasing for years would not care to subject himself to more of it if it could be avoided.

But even he could not resist tormenting the old fellow just a little.

"Squire," he said, "we'll make your wedding so quiet that not even the birds will hear, and quicker than a squirrel frisking up a tree. Just how quiet do you want it, Mrs. Gray? I guess the Squire would want you to decide that," he said, turning to the bride-to-be.

Then with a twinkle in his eye, he jested, "It's funny the

Squire has been 15 years getting around to asking you and now that everything is sewed up tight he gets in a big hurry."

The widow laughed appreciatively, but for once seemed not to have an idea in her head. It was as though she had won her heart's desire and had nothing more to ask of the world.

But not so with her chosen mate. While she fumbled for an answer, he broke in earnestly. "Wal, now, you know many a time a man's thought he had a gal jist 'cause she's promised him ter be his'n, an' then been left a standin' all alone ter the altar. Not that I think Molly'd do that ter me, but le's jist git this here weddin' over with, quick and proper."

"All right, Squire," agreed Grady seriously. "You get the license and have everything ready, and I'll marry you two weeks from today when I come again. Of course, you know I'm not a regularly ordained minister, but I asked the prosecuting attorney about the legality of any marriage I performed and he said as long as I had regular missionary charges I had a perfect right to officiate at marriages. Yours will be my first wedding."

"Wal, now, I'se right proud o' that," the Squire returned, patting the teacher affectionately on the shoulder, "an' I reckon yore knot'll stay tied as tight as any. We'se all mighty thankful for the he'p you been a givin' us here at Oakridge. The Lord bless yo'uns fer hit."

"Glad to be of service," Rogers acknowledged. "Now you be ready Sunday and right after church I'll tie you to that widow so tight you never will get loose."

More than a houseful of folk turned out for church that Sunday but the prospective bride and groom were so nervous they didn't notice. The Squire was slightly deaf and always sat near the front to hear the sermon. He didn't know how many folk sat behind him.

Rogers found preaching hard work that afternoon. His listeners endeavored to give their attention but an air of expectation filled the room and he was relieved when the hour for the wedding arrived. He was not without a feeling of excitement himself, but he had prepared his part of the ceremony well and felt fairly sure of himself. Everything went along smoothly in accordance with the well-laid plans.

The aged groom held himself proudly while Rogers pronounced them man and wife. But when it was over, he seemed to have lost his nerve. He did not move. While his bride wet her lips and eyed him expectantly, he looked helplessly at his feet. The tense and embarrassed guests leaned forward, waiting for something to happen.

"Give him a shove," someone whispered loudly.

Finally Rogers burst out, "What's the matter with you, man? If you're not going to kiss her, I will!"

But as he puckered his mouth toward the white-haired bride, who was old enough to be his mother, her husband's wits abruptly returned.

"Now that air's enough, Brother Rogers – you done yore duty. I was jist – jist a thinkin', that's all."

And, pushing Rogers aside, he gave the new Mrs. Morgan a resounding smack.

The guests relaxed noisily. But they were not through with the newlyweds. Both had lived in Oakridge all of their lives, and the romance of the pair was known to everybody in the ridge area. It had been all right for them to have a quiet wedding, but they would also have to have a charivari.

Joe Bates, the boy who ran errands for the Squire, organized the affair. He and his friends, with the aid of the mail carrier, Rosie, managed to tell everybody living between Lake City and Clear Springs to come to the schoolyard at Stony Point on Monday night. From there they would go in a body to the Widder's house. (She would always be "the Widder" to her friends and neighbors.)

The Squire had been quick to move his hog, table, kerosene lamp and three chairs to his bride's home. She had a much finer house than his. She also owned 30 acres, six hogs and a flock of chickens. Both had decided it would be more practical if he came to live there.

The people on the ridge knew that the Widder's shelves were stocked with her famous goodies, and that the Squire had celebrated his wedding by spending most of his Spanish-American War pension check on candy and treats. A charivari for this couple would be a satisfying one indeed.

So it was with eagerness that nearly everyone on Reed's Ridge who could walk or ride started up the trail to the Morgans' on Monday night. Ruth Barnes had offered to stay with Tommy so Grady Rogers borrowed a horse from Cliff Montgomery and rode along with him and Annie.

Many teams and wagons brought whole families. Young men and their sweethearts came on horseback, riding double. The neighbors within a 5-mile radius of the schoolhouse had walked, and nearly all the men carried guns. These would be used to shoot the volley to open the charivari. Cowbells and fox horns abounded in the crowd, and two men in a wagon carried a large musical saw.

As they approached the Widder's house, the organizer, Joe, jumped up in a wagon and yelled for silence.

"Folks," he shouted, "hit's only a quarter of a mile down ter the Widder Gray's. Le's leave the horses an' wagons here an' go jist as quiet as we all kin. When we gits there, surround the house an' ever'body git ready. When I yells, 'Le's go!' ever'body with guns, shoot. Then the rest o' yo'uns chime in with yore horns an' bells an' sech-like. Make all the noise yo'uns kin."

Everybody agreed to do as bidden but they needed no instructions. Charivaris followed the same pattern always and they all knew what to do. In a few minutes they started as quietly as possible down the last fork in the trail. With hardly a crack of a twig they surrounded the large cabin.

"Hit's all dark inside," someone whispered. "Reckon they

done found out 'bout this here charivari an' run away?"

"No. We seen 'em ter home jist a little while ago. An' look – they's smoke comin' out o' the chimney."

"Le's go!"

Joe's shout broke through the night and was followed immediately by the explosion of guns and the din of cowbells, fox horns, the musical saw and yelling voices. The clamor continued for nearly 15 minutes. But still no light appeared in the cabin.

"Le's smoke 'em out!" a male voice shouted.

And no sooner was the suggestion made than a nimble-footed young man climbed to the slope of the lean-to of the cabin via the rain barrel. From there he leaped up on the roof and seized the ridge comb just back of the exposed flue of the fireplace. Four other boys passed him a huge bucket of water and a wide board. With a grunt, he dumped the water down the flue and placed the board on top.

The waiting crowd heard a loud hiss as the water landed on burning logs and live coals. Gleefully they pictured the house being filled up with smoke and steam. The Morgans would have to come out now, unless they had stopped breathing.

"Yo'uns wins," the Squire coughed, "we'uns heerd yo'all war a comin' jist at the last minute, so we tried to make like we warn't home. But yo'uns got us beat, so come on in. I'll fetch in some dry wood offn the porch, fer we'uns'll have ter kindle 'nother fire."

Laughing and shouting, the crowd poured in and helped the half-strangled bride open the windows to let out the fumes. In a little while a new fire was lit in the fireplace, the windows were closed and the fun continued.

At 10 o'clock Grady Rogers decided it was time for him to go. Others felt the same way, so the embarrassed bride and groom stood in a corner while everybody filed by to shake their hands and congratulate them.

Give Me Thy Vineyard

As Rogers stepped out into the night, Rosie Gurney spoke to him:

"Yo'uns come horseback, didn't yo'?" she asked.

"Why, yes, Rosie, I did. With Annie and Cliff Montgomery. Why?"

"I'd like ter ride back with yo'uns. Pa couldn't come an' he made me promise I'd git somebody ter ride back with me. I tole him I'd ask yo'uns."

"I'm glad you did, Rosie. I'll tell Cliff that I'm going with you by Clear Springs. They probably will want to go back the way we came."

Rogers returned from delivering his message and they went for their horses. He untied Fred, and helped Rosie into the saddle, where she waited while he got ready.

"Yo's a ridin' down the road with me ternight, Rosie," a voice commanded as a horse and rider came up.

"No, I'm not. I'm goin' 'long with Brother Rogers an' yo'uns kin ride by yorese'f, Clark Harmon," Rosie returned tartly.

"Yo're ridin' with me an' the parson kin go on, fer we'se a ridin' slow," the young man repeated. "I wants ter talk ter yo'uns."

"Just a minute. Didn't you hear Rosie say that she was riding with me?" the teacher inquired.

"Yo'uns keep out o' this here or I'll smash yore face in fer yo'uns," Clark said angrily, dismounting.

"Clark, I certainly don't want any trouble with you, but I must insist you do as Rosie wishes. She does not want to ride with you. I should think that would be enough for a gentleman, but I take it you are no gentleman."

"No, I hain't!" the bully exploded, as he suddenly swung a vicious right fist at the teacher's face. The suddenness of the unexpected blow caught Grady off his guard. Clark's fist landed on his mouth with such force that it knocked him flat. He arose slowly, stunned.

"You cowardly fool. You should be given a sound thrashing," he declared, turning to his horse.

"Why don't you try hit, Parson?" Clark taunted.

Grady Rogers accepted the challenge so suddenly that his first blow landed on Clark's nose before Clark knew what was happening. With a roar he lunged at his assailant.

Rogers had been a clever boxer in college. Clark outweighed him by 50 pounds but Grady was faster, though he was no match for the bully in strength.

Grady stepped aside quickly and drove a hard right into Clark's ear, and followed it with a stunning left hook to his snarling mouth. This blow knocked Clark to his knees. Grady swung a vicious right, with all the force of his rapidly moving body behind it, that landed just under Clark's chin as he rose. He fell flat on his back and lay still.

Grady mounted his horse and turned to Rosie and said, "Let's go."

"Brother Rogers, where did yo'uns larn ter fight? Yo' shore give him a whuppin'!" she exclaimed admiringly.

"I've been a fool, Rosie," Rogers commented bitterly. "If Clark hadn't been half drunk he could have killed me."

"Don't blame yorese'f nary a bit, Brother Rogers. Clark's jist as mean sober as he is drunk. He's been a spilin' fer somebody ter lick him fer a mighty long time. Only he didn't think they war anybody cud do hit, since Hiram's been away."

"Just the same, Rosie, I wish it hadn't happened," Grady Rogers said soberly. "It looks bad for a man to fight, especially when he tries to preach, too."

"Don't reckon nobody'll hold hit agin yo'all fer a lickin' none o' them Harmons. They shore has hit a comin' ter 'em."

By the time they reached the Gurney place, Rogers' hand was paining him uncomfortably. He told Rosie about it and she was much concerned.

"Better come in an' let Pa look at hit. They might be some

bones broke," she said.

"Oh, it can't be that bad," Rogers replied. "But it does seem to be swelling."

"Wal, come in anyway an' I'll make a pot o' coffee."

They entered the cabin and Rosie awakened her father to tell him about what had happened. John Gurney examined Rogers' hand and declared there were no bones broken.

"But yo'uns best soak hit here in a pan o' hot water an' vinegar ter take the swellin' out," he said.

Rosie had kindled the fire and already had set the teakettle and coffeepot on the stove.

"A fightin' parson, eh," John drawled.

"Yes, John, I lost my temper. I should have known better."

"Oh, I don't know," John continued slowly. "I feel right proud o' yo'uns. Jist 'pears ter me like a fightin' preacher what takes his own part when he has ter is a right handy man fer the Lord."

"Wal, I shore hopes he knocked some o' the meanness out o' Clark Harmon," Rosie said, placing cups of coffee before the men.

The teacher remembered that Ruthie Barnes was sitting up with Tommy and he rose to go, declining John's pressing invitation to spend the night.

Give Me Thy Vineyard

Give Me Thy Vineyard

Give Me Thy Vineyard

Chapter 24

*A*S GRADY ROGERS rode home alone from the Gurney cabin, he took himself severely to task.

What a fool I've been, he thought, *to get myself involved in these community affairs. Here I've made an enemy of the Harmons, notoriously, the most dangerous characters on the ridge. And all for what?* Rogers wasn't sure he knew the answer to that question.

He tried to straighten things out in his mind. Rosie Gurney was a fine woman; of that he was sure. She had been very kind about helping out with Tommy. Rogers appreciated that. No doubt she was responsible for much of the boy's progress in recovering his health.

But what of Hiram Jackson? Was he guilty or not? The teacher had tried to find out by questioning people on the ridge, but none of the answers were direct. Some intimated he was guilty, others that he was innocent, but all agreed emphatically that he was justified.

Rogers himself was inclined to believe the man was innocent, especially since Hiram and Rosie had been coming to his cabin. He supposed Rosie had persuaded him to this conclusion.

He wanted to help them but what could he do? What could anybody do?

Cliff and Annie were waiting to take their horse when the teacher reached home. Ruthie Barnes had ridden on home with her husband.

Rogers went to bed as he had many other nights lately, wondering how he could help Rosie and Hiram.

The night after the charivari, Annie and Cliff came to call. They gossiped about the affair until Tommy fell asleep. Then Annie spoke out what was on her mind:

"Me an' Cliff's been a thinkin' hard terday, Brother Rogers, an' we thinks hit air plumb dang'rous fer Tommy ter stay here days alone now that you has had that fight with Clark Harmon."

"But, Annie," expostulated Grady Rogers, "if I can't leave Tommy alone, I'll just have to take him and go someplace else. And he is getting so much better!"

"We'uns thought o' that, too," Cliff began.

"Yes, Brother Rogers," Annie broke in, "we shore has. An' this here is what we'uns thought ter do. I'se got a exter room an' iffn yo'all an' Tommy wants ter move in hit then yo'uns kin finish the school an' Tommy'll be safe."

"Why, Annie, I just don't know what to say. I know it was very foolish of me to incur the enmity of anyone with the reputation of the Harmons. But even they wouldn't harm a sick little boy, would they?"

"No tellin' what them lyin' Harmons would do, Brother Rogers," Cliff Montgomery again interposed. "This here cabin might jist nacherly burn down someday an' that little feller in hit an' nobody'd ever know who done hit."

Rogers shivered and glanced anxiously toward his sleeping son. He knew now he would never dare leave Tommy alone a minute.

"What a fool I've been," he said.

"Now don't chide yorese'f none," Cliff said. "Yo'uns jist done what nacherly had ter be done."

Grady sat with bowed head, searching in his mind for a solution to this grave problem. Finally he said:

"Annie, I don't know what to say. You are very kind to

offer us a place to stay, but I hate to inconvenience you. There are so many angles to this thing. If I only had a little time to think it out. There's one thing sure, though, I can't leave Tommy alone anymore."

"Shore yo' cain't. An' we'uns knowed yo'd have ter have time ter 'cide what ter do, so Ruth Barnes said she'd take turns with me a stayin' with Tommy rest o' this week."

"I'll accept that offer," Grady agreed, "but please don't say anything to Tommy about the fight I had with Harmon."

"No, of course not. Ruthie an' me jist thought we'd let on ter him that we'uns come over ter work up yore apples."

Grady smiled. Annie surely had a way of smoothing everything out for folks. But before he could open his mouth to speak, Annie rattled on:

"An' hit's the plain truth, too," she said. "Them apples air a wastin'. John kin fetch our big kittle 'long in the mornin' an' we'uns kin pare an' cook 'em inter apple butter whiles we'se here."

"That will be wonderful, Annie. I have dried and canned quite a few of those apples, but I hadn't thought to make butter, too. And I love it in the winter, with hot biscuits and butter. I can see Tommy is going to have a fine time," he finished.

"We'uns'll shore take good keer o' him, Brother Rogers. He's sech a little feller. Seems like he orter have a mother," she said plaintively.

Cliff Montgomery shifted uneasily and Grady Rogers jerked his head erect.

"Why, Annie, I do the best I can for him," he defended. "I know I have to leave him alone a lot, but I stay with him all I can. I've always tried to make up to him for the loss of his mother. He reads good books and I've taught him about God and to say his prayers. He has a bath every morning before I go to school and on Saturdays I wash and iron for both of us. And surely the food I prepare for him is all right for he is gaining right along." The teacher seemed unable to stop, as though he were trying to convince himself as well as his listener.

"Oh, yo'uns does all right by him," Cliff Montgomery said. "Annie, we'd best be goin'."

"'Course yo'all does good by him," Annie agreed, ignoring her husband's suggestion. "'Tain't yore fault he's a ailin'. An' yo'uns teaches him right, too. A body kin tell that by his nice ways."

"But," she continued, "they jist hain't nary man kin do fer menfolks what a woman kin do."

An awkward silence followed this irrefutable statement.

"Annie," her husband said, "leave Brother Rogers 'lone. Hit's none o' yore bizness."

"Hit is my bizness, Cliff, an' yor'n, too. Brother Rogers is right clost ter us now. We'uns ort ter tell him what's best fer him."

"But we'uns don't know what's best–"

"Wal, I does, an' I'se a goin' ter tell him. Brother Rogers, yo'all needs a woman yorese'f. Yo're jist too good a man ter be a livin' lonely 'thout ary woman."

"I can't support a wife," Rogers said sharply. This conversation seemed a little ridiculous. After all, this really was none of Annie Montgomery's business.

"The right gal'd be willin' ter marry yo'uns 'thout no money."

"Well, I haven't found the right girl yet."

"Right shore yo's been a lookin'?"

"No," Grady admitted, "I haven't."

"Rosie Gurney'd be doin' a sight better for herse'f iffn she tuck up with some good man an' stopped a pinin' fer Hiram."

Cliff laughed at Annie's illogical argument. She had finally got around to what had been on her mind all of the time. Rogers smiled ruefully.

"I'm afraid Rosie is like a lot of the rest of us," he said dryly. "What she should do and what she will do are two entirely different things."

His neighbors rose to go.

"We'uns'll be over in the mornin' ter look arter Tommy." Annie sniffed, wondering if her recently opened campaign would bear fruit. "Yo'uns kin make up yore mind what ter do by the last o' the week."

She followed her husband through the door.

After they were gone, Grady Rogers sat for a long time, thinking. As always, his greatest concern was for Tommy. He had been getting better so fast these last few weeks. He was able now to come to the table for his meals and while it was still necessary for him to spend most of the time in bed, he could get outside for a little while on pretty days.

And he was happy here! Happier than he had been since his illness. Grady thought that had helped him more than anything else.

But would he be as happy staying at Montgomerys'? Or what would the shock of having to leave the ridge do to him?

Rogers recalled the things Annie Montgomery had said to him. He didn't know whether he should feel indignant or grateful. Certainly she was his best friend and confidante. He had gone to her in times of loneliness and bewilderment. Her advice had always been good and helpful. But he knew she had a way of managing the affairs of those she loved and he was frightened at her taking a hand in his private life.

He thought of the roundabout way she had gotten to Rosie Gurney. Not that what she had said about the girl wasn't true. Rogers knew she was a fine young woman with a single-minded purpose and devotion. Too bad things had to be like they were for her. She would make a fine wife.

Grady thought she was very attractive, too. Of course, her speech and dress were a little crude. He wondered what she would be like transplanted to the city, dressed in nice things.

Give Me Thy Vineyard

"Nope," he decided almost audibly. He had never seen city ways that could do much to improve the looks of such a girl as Rosie. It was like comparing a regal lily from the hothouse with a wild rose: the lily cold, formal and forbidding; the rose sweet, and warm, and inviting. Rosie flowered much nicer in her native environment. It was best for her to marry Hiram and he hoped someday she could do that.

The teacher sighed and looked at his son, sleeping restlessly on the bed. Poor Tom, with his big mind and little body, and worry about dying. It wasn't that he was really afraid to die. He was just afraid of not living. He knew that God was in the Other World and that it was beautiful there. But he was so pitifully eager to see all of the things he had heard about in this world.

Annie Montgomery was right. He should marry again. But where would he find a woman that could satisfy him in every way as Betty had – Betty!

He realized with a shock that he had been thinking very infrequently of his wife since coming to the Ozarks. The change had been good for him as well as for Tommy. It was bad for a person to continue to live in that part of his life that was already over.

He undressed and went to bed. As he drifted off to sleep he thought of Rosie Gurney. They had one thing in common – their feeling for God. They both knew what faith meant, he and Rosie. Once she had told him that at times she felt she would go crazy with wanting Hiram, and worrying, but that God had always seemed to be with her and had kept her on the right track. Rogers wondered drowsily if she would always go on waiting for Hiram, or would there come a time when she would lose faith and turn to someone else?

Give Me Thy Vineyard

Give Me Thy Vineyard

Give Me Thy Vineyard

Chapter 25

GRADY ROGERS went to the store at Clear Springs for his mail and groceries on Thursday after his fight with Clark Harmon.

"It has been a lovely day, hasn't it, Dave?" he said to the old storekeeper. "The air is just right to make one feel good. Makes you glad to be alive, doesn't it?"

"Hit shore does," the storekeeper agreed. "Take hit winter, summer, the whole year 'round, this here's the best place ter live in I ever seen." The old man failed to recollect that in all his lifetime he had never traveled more than 100 miles distant.

"I hear yo'uns had a run-in with Clark Harmon," Dave commented.

"Yes, Dave. I'm awfully sorry it happened."

"Yo'all don't need ter feel sorry. But yo'd better keep a sharp lookout frum now on. Yo're lucky yo'uns didn't git yorese'f kilt."

Rogers knew the old man told the truth. "I'll be careful, Dave," he said. Then he ordered his groceries and hurried home.

It had been Ruthie Barnes' day to stay with Tommy. She had their supper partly prepared when he got home. All he had to do after she left was to make the biscuits. First he visited with Tommy and then went to the spring for water, before beginning his biscuit-making.

Give Me Thy Vineyard

He had been doing his own cooking for years so the construction of his baking was more or less automatic and required little concentration. But the perplexing problems weighing heavily upon him absorbed his complete attention. So rapt was he that he jumped when Tommy called suddenly, "Hey, Dad, someone's hollering outside. Hear him?"

Rogers listened. Sure enough, he heard a distant "Hallo."

"What's going on?" he muttered as he opened the door. Tommy was up on his knees looking out of the window.

They listened and again came the "Hallo, there." Then, down the trail, Rogers saw a stranger astride a horse.

"I want to come up!" the man shouted.

"Well, why don't you?" the teacher called back.

"Is it all right?"

"Certainly it's all right."

The man rode the horse up near to the cabin and dismounted. Rogers noted that he was well-dressed and bore every evidence of being city-bred.

"I thought you might have a dog, and I was afraid to venture near," he explained. "I have heard that nearly every home around here has a watchdog and that many of them are savage." The man laughed awkwardly.

"Oh, don't worry about that. We don't have a dog. We don't need one." He smiled. "My son and I don't have anything anyone would want to steal. Come in." He extended his hand, which the stranger shook precisely.

"My name is Clarence West. You're Grady Rogers, I hope?"

"Yes."

"I've had a difficult time finding your place, Mr. Rogers. Had to take a horse. They told me I couldn't get here in my car."

"These hills are no place for a car, Mr. West. Won't you come inside?"

West eyed the little cabin hard and curiously, seeming to be making mental notes of the two kerosene lamps, the little stove and the old table. When he saw Tom, who was staring at him, he walked over to the bed.

"You must be Tommy Rogers."

The boy continued to stare without speaking. He had decided that he didn't like the short dapper man.

"Yes, this is Tommy, Mr. West. But how did you know?"

The man smiled as he answered, "It's my business to know. Let me introduce myself further. I'm an attorney for the United Electric Company. I came to discuss business with you."

"Business?"

"Yes. And of an important nature. I–" He sniffed. "But are you preparing supper, Mr. Rogers? I'm sorry. I didn't mean to come while you were eating. It took me so long to–"

"That's perfectly all right. Won't you join us?"

The lawyer sniffed again. "Smells good. Thanks. I guess I will. But first I have something for Tommy."

He drew a package from his overcoat pocket. "Had to fold it, but I guess it's still suitable."

"Oh, look! A picture book and a paint box! Thanks a lot, mister."

Tommy temporarily forgot his suspicions as he looked the gift over.

"This is very kind of you, Mr. West, but I don't see–"

"Think nothing of it. I knew your child was bedridden, so I took the liberty." He sat down, his small black eyes again taking in every detail of the room.

What was it all about? Rogers wondered as he set the table. What business could he have with the electric company? He smiled inwardly as he thought, *Maybe they're going to give me special low rates for electricity.*

As soon as Rogers sat down, West reached hungrily for a biscuit, buttered it and started to take a bite. But he stopped in embarrassment when he heard Tom ask to say grace. Surreptitiously, he placed the biscuit behind his glass and bowed his head.

"All right, son," Rogers said.

"God is great, God is good. Let us thank Him for our food. Amen."

West peered at Rogers from the corner of his eye and waited. The teacher lifted his head and smiled kindly at his guest's discomfiture. It was obvious that West had not thanked God for a meal for a long time.

The men engaged in small talk while they ate. Rogers was intensely curious over the reason for West's visit, but he waited the man's time. Finally, at the end of the meal, the lawyer said:

"As I told you, Mr. Rogers, I represent the United Electric Company. I came to you because of your reputation for honesty and truthfulness."

"Really?"

"Yes. I need some information and I know you are the one who can give it to me right."

"What kind of information?"

"About this outlaw, Hiram Jackson."

So that was it. Rogers saw Tom making wild signals at him from behind West's back.

"Why should I know anything about him, Mr. West?"

"Come now. We know you're his friend."

"But almost everyone is his friend. The hill people have been his friends since he was born. Why don't you–"

"We happen to know he's been coming to your cabin."

Rogers was jolted. Who had told? Only Hiram, Rosie and Tom, beside himself, knew and they would never tell. Maybe the lawyer was bluffing.

"If you know that, why haven't you sent the sheriff to pick him up?"

West smiled thinly. "You're smart, Mr. Rogers. So I'll credit your intelligence by being completely honest with you. Naturally, I expect that you will be honest with me. Our informant saw Jackson going through the woods from your cabin late one Sunday night. But by the time he got to us to tell us, and by the time we found the sheriff, it was the next day. You do admit, then, that Jackson has been here?"

"I admit nothing, Mr. West. I'm not on trial." Who had spotted Hiram? he wondered. It must have been one of the Harmons. Only they feared him enough to do a thing like that.

"I'm disappointed in you, Mr. Rogers," West said, leaning back in his chair. "I was sure that you, coming from the outside, wouldn't be tainted by this local 'code of the hills' nonsense. I was sure you'd have a true sense of justice."

"I beg your pardon?"

"I'll give you a little background. You knew that United built the dam across Spring River. You probably also know that we bought all the land in the lake bed. The resort land and beaches are ours, too. Therefore, you can see we have a lot of money invested here."

Rogers nodded.

"My company is planning two other dams in the Ozarks."

"So I've heard."

"Then you must have heard, too, that the hill people are opposing us every inch of the way. It's the same sort of thing we had here four years ago – when one of our most valued men was murdered." He leaned toward the teacher. "Hiram Jackson committed the murder, Mr. Rogers. He shot a man in the back in cold blood. And you're protecting Hiram Jackson. You who have become a preacher and–"

"I don't believe Hiram committed that murder, Mr. West," Rogers interrupted in an obvious attempt to keep calm.

"Whether you believe it or not, he was tried and convicted. And the people around here are protecting him. There may even be more killing. That man is a symbol of rebellion. If there's going to be any more progress in the Ozarks, he's got to be captured. Don't you see that?"

"No."

"What?"

"No, I said."

"But I can't understand it." The lawyer's glittering eyes scrutinized him. "Aren't you interested in progress? We hold plans for the development of this whole area."

"Maybe the people around here don't want the country developed, Mr. West, at the price they have to pay."

"At the price *they* have to pay? We paid them plenty for their land, often more than it was worth."

Rogers sighed wearily. "Yes, you paid them, but in most cases it wasn't nearly enough. And even if it were, what could they do with the money? They don't want to go to the city. They're farmers – have been for generations."

"We gave them enough to buy new farms."

"If that were true – and I think your conscience will tell you it isn't – you must realize that most of the tillable soil around here was in the area you flooded."

"But now they have electricity. They could build farms twice as productive as the ones they had before with electric power to help them. It's just that they're too lazy..."

"That's not true either, Mr. West! Your company charges such high rates for electricity that most of these people can't touch it. Surely, electric power would help them develop the soil, but your rates won't let them buy it."

"Mr. Rogers, United Electric Company isn't a government project. We have a right to make a profit."

"You have a right to a fair profit. But what you're doing is nothing but taking advantage of a situation and you know it. The people in the larger towns can afford to pay your prices, but these folks here have been left in much worse shape than before you came. If you're interested in progress, give them cheap electricity, then see what happens!"

The lawyer smiled with his teeth. "Well, Mr. Rogers, I didn't realize that you felt so strongly about this. But if you remember, I came here to talk to you about Hiram Jackson.

Let's get back to that."

"I think I made my position clear, Mr. West."

The lawyer stood up and eyed him. "We will capture Jackson sooner or later, Mr. Rogers, but we would prefer it to be sooner. We're cracking down now, because of those new dams. We're going to raise the reward for him from five hundred dollars to two thousand."

"That's a lot of money."

"I know. And we wanted to give you the first chance to get it."

"I beg your pardon."

"I'll pay you the two thousand dollars right now, Mr. Rogers, if you'll tell me what you know about Jackson's habits – and where we can find him."

"I'm not interested." Rogers stood up. "And now, if–"

"Wait a minute," West interrupted. "Let me finish. Naturally this transaction would be held in strictest confidence. The hill people will never know the source of our information."

How little West understood hill people, Rogers thought, realizing by now at least a hundred of them must know of the lawyer's trip through the hills and his destination. He pictured the bitterness and probable revenge of these people toward anyone, especially an outsider like himself, who betrayed Hiram. He pictured Rosie's black, accusing stare.

"Daddy!" Tom's voice cut sharply through his thoughts. He'd almost forgotten about him. The poor child must be going crazy.

"Excuse me," Rogers said to West, "I forgot to bring him his – his – er – medicine."

Filling a tumbler, and fumbling in a box for an aspirin, he bent over the boy and helped him to a sitting position.

"The secret, Dad! Rosie's secret!" Tom whispered urgently, nearly knocking the water out of his father's hand in his excitement.

Roger's nod was barely perceptible. "Don't worry," his lips

said. "Now go to sleep," he said out loud.

When Rogers returned to the table, the lawyer was counting out money. "I'm a man of my word, Mr. Rogers. I want to pay you immediately."

Rogers' mouth hardened. "I told you I wasn't interested."

"Come now, Mr. Rogers. Two thousand dollars will do an awful lot for your boy. Might get him on his feet before–"

"Just who do you think I am, Mr. West – Judas? You were right earlier. Hiram is my friend. Do you think I'd sell him out?"

"As a religious man, Mr. Rogers, you should recognize the fallacy of your analogy. You wouldn't be 'selling out' a good man. You'd be bringing a criminal to justice."

"I don't see it that way. And I'd like to end this discussion now. I'm not interested and never will be. The thing you and your company cannot understand is that there are people who do not have a price. You see only the Judases who will sell out, but you fail to recognize the fact that for every man who had a price there were 11 who did not."

"Now one more thing, Mr. Rogers. You have practically admitted that Hiram Jackson comes here with your knowledge and consent. Do you know what the penalty is for harboring a fugitive from justice?"

Rogers was a little taken aback. He had been well aware of the chance he had been taking all along. How should he answer this? Then he thought of the stories Jim Logan had told him. He would answer bluff with bluff.

"I hardly think your company is in a position to talk either of honesty or justice, Mr. West," he said icily. "What about some of the nefarious practices you have dealt in the past?"

"Just what for instance, Mr. Preacher?"

"Well, there are your top men who were convicted of criminal fraud. And if that isn't enough I'd like to remind you of a little matter of blackmail against a state legislator who also happened to be a preacher. Money, power and political pressure in high places secured pardons for the officers of your company, but you consider a hillman whose conviction is questionable, an outlaw, a symbol of rebellion."

It was a shot in the dark, but the blow struck home. The company representative made a brave attempt to look blank, but traces of distress and confusion betrayed him. Where had this schoolteacher heard of these things? Such information could prove very dangerous in the hands of the natives.

"Well, Mr. – Mr. Rogers," he stammered, gathering up his money, "if you have decided to go along with these ignorant hillbillies I guess we can't do business."

Rogers was silent as he watched his guest fold the paper money and put it in his pocket. The man reached for his hat and made for the door.

"Just as a parting suggestion," Rogers said to him, "don't you think that is an awful lot of money for a stranger to be carrying in these hills? Men have been killed for less."

West stopped dead in his tracks, as he thought of the murder of their company adjuster four years ago. His face paled.

"Thanks," he mumbled nervously. "Thanks very much for warning me."

He rushed from the cabin and jerked his horse loose. Tommy and his father laughed while they watched his well-padded body jostling up and down in the saddle, like a storm-tossed boat at sea, as his horse flew down the road.

Give Me Thy Vineyard

Give Me Thy Vineyard

Chapter 26

G RADY ROGERS didn't debate with himself any further about what action to take. He knew he must accept the invitation of the Montgomerys to move to their place. He must also get a warning to Hiram that he had been seen going from his cabin.

Grady explained his decision to Tommy and the next morning when Annie came he repeated it to her.

"I didn't want to do it at all when Daddy first suggested moving to your place," Tommy observed to Annie Montgomery. "But I guess there just isn't anything else to do. The weather is getting cold and there isn't any way for me to keep the fires burning while Daddy is away all day."

"Yo're right, honey," Annie agreed. "Hit's a heap better fer yo'uns thisaways. An' my boys is jist a pinin' fer yo'uns ter hurry up an move."

"Will tomorrow be too soon, Annie?" Grady wanted to know. "It will be Saturday and a good time for me to get things settled."

"Nary a bit too soon, Brother Rogers," that good lady replied. "I'se got the room all ready fer yo'uns. Now yo'all jist go on off ter school an' don't worry 'bout things none."

The bewildered teacher was so grateful to be able to leave his son in such capable hands that he couldn't resent Annie's officiousness. He felt greatly relieved as he hurried down the trail that led to the schoolhouse.

Give Me Thy Vineyard

At school that day the children began asking their teacher if they could have a Christmas program.

"Why, yes," Rogers answered.

"An' a tree, too? We allers goes in the woods an' cuts one."

"We'll set up a tree and trim it with strings of popcorn and colored paper chains," the teacher promised.

"An' some little red berries," piped up an 8-year-old.

"Berries?" Grady asked. "Oh, you mean those red berries I see growing on bushes in the woods."

"Yes, we'uns allers does string 'em fer the tree."

"Well," their teacher laughed, "if you have always done it then we'll keep on doing it. We will start on the program Monday."

The teacher listened to the children reciting their lessons only with his ears that day. His mind was occupied with things that had been going on outside the schoolroom. His fight with Clark Harmon, Tommy's danger, Mr. West's visit. And Hiram. How long could he escape with a price of $2,000 on him? Someone knew he had been to the cabin. Who could it be that would tell? The Harmons, of course. Grady must send Hiram a warning. He wouldn't dare come to the cabin again.

The long, anxious day finally dragged itself to an end and the children were liberated for the weekend. Grady hurried home to relieve Annie Montgomery and to get their things ready for the move tomorrow.

Saturday dawned with the kind of weather they had hoped for. By the middle of the day, when Cliff drove over in the wagon for them the sun was shining bright and warm. Tommy was excited with eager anticipation at the change in their program of life, but his father didn't share his enthusiasm. He had enjoyed their simple, quiet life in the cabin. However, for the time at least he knew they had no choice but to accept the Montgomerys' kind offer to shelter them.

As soon as Tommy was comfortably settled, his father made a trip to Clear Springs. He had to get a message of warning to Hiram. He didn't know when he would see Rosie, but he knew the fugitive came to Dave's store on Saturday nights.

When he reached the store it was full of people, so he waited around until the last one had gone. Then he told Dave of the move he had made and of Mr. West's visit.

"Plumb glad yo'uns moved that little feller out o' the way o' danger," Dave commented. "Them Harmons won't stop at nuthin' ter git even. An' I'll tell Hiram somebody's tole 'bout him a goin' ter yer cabin. Don't think many folks knowed 'bout hit, but reckon if the Harmons knowed hit they'd shore tell!"

"Will you tell Hiram about their raising the reward, too?" Grady inquired.

"Nope. Don't reckon hit would be good fer him ter know thet. He might git panicky an' do somethin' he hadn't orter."

"Tell Rosie I've moved and she won't need to look after Tommy anymore," the teacher said as he turned to leave the store.

Then he thought of something else.

"Oh, yes, Dave, I nearly forgot. I want you to order me 75 pounds of candy and six dozen oranges for Christmas treats."

Dave stared blankly for a minute. "Yo'uns don't have that many young'uns in school, does yo'?" he asked.

"No, but I made a list of all the little children in the district who are not old enough to start to school. There are almost as many of them as there are pupils. And then there are several old folks who won't have much Christmas, like Grandpa Benson and Granny Smith. I shall prepare treats for all of them."

"All right, I'll fix it up fer yo'uns." Big Dave agreed, making a mental note that he would sell this to the teacher at less than cost. Rogers couldn't afford to spend nearly half his month's check for other folks' Christmas.

The children worked happily the intervening two weeks until Christmas. With their teacher's guidance they made clever invitations to carry home to their parents asking them to the Christmas party. They learned recitations and songs and tried hard to speak and sing just as their teacher wanted them to. Grady taught them the Christmas story and showed them how to dramatize it. The girls were delighted with the chance to act, and wear lovely costumes, but the big boys felt terribly self-conscious dressed up in fancy robes and headdress. They were glad Joseph and the shepherds had no speaking parts.

Grady had had quite a time with those costumes. Finally Annie suggested coloring some sugar sacks. She knew several ways of making dyes. So one day she and Ruthie Barnes made the children's costumes.

They set up the tree and decorated it two days before the program which was to be given the afternoon before Christmas Day. Most of the parents came, except Tobe Alton and Cliff Montgomery, who stayed with Tommy. The party was a thoroughly enjoyable affair and they were all generous in praising the teacher and his pupils.

Grady gave his pupils their treat, wished them all a "Merry Christmas" and dismissed them for a week's vacation which the school board had suggested.

Tommy and Grady ate Christmas dinner with the Montgomerys. Annie cooked a turkey with dressing and made giblet gravy. Ruthie and Zeke Barnes and Fred spent the day with them. Tommy was feeling his best and all aglow with excitement. Rosie came by in the afternoon and brought Tommy a gift from Hiram. She set a little box-like cage on the floor before him. It was made from an 18-inch length of hollowed-out log about 12 inches in diameter. The ends were closed with a securely fastened latticework of strong hickory thongs.

Tommy squealed and clapped his hands. "What is in it, Rosie?" he cried. "Tell me quick."

"I'll show yo'uns," Rosie said gladly, pulling a squirrel from the cage.

"Oh," was all the boy could say as Rosie brought the little animal to him. "Oh," he repeated. "Did Hiram catch it in the woods?"

"Yes, he did," Rosie said, noticing the teacher wipe his eyes. She wanted to cry, too.

"Hiram caught hit an' has been tamin' hit in his cave fer yo'uns. He fetched hit over an' left hit at Uncle Dave's fer yo'uns."

"And all I've got for him is this bag of candy and an orange," Tommy said sadly.

"Oh, Hiram'll love hit," Rosie exulted, "an' he'll love yo'all, too, fer 'memberin' him."

"I remembered you, too, Rosie," Tommy cried gaily. "Daddy said I could give you this new book."

"Oh, Tommy," she said, hugging the boy to her. "Yo'all shouldn't give me yore new book." She opened the package. It was *Pilgrim's Progress*.

The next day Grady Rogers persuaded Annie to let him take Tommy with him to spend their week of vacation in the cabin.

Not that Tommy hadn't been happy with the Montgomerys. He loved Cliff and Annie and their three boys. The boys told him interesting things that happened at school which his father apparently didn't know about or thought unimportant.

But Rogers thought it would be nice to be to themselves again. He had a supply of groceries to last so he would be able to spend all of his time with his son.

They were very happy in their isolation for three days. The weather had turned cold with a rather strong wind blowing from the northwest, but they had plenty of firewood and several new books and magazines received as Christmas presents so they spent the short winter days happily reading.

Tommy woke up one morning with a headache and no appetite. He rested in bed all morning. At noon his father wakened him to eat his lunch. He still wasn't hungry. Grady became alarmed and felt his head. It was hot. By mid-afternoon his fever was raging and Rogers ran all the way to the Montgomerys' for Annie. She was bathing two of the boys, but she left them in the tub to care for each other and ran to the cupboard for a bottle of herbs, good for "layin' the fever." She walked as fast as her stout legs would carry her to Rogers' cabin.

As soon as Cliff could understand what Rogers was saying, he saddled a horse and raced recklessly along the narrow, twisting 14 miles to Hartstown for the nearest doctor.

Then Rogers hurried back home overtaking Annie halfway there. He entered the cabin and tried to appear calm so as not to alarm Tom. The child was in a troubled sleep and Rogers and Annie sat by his bed watching him. When he opened his eyes they gave him some of the homemade medicine.

Annie fixed supper for Rogers but he couldn't eat. He knew his son was growing worse. His face had turned yellow and he was spitting blood.

It was nearly midnight before Cliff arrived with the doctor. He examined Tom quickly, but thoroughly. When he was finished he motioned Rogers outside.

"I'm sorry to tell you this, Mr. Rogers, but your boy is dangerously ill. Probably won't live more than a couple of days."

Rogers stared at him. He knew he hadn't heard the man right.

"What is it, Doctor?" That was his own voice, but it was coming from someone else. Someone who was alive and able to talk.

216

Give Me Thy Vineyard

The doctor was saying to him, "Pneumonia. His already weak lungs are working themselves to death. I've given Mrs. Montgomery something for him. It will ease the pain. I'll give him something else to make him stop coughing." He put his hand on Rogers' arm. "I wish I could do more. I feel so–"

"Can't we get him to a hospital?"

"The nearest one is in Springfield. He'd never be able to stand the trip."

"You mean there's nothing for us to do except wait?"

The doctor stared at the ground. "There's nothing medicine can do. Only a miracle can save your son now. I've seen miracles in my thirty years of practice here in the hills. You are a religious man. Perhaps prayer–"

"I'll never stop praying as long as he breathes," Rogers said devoutly. "If only I hadn't brought him here. If I had kept him near a doctor. Perhaps he has had too much exposure."

"Now, Mr. Rogers, you must not blame yourself for any part of this. You have done what you thought was best. No man can do more. Besides, this or something else would have occurred sooner or later. And even if by some miracle the boy does get better–" He couldn't go on. Things like this were always hard for him.

"If he does get better, what then?" Rogers prompted.

"He couldn't live more than five years. And he'd be suffering all the time. Maybe God in His infinite mercy knows that it would be better if–"

"He won't die," Rogers declared. "I won't let him."

"You may be right," the doctor answered. "I don't believe enough in miraculous healing – yet, I don't know. God's wonders are out of my sphere."

For two days and nights Rogers and Annie sat by the bed. Rogers sent a continual petition heavenward for help. He didn't think he should ask that Tommy's life be spared. God knew best about that. But he asked for two things: that he be given grace and strength to submit to God's will and that his child be called upon to suffer as little pain as possible.

Rogers thought in the two days' vigil that he had prepared himself to give Tommy up. But when he saw his time was very near, he felt he could never give him up. He wanted to gather him in his arms and hold him by sheer force.

The word had gotten around that the teacher's son was gravely ill, and the cabin was filled with sympathetic neighbors, offering to do what they could. Rogers hardly knew they were there except that he felt comforted to know so many cared.

In his moments of lucidity, Tom had asked for Rosie and Hiram. But Rosie was in Lake City, more than 20 miles away. And Hiram – how could anyone say where he was? The fugitive probably did not even know that Tom was sick, and Rogers reflected it was better that way. He might try to come and see the boy of whom he had grown so fond, and then there would be trouble from all sides. He, Rogers, felt he had trouble enough.

Suddenly Tom opened his eyes and looked at his father.

"Hi, Dad."

"Hi, son." Thank God he was rational. "Want some water?"

Tommy shook his head slightly and closed his eyes again.

In a few seconds his painful breathing stopped altogether.

The people in the cabin stirred and looked at each other. Many began to weep openly. Annie Montgomery opened the door of the old-fashioned clock and stopped the hands at the hour of death. Then she removed her apron and draped it over the mirror of the dresser. An old, old custom of pioneer people.

Rogers turned to the women.

"His things are in there," he said, pointing to a small chest. "You know what to do." Then he went blindly toward the cabin door. Cliff Montgomery reached out to stop him, but his wife said sharply, "Let him go, Cliff. He needs ter git out now."

Rogers stepped out into the blackness of the night.

Give Me Thy Vineyard

Give Me Thy Vineyard

Give Me Thy Vineyard

Chapter 27

*T*HE TEACHER STRUCK OUT into the thick, trackless woods behind the cabin, not seeing or caring where he was headed. All he knew was that he had to get away from the place where this thing had just happened.

He had to make himself believe it really had happened. That he was not having a bad dream, from which he would soon wake up. No, he would never wake from this. He would always go on with that raw aching spot around his heart.

He had spent hour after hour in prayer to prepare himself since the doctor's visit. But he supposed one could never fully prepare to let a loved one go. It had been the same way with Betty and his mother, the only women he had ever loved. And now Tommy. Why was he called upon to give up everyone he loved and needed so much?

Aimlessly he walked in the darkness of the woods, bumping into trees and tripping over underbrush. He had to get away. He had to find God. Only God could ease this pain. What did a man do in an hour like this without faith in God? "God giveth and God taketh away." Someway Grady would have to reconcile himself to God's will.

On and on he pushed his way, breathing in great gulps. This was how Tom had felt, fighting for air with bands of fire cutting his chest. He tripped and fell, cutting his hand on a sharp stone. But there was something good about the pain.

Give Me Thy Vineyard

Something forced him to his feet and deeper into the woods. Tom had always wanted to walk through the woods at night. He liked the night sounds. He was such a good child. Whose fault was it that he never had a chance?

Whose fault indeed! Rogers could only blame himself. He was God's reason for taking Tommy away. He had no right to the boy who was dying for a home, while he, his father, had been waiting to fall in love.

Love, Rogers thought bitterly, *love brought Tom and killed Betty*. And now Tom, too, was gone. Poor little Tommy, so brave and patient and good. How right Annie Montgomery had been. The little fellow did need a mother. Had always needed one. No wonder she had been so indignant.

But a man didn't marry a woman to have a nurse and companion for a sick child. Even if he had found someone to take Betty's place he couldn't have asked her to take on that kind of responsibility.

Hour after hour Rogers circled around in the woods. At last he came upon a well-worn path. He wondered vaguely where it led. He was so tired. He staggered up the trail and fell upon his knees beside an old log. He was oblivious of his surroundings. For a long time he knelt there, his brain tired, too numb for thought. Finally he began to talk to his Maker. He poured out all the hurt and anguish of his tortured soul to God alone, who could hear and heal.

Grady rose and sat upon the log and wondered how long he had been there. It might have been a few minutes or it might have been hours. He had lost all sense of time.

But the darkness of night was releasing its grip on the hills as the first streak of light heralded a new day and Grady saw where he was. The cliff behind the Montgomerys' house. It was here that he first found rest and peace in the quiet beauty of the hills. It all seemed so long ago now.

But he had never seen it early in the morning. It seemed to have a different meaning. When Rogers first gazed out on the scene before him, he thought he saw a new beginning – new life for him, new hope for Tommy. But it had meant the end for Tommy. What for him? Grady Rogers looked straight ahead for a long time. *This must be the beginning for me,* he thought. *Tom's purpose here is done and God in His mercy took him Home. He still has work for me to do. I must find what it is.*

Grady Rogers turned into the trail toward his cabin breathing this prayer, "Not my will but Thine, O God." Halfway down the hillside he met Cliff Montgomery.

"I thought I'd find yo'uns up here, Brother Rogers," Cliff said. "Some o' the folks war a gittin' oneasy 'bout yo'all."

"I'm all right now, Cliff. And I certainly do thank all of you for your kindness."

Montgomery nodded sympathetically.

"I'll take Tommy back home to be buried by the side of his mother. I suppose there isn't an undertaker closer than Hartstown, is there?"

"They hain't none closter than Springfield," his neighbor said grimly.

"But, Cliff, what am I going to do? If I move Tom – if I take him home – he'll have to be – embalmed." He tried to keep his voice firm and even.

"Yo'uns jist cain't take him away, Mr. Rogers. Yo'll jist have ter lay him away here."

Rogers looked stunned. He hadn't thought of the impossibility of taking his son home for burial.

"I guess you're right," he said dejectedly.

They had reached Cliff Montgomery's place. Cliff made an excuse to do some chores and look after the young'uns so Rogers went the rest of the way to his cabin alone.

In his absence kind neighbors had gone about doing what there was to do.

Annie Montgomery had begun by tearing an old pillowcase into strips. Then, closing the dead child's mouth, she placed a strip below the jaws and tied it on top of his head. With another strip she tied his hands across his chest.

Taking two pennies from her husband, she laid them on the boy's eyelids to hold them until the coldness of death would take their place. Then she and the other women gently washed the body and dressed it in clean clothes which they found in the dresser.

The men placed two chairs side by side about 4 feet apart, filled the space with an oak board and placed an old quilt on it. They then draped a blanket over the backs of the chairs and smoothed it over the quilt, letting it hang to the floor. They lifted the child to this bier and waited for rigidity to set in.

The people hardly dared look at each other while they performed their tasks, for they all stood in awe of death. They believed that God, for some reason or other, took their loved ones from them with His own Hand. Therefore, the advent of death brought them into a nearness of His Presence. So they spoke only when necessary, and in hushed tones.

After covering the body with a clean sheet, the women pulled the covers from the bed and carried them into the yard to the clothesline. It was a relief to get out into the open air where they could sniffle unreservedly.

"'Course, 'twas better for the little feller ter go, him bein' so puny he couldn't get out none," said Mrs. Morgan, wiping her eyes.

"But his pa'll miss him more'n if he war a pert young'un. 'Pears like when yo're a lookin' out fer a body all a time yo' misses 'em a sight worse when they's gone," Annie declared.

"But iffn hit's the good Lord's will fer him ter go ter his Maker, then hit's better thataway. His pa'll git over hit." Mandy Ames knew what she was talking about. She had lost her only child five years ago.

"But, say," Ruthie Barnes reminded them, "where is Brother Rogers, nohow? He should o' been back by now."

Annie Montgomery frowned. "I'se worried 'bout him, Ruthie, no foolin'. It war natural fer him ter want ter git out alone in his moment o' grief, but he's been gone fer hours."

The men were also concerned about Rogers. They had taken down the bed and placed it in the back yard where it would stay until after the funeral, and had hung the feather tick over the fence. But while they worked they wondered if some of them should go out and look for the teacher. They didn't know that Cliff Montgomery had already set out on that mission.

The neighbors were just finishing their breakfast when Rogers came in out of the swirling morning fog. One of the women quickly poured a cup of coffee and the men pushed a chair under him. His face was deathly pale, and his bloodshot eyes blinked painfully. There was a cut on his hand and blood on his chin and shirt; his clothing was torn and disheveled.

"Yo'd best have another cup o' coffee, Brother Rogers. Hit'll make yo'uns feel better."

He forced down the second drink and sat quietly for a moment trying to pull himself together. At last he said, "I'm ready to have the funeral tomorrow. At 10 o'clock, I guess." He looked tiredly around. "Is there someone who can make a casket?"

"Yes," said Annie, "we'se got good dry walnut and cherry laid away in the stable. Cliff's right handy at makin' coffins. He'll git right at it."

"Somebody'll have ter go ter Hartstown," Annie continued, "an' git the cotton battin' an' crepe fer covers an' linin'. Then they's got ter be handles an' stuff. Hit'll cost 'bout eight dollars."

"Me an' my boy'll go an' fetch hit fer yo'uns, Brother Rogers," volunteered quiet Sam Bates. "We'uns knows what yo'll be a needin'."

Rogers looked away from him, remembering that two of

Sam's boys had been drowned last summer.

Rising from his seat at the table, he asked about the grave.

"Brother Rogers, yo'uns jist leave all o' that ter us. We'll git ever'thin' all ready iffn yo'all'll tell us where yo' wants ter berry him an' who yo'uns wants ter do the preachin'," Annie directed.

"I guess the little graveyard between here and Clear Springs will be all right. We'll have the funeral at the schoolhouse. You will know best about the preacher."

"I'll send Fred Barnes ter fetch Brother Honeycutt," Annie decided. "An' I'll pick out the songs."

Rogers went through the funeral as if in a trance. He scarcely heard the sermon or the songs. He sat like one turned to stone. When he moved it was as if he were dead.

Finally his neighbors lowered the handmade casket into the grave with a heavy pair of harness lines. Then Rogers turned and walked away.

Rosie Gurney stood with the other women by the side of the grave, sobbing softly.

"Jist 'pears like Brother Rogers is a needin' a woman now worser'n ever," Annie Montgomery said.

Give Me Thy Vineyard

Give Me Thy Vineyard

Give Me Thy Vineyard

Chapter 28

*T*HE FULL MOON was plowing its way steadily through the broken clouds as two armed guards paced slowly along the top of the dam. Four times during an hour they met at the white line that marked the center of the structure, talked for a moment, and then turned back. But at their fifth meeting they stopped for a longer time.

One of the guards was thin and jumpy, and the creases in his new uniform had not yet straightened themselves out from wear.

"This walking sentry all night is foolish," he complained. "These hillbillies are too stupid to know how to damage turbines."

"Don't kid yourself. They're not so stupid that they don't know what a couple of sticks of dynamite can do. They're still plenty sore, you know, because of the company taking their farms and flooding them."

"So I heard."

"Two years ago someone blew up a transformer unit at the power line. We never knew who did it. It was a dynamite job and cost us plenty of money. Nope. Until these people get used to the idea that we're here for their own good, they've got to be watched."

"Why doesn't the company catch this hillbilly Jackson I've been hearing so much about? The fellows were telling me he's the guy that's stirring everybody up."

"Well, I don't think he's really doing much, if anything. He's not smart enough. But the people have built him up in their own minds as a sort of god, fighting the company at the risk of his own life. You know the sort of thing. That's why he's so dangerous to us. The company's been trying to soft-pedal our attempts to catch him, so the other hillbillies won't get too excited, but now we're going to get tough. We've made that sheriff promise to get on the ball – he's been stalling around all these years – and we've raised the ante on the reward for Jackson. It's up to two thousand now. We'll get him."

The new guard had a romantic soul. He smiled. "You know, this business reminds me of the Jesse James stories I used to read when I was a kid."

"You're not far off. The railroads right here in this state were the ones who had all that trouble with Jesse James. They condemned the land, too, and the people hated them."

"Yup. And so the people sympathized with Jesse and protected him. But the railroads kept raising the reward money until it hit five thousand. That would equal ten thousand now and one of Jesse's own friends killed him and collected."

His companion nodded. "That's what we hope will happen again. That guy Jackson's a thorn in our side, and two thousand dollars is like a million down here."

"Well, guess it won't be long now. Have we got time to talk any more?"

"No, but let's stay here a minute more anyway." He liked to talk. "You know," he continued, "someone's already turned down that two thousand cold?"

"They have! Who's the sucker?"

"A schoolteacher. A religious guy with a sick kid. He comes from the outside and West thought he'd be only too happy to spill what he knew about Jackson and take the money. West went to him before we posted the reward notices and counted the money right out under his nose, but he wouldn't touch it. He's become just like the rest of them."

"Hmm. Maybe no one will talk?"

The other guard looked at him knowingly.

"Well, if not, maybe we won't need talking."

"What do you mean?"

The older one hesitated. "Oh, I guess I can tell you. But you'd better keep your mouth shut. This is still sort of a hush-hush deal." He leaned closer to his companion. "This afternoon a hillbilly named Clark Harmon came into the office and said he'd show us where Jackson digs roots. The boss almost fell over."

"Who's Harmon?"

"He's a shifty sort of guy. Four years ago he saw Jackson running away from where our man was murdered and testified against him. His brother was with him and testified, too, and since then the people here have hated them."

"But what suddenly made him decide to squeal now? Don't tell me he just found out where Jackson digs roots. I heard that everybody around here has known Jackson's hideout for years but won't talk."

"Harmon might not have known before, because, like I said, no one will have anything to do with him. But he's been scared stiff that Jackson will take revenge on him for testifying, so he's always been on the lookout for him. The two thousand must have spurred him on a bit. He saw Jackson going away from this teacher's cabin one night."

"Why doesn't he kill Jackson himself?"

"Well, it seems that he's afraid to get within shooting range of him. Jackson always has a dog with him and Harmon thinks the dog is a devil. Superstitious, I guess. And besides, Jackson's a better shot than he is, and he might shoot back."

"Then what's the deal?"

"Harmon will come here early tomorrow morning and one of the boys will go back into the hills with him. Harmon says he'll take him to a secret place across the valley from the hill where Jackson digs roots. From there our man can try for a long shot, either at the man or the dog. This'll give us a good chance to test one of those new Savage .303 high-powered rifles with the long-range telescope sights."

"Pretty good."

"Right. I think we've got him where we want him now. But, you know, this guy Harmon wanted the whole reward for his work. We finally got him to agree to take five hundred dollars if we kill the dog and a thousand dollars if we get Jackson."

"Why don't we give him all of it if we get Jackson?'

"Why should we? He's just a stool pigeon. If he'd do the dirty work himself he'd be welcome to it, but the guy who does the shooting deserves some credit, too."

Give Me Thy Vineyard

Give Me Thy Vineyard

Give Me Thy Vineyard

Chapter 29

*H*IDDEN BY THE UNDERBRUSH, Hiram knelt on the ground digging industriously at a clump of goldenseal roots. It was Saturday and tonight he would go to Big Dave's store for supplies and a letter from Rosie. He had not seen the girl for more than two weeks and he was worried. In her letter last Saturday she had told him to be extra careful. The sheriff was really looking for him now, she said, and she didn't dare meet him during the day.

Dave, too, had expressed anxiety about him, but had changed the subject when Hiram had tried to press him for details. What was happening on Reed's Ridge anyway? Ever since poor little Tom Rogers died, Rosie had been so strange and quiet, as if she were holding something back. And yet it would seem that everything was all right. The election was over. The deputy had been elected sheriff by the hill folks because both he and the old sheriff had promised to keep hands off Hiram. The old sheriff had promptly been appointed deputy and Hiram hoped that with the two officers on his side as they had promised, he might have more freedom of action now. And yet he didn't.

Dave had muttered something puzzling about a double cross and the reward. What was it? The reward had never seemed to tempt the law before. Did the officers want it now because they were sure of their jobs for another two years? But it didn't make sense. Why hadn't Dave told him the whole story?

Hiram shook his head and then quickly began to fill the sack with roots. He whistled for Bullet who lay on a boulder a hundred feet away. Through the underbrush he could see the big dog rise and stand for a moment, silhouetted against the sky, when a rifle shot blasted his thought and he stood stunned as Bullet toppled from the boulder.

Still clutching the sack of roots, he plunged after Bullet, who was rolling over and over down the side of the steep cliff. The dog's descent was finally stopped by a heavy clump of brush and Hiram was able to reach him. He was alive but covered with blood.

"He'll make a fine trail of blood fer them ter foller," Hiram muttered savagely, ripping off his shirt and wrapping it tightly around the dog's body. "There. This'll hold us fer a little bit nohow."

Then picking the animal up, he ran with him, stooping as low as he could, in a zigzag line along the side of the mountain. In a heavy thicket he turned to the right and made his way upward. Then he crossed the crest and descended the opposite slope. Halfway down he turned south, following the narrow protruding ledge of granite rim rock. Turning downward again, he entered the wild dark canyon which was his front yard.

Here he stopped for a minute to catch his breath. Bullet weighed about 75 pounds and was a dead weight in his arms. Had they crippled the dog, he wondered. Maybe he would even die. With his mind confused, Hiram started out again as fast as he could move. In a short time he had pushed his way through the tangle of sumac, buckeye blackberry and grapevines which covered the canyon and was crawling down the tunnel and into his cave.

Gently he laid Bullet on his own bed. Quickly he lit a fire and then pushed a big rock into the tunnel opening. Even in his anxiety he did not forget to stuff up the cracks with rags. This was automatic with him now.

And then, placing a lantern near the dog, he examined the wound carefully.

"Shot yo' plumb through, jist back o' yore front leg. Now lay still, 'cause I'se goin' ter clean hit out."

The dog whined and weakly nipped at Hiram as he cut the flesh and burned out the wound.

"Iffn I ever find out who shot yo'uns, Bullet, I'll shore kill him. But killin's too good fer anybody what would shoot a dog. Hit's that reward what's behind hit. Five hun'erd dollars is so much money, they's pappies what would kill their young'uns ter git hit." He shook his head. "But no one 'roun' here could o' done hit. We'uns don't pack long-range rifles. The shuriff must o' got somebody from the outside. Or else hit war somebody from the 'lectric."

With a sigh he finished tying up the dog's wound. Then he went to the little underground stream and filled a bucket of water. Every little while he put cold compresses on the wound and fed the dog water. He tended the half-conscious animal like a baby, for he knew that without Bullet his own days were numbered.

Bullet fought for life. With glazed eyes and tongue hanging loose, he whimpered continually and tried to move.

Give Me Thy Vineyard

Give Me Thy Vineyard

Chapter 30

*B*IG DAVE GURNEY had just completed his bountiful bachelor breakfast when Rosie opened the kitchen door and walked in. Big Dave slept late on Sunday mornings, for Saturday's business was always heavy and closing time found him "plumb tuckered out."

Rosie was wearing a neatly starched white blouse and a green knitted skirt. A heavy jacket completed the ensemble. She was carrying a small Bible, for she was on her way to church at Stony Point. Rosie had long made it a habit to stop in at her uncle's every Sunday morning to pick up the message which Hiram left for her the night before.

But this time, instead of booming a greeting and teasing her about Hiram's scrawled note, Dave looked at her anxiously and motioned for her to sit down.

"I'se afeard they's somethin' wrong, Rosie. I waited ter the store till after 11 o'clock last night, but Hiram never showed up. Thar hain't no message fer yo'uns this mornin'."

Rosie caught her lower lip between her teeth and her black eyes widened.

"Uncle Dave, I told yo' we should o' let Hiram know 'bout the reward a goin' up. Maybe the shuriff er somebody from the company er even one o' the folks 'roun' here shot him an'–"

"Whoa, Rosie! Now jist a minute. Don't you think if they got Hiram we'd know 'bout hit? They couldn't keep a thing like that hid. Yo' all is a gittin' too excited, gal."

"Wish yo' hadn't o' mentioned that sneakin' little shuriff. Jist hearin' 'bout him riles me up. I cain't git over his doin's. Before th' 'lection a promisin' if ever'body here'bouts would vote fer his deputy he'd let Hiram be. An' now that the 'lection's over things is worser'n ever."

"But what 'bout Hiram, Uncle Dave?" The big man frequently got lost in his own thoughts and had to be led back to the subject at hand.

"Hiram? Oh, shore, shore. Now don't yo' worry none, gal. Now that I think 'bout hit a little, seems ter me Hiram's jist bein' extry keerful like we'uns tole him ter be. Maybe he got wind that the shuriff war a hangin' 'roun' the store last night an' kept away." He wagged his head up and down on his fat neck.

"Yo' warn't talkin' thisaway when I come in, Uncle Dave," said Rosie shrewdly. "Yo'uns seen me git all het up so yo'uns is a tryin' ter make me feel better now. Yo' is worried an' yo'uns knows hit. Now be straight with me; what air yo'all a thinkin'?"

Dave was too honest to resist his niece's direct gaze.

"Yo'uns knows me too good," he mumbled. Then, with a sigh, he settled heavily back in his chair. "Yo're right. I is worried 'bout Hiram. He knows these hills better'n anybody else, but I'se jist afeard he cain't stay hid when folks kin git two thousan' dollars fer him. Honey, that's why I'se glad we didn't tell him 'bout the reward a goin' up. It might o' made him so nervous he'd do somethin' wrong."

"'Nother thing, Brother Rogers had a set-to with the lawyer fer them fellers at the dam. He offered Brother Rogers the reward to tell 'em what days yo' an' Hiram met at the cabin when Brother Rogers war gone preachin'."

"Yes, Rosie, I'm scart they's a goin' ter git Hiram fer shore now."

"Oh, oh, Uncle Dave, then they know 'bout me seein'

Give Me Thy Vineyard

Hiram? Yo' think they got him now nohow?"

"No, Rosie. I war bein' straight with yo' afore. I'se oneasy 'bout why he didn't come by last night, but I'se sure they hain't got him. Like I said, we'd know fer sartin' iffn they did."

Rosie left her uncle's house a few minutes later deeply concerned. What should she do? Should she go to Hiram's cave and see if he was there? But it was broad daylight, and people would be on their way to church. That would be taking too much of a chance.

Someone might see me an' foller me, she thought. *Them low-down Harmons is always a snoopin' 'roun' on Sundays. No, hit's best that I goes straight on ter church. Then I'll talk this over with Brother Rogers. He's smart. He'll tell me what ter do.*

So Rosie went to church. But as she rode slowly along, a plan was gradually emerging from the confusion in her mind.

There were many people in the schoolhouse when she arrived, although it was still some time before Sunday school would begin. Hill folk like to go early to public gatherings in order to visit and talk.

Rosie tried her best to appear at ease. But she had to make such an effort to respond to the greetings of the crowd that she excused herself as quickly as she dared and stood in a corner by herself. She saw Rogers standing near the big black stove, surrounded by people. It was impossible to get to him now.

At 10 o'clock the services began. Rosie hardly heard what was going on. Where was Hiram now and what was he doing?

What could it have been that kept him last night? Oh, how could these folks sit around so calmly when she was bursting inside? Suddenly she hated them for their easy, happy lives, while she and Hiram had to – she stopped and reproached herself. What sinful thoughts! And at meeting, too. She

241

asked God to forgive her.

Sunday school lasted one hour and worship and preaching another, but both hours were wasted on Rosie. She squirmed and chafed with impatience. Then church was over and she flew to Rogers as he left the teacher's desk. She had to get to him before anyone else did.

"I wants ter talk ter yo' alone. Hit's real important. Kin I go home with yo' ter yore cabin?" Rosie poured this out in a rapid undertone.

Rogers looked at her sharply and nodded assent as people began to crowd around him.

Grady Rogers had changed in the month since Tom's death.

His body and face and hair had grown thinner and his blue eyes were cloudy.

He had packed to leave Stony Point soon after the funeral, but the hill folk had begged him to stay. At first he refused, but they kept at him with their pleading. The school needed him, they said, and the community needed him. They would raise his pay to 30 dollars a month; they would take him in to live with any of them; they would do anything he asked. Finally he agreed to stay. But not for long, he told them.

He moved back to the little cabin. Something held him there. But now his friends seldom left him alone. There always seemed to be company in the house, or people coming in wagons to take him to their homes for meals. Maybe this social life was good for him, maybe not. He never had time to think about it. He never had time to think about much of anything anymore.

And now Rosie wanted to see him. He was alarmed by the urgency in her voice. What was up? Politely, but as quickly as possible, he declined invitations to dinner.

At last everyone was gone and he and Rosie started down the trail to his cabin. Rapidly she told him of Hiram's failure to come to Dave's store.

"I didn't know who else ter go ter but yo'uns," she said. "Uncle Dave jist sets aroun' an' tries ter pertend he thinks ever'thin'll be all right, an' my pa – well, yo' know, Brother Rogers, he ain't so set on Hiram nohow. He wouldn't want me ter be a takin' no chances."

"What do you plan to do, Rosie?"

She leaned toward him. "I'se goin' ter hunt him up ternight when hit gits dark an' nobody kin see me go, 'cause I jist know somethin's happened ter him. I feels hit. Iffn Hiram couldn't git ter the store last night, but still war all right, he'd o' left me a message with the Altons er some o' the other folks he trusts. But somethin' kept him from goin' no place." She bit her lip and frowned distractedly.

However, she began to relax as she listened to Grady Rogers' low, calm voice.

"If I were you, Rosie, I'd tell your father what you just told me. The thing you're planning to do is dangerous. Someone ought to go with you." Rosie nodded her head in silent agreement. She knew he was right. "Do you want me to go with you?" Rogers inquired gently.

She frowned, hating to refuse him.

"I don't think so, Brother Rogers. No one but me knows Hiram's hidin' place. Now don't look like that, please. I knows yo'alls a friend – one o' the best we's got – an' so does Hiram. But not even Tobe Alton knows exactly where Hiram stays. An' 'sides, hit's a long ways from here, through wild an' dangerous country. Yo' cain't go a horseback. Only we'uns who's been a livin' roun' here all our lives could sneak roun' them hidden trails an' through no trails at all without makin' no noise." She eyed him, hoping he would understand. He did. "I guess you know what you're talking about, Rosie. But I still say, don't go alone. It's too risky now with that reward raised. You can't tell who might be following you."

Reluctantly, Rosie respected his advice. She told her father that she was going to look for Hiram that night. At first the usually mild John Gurney exploded, pounding on the table and forbidding her to leave the house. But after she had cried and pleaded, and then stubbornly declared that she would go anyway, he gave in. He had never been able to refuse his daughter anything. But he insisted on going with her, and to his surprise, she agreed after only a short argument. Rosie again remembered Rogers' advice.

As soon as night fell, father and daughter, each carrying a gun and fox horn, left the house. After first making sure that no one was around, they cautiously crossed the river and made their way up Turkey Range. Under a large tree at the edge of a high, bald peak, they stopped to get their breath. Rosie looked around. In the rising moonlight she could see for miles.

"I think this air fur enough fer yo'uns ter come with me, Pa," she said softly. "Hiram's cave hain't too fur from here, an' this air a good place fer yo'uns ter watch iffn anybody's a comin' from ary side."

Gurney nodded. He was tired out.

"All right," he agreed. "But iffn yo'uns hears one blast out o' this fox horn, yo' freeze right where yo're at an' git yore gun ready."

"Yes, Pa. An' iffn yo'all hears a noise from me, yo'uns come a runnin', cause I'll be a needin' yo'."

Carefully Rosie made her way down the western slope of the range and along the wild canyon. It took her an hour to reach the limestone cliff which housed Hiram's cave.

Her hands shaking, she parted the familiar thick bushes and crawled into the pitch-dark tunnel. He was there. He had to be, because the cave opening was sealed from the inside. Thank God.

"Hiram. Hiram. Hit's me, Rosie," she called in a tense, low voice.

No answer. She repeated the call, a little louder.

Finally his muffled voice came to her and her heart banged.

Give Me Thy Vineyard

"Jist a minute."

Hiram pushed aside the rock and Rosie crawled blinking into the lantern light of the cave room. Quickly he replaced the rock in the passageway and stared at her.

"Hit war dangerous fer yo' ter come ternight, Rosie, 'thout me a knowin'."

Ignoring his scoldings, she ran to him and peered eagerly into his face. He seemed to be fine, just fine. She moved closer.

"Yo'uns mad at me, Hiram?"

"Wisht I could be. I shore been missin' yo', gal."

"An' I been a worryin' 'bout yo'uns cause yo' didn't go ter Dave's las' night. I would o' come sooner, but I was afeard ter till atter dark. Pa come with me ter the top o' the range. He's a watchin' now. What happened noway? Air yo'uns all right?"

"'Tain't me, Rosie, hit's Bullet."

"Ohh– – –" She saw the dog, his head nearly hidden by a large blanket.

"Hiram – what happened?" She dropped to her knees and stared at the suffering animal.

"Somebody shot him from clean across the valley, ter the other side o' the range. I didn't dare leave him ter go ter Dave's las' night. He's orful sick. I'se been keepin' cold rags on both his sides. The bullet went plumb through. He don't eat nothin', jist lays there a sufferin' an' a loppin' up cold water. Hit's nearly two days now an' he's still bad. There hain't nothin' a body kin do, only jist wait. Iffn he kin hold out three er four days more, I reckon he'll git well."

"Pore Bullet." Rosie gently patted his head. "Kin I bring yo'uns some stuff fer him from the store?"

Hiram shook his head vigorously.

"I don't want yo'uns comin' here agin, Rosie; hit's too risky, now that they'se a gunnin' fer me. But tell Tobe Alton ter put some o' that air liniment an' some bread in the old holler tree we knows 'bout on Gobbler's Knob. I'll try ter git

245

hit termorrer night."

"Honey, kin yo' trust Tobe fer sure?"

"He's my best friend, hain't he?"

"Yes, only I git a funny feelin' 'bout him sometimes. He looks kinda sneakin'."

"An', oh, Hiram, I plumb forgot. Yo'uns don't know 'bout the reward – they done raised hit ter two thousan' dollars! An' even Tobe might go fer that."

"What!"

She looked at him, frightened by the expression on his face.

"Honey, Dave tole me not ter tell yo'. I forgot." She shook her head. "They wants yo' orful bad, Hiram. They's tryin' ter git ever'body a gunnin' fer yo'uns."

Hiram sat down and stared at the fire. For several minutes he said nothing.

Rosie, afraid of his thoughts, knelt beside him and put her arms around his neck. But suddenly, like a stranger he took them down and shook himself free of her.

"Why, Hiram?! What is yo'all a doin'?"

"Rosie, hit better be all over fer us, right now. They jist hain't nothin' ter look fer no more. Iffn Bullet dies they'll git me shore, an' I'll never git out o' the pen. An' even iffn he don't die, them fellers'll never git me 'thout a fight. I shore 'lows ter do some killin'."

"Hit'll never come ter that. Hit cain't." Rosie cried passionately.

Hiram moved close to her and took her in his arms, flaming at the closeness of her. He kissed her again and again.

Suddenly he released her and pushed her roughly from him. Rosie, hurt and stunned, staggered before him. Then, recovering herself, she turned to face him, her face aflame with anger. But before she could say a word, Hiram was speaking in a tight, hard voice, from his towering height above her.

"Rosie," he began, "I'se got somethin' ter say ter yo'uns an'

I wants yo'all ter listen till I gits through. Then I wants yo'uns ter clear out o' here an' I don't want ter ever see yo'uns agin."

Rosie gasped. "Why, Hiram Jackson! Yo're outer yore haid," she exploded.

"No, I hain't outer my haid," Hiram retorted. "Yo'uns jist hesh till I finishes. Then yo'll know I'se right. Rosie, when Bullet gits better so's I kin leave him er he dies, one t'other, I'se a goin' ter go out o' here an' do some killin' an' hit's 'bout time. I'se listened ter yo' an' Dave an' that preacher friend o' yo'rn 'bout long 'nuff."

"Why, Hiram, he's no friend o' mine. Leastways he's a friend o' yo'rn, too."

"He is too a friend o' yo'rn, Rosie. Yo'all jist fergit all 'bout me now an' yo' makes up ter that air preacher. He's already in love o' yo'uns. Anybody kin see that an' yo'all talks alla time 'bout him a bein' so good an' nice. He'd suit yo'all jist fine, Rosie. I hain't never been good 'nuff fer yo'uns, gal, an' I knows hit, but that preacher'll jist nacherly make yo'all a good husbin."

Rosie was too crushed to utter a sound. Hiram's words infuriated her. It was hard to tell whether the hard choking lump that rose in her throat was from fury or heartburst. She stared at Hiram as though she had never seen him before. Indeed he was a stranger to her in his present condition. His hair was tousled, his clothing rumpled and dirty and his eyes bloodshot from sleeplessness. Fear glowered from a face that revealed nothing but hatred and rage and suspicion. He looked like an ugly giant to Rosie as he stood with widespread legs and clinched fists before her. She shrank from him and knew only that she wanted to get away as fast as she could.

Wildly she ran and tugged at the log that blocked the opening of the cave. Hiram kicked ashes to cover the flame of the fire and blew out the lantern. In the darkness he moved to the cave's entrance and removed the log that closed it.

As Rosie darted past him to crawl out to freedom, he reached out and grabbed her. He drew her roughly to him and kissed her with such ugly, savage passion that she was reminded of her unpleasant encounter with Ray Harmon. This wasn't the impatient, stubborn Hiram she had always known. This was a brutal beast from whom she must escape.

More frightened than she had ever been in her life, Rosie struggled with what strength she could muster to free herself, beating upon Hiram as hard as she could with clenched fists. As suddenly as his arms had imprisoned her, Hiram released her from his grasp.

"Go," he whispered hoarsely. "Go as fast as yo' kin, Rosie."

The frightened and bewildered girl needed no second bidding. Dropping to her knees, she crawled through the opening as fast as her feeble strength would carry her. Once outside she forgot to be cautious and ran through the dark canyon as though pursued by demons.

At last she stumbled and fell to the ground exhausted. For many minutes she lay there half-stunned, half-conscious. She was more miserable than she had ever been before in her life and wished with all her heart she could die. Then she thought of her father waiting for her up on the ridge and her heart was filled with contrition. How good and patient he had been with her always! And how right he was, too! Hiram wasn't good enough for her. He wasn't good enough for anybody. At last she saw him as he was – a stupid, ignorant brute. She hoped she never would see him again, and she didn't care what happened to him.

Maybe he had killed the adjuster. For the first time she permitted her faith in Hiram's innocence to waver.

Her thoughts turned to Grady Rogers. Hiram had said he was in love with her. Rosie wished it were true. But, of course, it couldn't be. Any girl Brother Rogers loved would have to be refined and pretty and educated. Rosie felt her inadequacy and flushed. No, Hiram had just said that because he was jealous.

Jealous! Rosie sat up. That was it. Hiram didn't hate her. He didn't mean the things he had said. He still loved her and he was jealous of Grady Rogers. And he was scared, too. Scared of the things that could happen to her.

Rosie's heart sang. What a fool she had been! Why had she let Hiram talk so wildly? Why hadn't she made him hush and listen to her? Why hadn't she made him understand how much she loved him and how they must be patient a little longer and let God work out things for them in His own way? She felt like running back to Hiram and telling him all of these things, but her better judgment told her to rejoin her waiting father and come back and talk to Hiram at another time. She needed time to think things over and to pray for guidance.

Give Me Thy Vineyard

Give Me Thy Vineyard

Chapter 31

GRADY ROGERS was very anxious to hear about Rosie's visit to Hiram's cave, so instead of going home Monday after school he hiked directly over to Dave Gurney's store. Rosie hadn't gotten in yet off the mail route, he learned from Dave. He had seen her that morning and she told him that she had found Hiram in his cave and that Bullet had been shot. The dog was likely to die, Hiram was nearly wild and he had never seen Rosie so unhappy and discouraged. Dave himself, Rogers noticed, was pretty grim. He didn't question the old man further, but decided to wait for Rosie.

She came in half an hour later and Grady was touched by her tired, spiritless manner. She pushed past him, scarcely speaking, and turned the mailbags over to her uncle.

Then she said in a weary voice, "Uncle Dave, I wants ter speak ter Brother Rogers alone. Kin we'uns go over ter yore house?"

"Shore, honey," her uncle responded. "Jist go ahead an' he'p yorese'f. Yo'all know I'd give all I got ter ease things up a bit fer yo'uns."

"Shore, I knows hit," Rosie said listlessly, as she passed through the door that Grady Rogers held open for her.

They stepped off the porch that ran across the front of the building and into the well-worn footpath that led to the front door of Dave's house. Once inside, Grady opened the drafts on the large round-bellied stove and filled it with wood.

Rosie set the coffeepot on and brought cups. Then they sat in the comfortable room facing each other. Rosie seemed not to know where to begin and her companion gave her plenty of time. Finally she said, "Did Uncle Dave tell yo'uns?"

"Yes. He said you found Hiram in his cave and that Bullet had been shot. Is that all, Rosie?"

"That's all I could tell him," Rosie said, "but I want ter tell yo'uns the whole story. Do yo'uns have time ter hear hit?"

"Take all the time you wish, my dear."

So the unhappy girl told him everything. How Bullet was shot, and was very badly hurt. How Hiram was filled with rage and hatred and fear. The cruel things he had said to her and the brutal way he had embraced her.

"But I don't believe he meant ary word o' hit, Brother Rogers. I think he's jist scared an' jealous an'–an'–kinda wild bein' shut up alone like he is. Ever'thin's been a gittin' worse fer him 'stead o' better fer a long time now."

"I think you are right, Rosie," her counselor said. "No doubt Hiram is jealous, because he is afraid. Fear is what makes jealousy, you know."

"I'se made up my mind what I'se a goin' ter do, Brother Rogers," she said, paying no heed at all to Grady's observation.

Rogers looked at her steadily. He caught a note of grim determination in her voice. "What will you do, Rosie?"

"Yo're not a goin' ter like what I tells yo'uns, Brother Rogers, but I kinda looks ter yo'uns ter understan'. I'se made up my mind ter go an' live with Hiram in his cave."

Rogers couldn't help being shocked. "Rosie," he exclaimed, "you don't mean it."

"Yes, I does, Brother Rogers. I means hit. Hiram's a goin' crazy up there all alone. An' they's only one thing that'll stop him from doin' somethin' awful. I'se a goin' ter him."

"Does Hiram know this?" Rogers inquired.

"No, he don't yet. I come away from him as fast as I could like I tole yo'uns. But I sent him a letter terday long with some liniment fer Bullet by Tobe Alton."

"Why did you send him a message? If you've made up your mind to do what you've just told me, why don't you just take your things and go to him?"

"'Cause hit's dangerous fer anybody ter go near his hideout now. He's liable ter shoot at any noise he hears. He'd never 'spect me ter come back agin."

"Does Tobe know where to find him?"

"Tobe puts his stuff in a tree they both knows 'bout."

For a long time Grady Rogers sat gazing at the leaping flames in the stove that could be seen through isinglass openings in the door. Rosie grew too uncomfortable to remain quiet.

"I knows yo'uns thinks hit's orful wrong, Brother Rogers, an' I reckons yo're right. But–"

The teacher raised his head and looked at the girl. "You know what this means, don't you, Rosie? And all of the risks you are taking?" he said seriously.

"Yes, I shore does. I'se thought about ever'thin'! An' I'se prayed an' prayed. They jist hain't no he'p fer hit."

"Does your father know? Will he let you do this thing?"

The girl nodded. "He knows," she said, "an' his heart is broke. He won't ever understan' er fergive me, I reckon."

"Well," Rogers finally offered, "if you are willing to try living with Hiram in his hideout, why don't you bring him to my cabin and let me marry you? Not that I advise you to do it. It's a very foolish thing for you to do and is bound to lead to more grief for you. But if you were married, your honor at least would be saved."

"We'uns cain't git married, Brother Rogers. Hiram can't leave his cave now. An' we'd have to have license an' witnesses. Hiram jist wouldn't take the chance. An' I wouldn't want him ter take so much risk either."

"He surely wouldn't ask you to make such a great sacrifice. A gentleman protects the honor of women – especially the woman he loves."

"I knows all that as much as yo'uns does, Brother Rogers, but Hiram an' me's not ever had a fair chance. We'se tried hard anuff, but we'uns both knows now that afore long Hiram's bound ter be caught. If they takes him alive, he'll go ter the pen fer that air murder he never done. But they won't take him alive, Brother Rogers. Hiram'll die a fightin' 'cause he'd ruther be dead than in the pen."

Rogers felt that all the things the girl said were only too true. What could he say to her, whose life had been turned into a tragedy by the sin of society?

"Rosie, I wish there were something I could do to help. I wish with all my heart I could change your mind about this mistake you are making. For it is a mistake, my dear girl. You will live to regret it."

"I'm sure I will, Brother Rogers. Someday I'll wonder how I ever could a been so weak."

"Not weak, Rosie. I know you are not making this decision in a moment of weakness. You have been strong and full of faith all of these months. Won't you and Hiram just try to be patient a little while longer? Surely help will come to you some way soon."

"I'se already writ that letter, Brother Rogers, an' I'se tole my pa. I hain't a goin' ter say nuthin' ter Uncle Dave until Hiram's sent me word ter come. Nobody else will know but yo'uns. Hit'll be a lot safer fer me if nobody knows where I'm at. Pa an' Uncle Dave kin make up a story ter tell folks. Nobody will 'spect yo'all ter know where I disappeared to."

Rosie stood up and moved toward the door. Grady Rogers rose and followed her outside. He wished so much that he could think of something that would turn Rosie from hurling herself headlong into certain misery. Finally, as they parted, he said, "Rosie, I believe if you will pray very earnestly that God will show you a better way than this."

"I cain't pray no more, Brother Rogers," the miserable girl

cried. "I cain't pray, ner think, ner hardly sleep, ner eat. But I just had ter tell yo'uns, Brother Rogers. I'd be a heap comforted if I knowed yo'all understan's an' don't think too bad 'bout me."

"I do understand that you are a very fine person, Rosie, and if you can't pray for yourself, I'll pray all the harder for you."

"Thank yo'all, Brother Rogers," she whispered and walked away as one going to her execution.

Grady returned home almost as heavily burdened by this brave girl's tragic problem as she was herself. How could he let her go on into such a dangerous situation? Why didn't John Gurney stop her? And then again, how could he stop her? What could anyone do? She had sunk into the slough of despair and hopelessness where no human hand could reach her.

All the next day as he listened to classes, thoughts of the tragedy in Rosie's life hammered at his brain, accompanied by the question: *What can I do to help her? What can I do?* When he dismissed school and returned to his cabin in the woods, John Gurney sat on the front doorstep waiting for him.

This is it, Rogers thought to himself. *Rosie has gone. It is too late to help her now.* His heart sank low.

"Good evening, John." He hailed his neighbor, trying to appear cheerful.

John Gurney stood up, but he didn't return the greeting. He scarcely raised his head and his voice was tired and broken as he said, "I had ter come ter see yo'uns, Brother Rogers. We's in orful trouble an'–an'–"

"Yes," Rogers said encouragingly.

"Well, hit hain't easy ter talk 'bout, but–but–hit's 'bout Rosie."

"Where is Rosie?" Rogers spoke sharply, feeling he couldn't wait another second for John to fumble around with words.

"Oh, she's home. I mean she will be when she gits in offn

the mail route. But, Brother Rogers, she's a aimin' ter do somethin' orful an' I cain't stop her." He lifted his head slightly and the pained look in his eyes caused Rogers to wince.

"I think I know what you are trying to tell me, John—"

"Yo' do? How'd yo'uns know?" Rogers' neighbor seemed incredulous, but at the same time relieved that he wouldn't have to relate the shameful plans of his daughter.

"Rosie told me herself, last night."

"Then hit's true. I hain't jist been a havin' a orful bad dream."

"John, you must stop her," Rogers said firmly. "She can't go and live in that cave with Hiram without being married to him. Or even if they were married, for that matter."

"I cain't do a thing with her, Brother Rogers. I talked like I never talked to her before. Jist hain't no use."

"Come on in the house, John," Rogers invited. "We can talk more comfortably there."

"Nope. I'll mosey on back home. I tole Rosie she could come an' go like she's allers done till she act'lly turns bad an' shames me. Then she cain't never come back no more atall. Sin is sin, Brother Rogers, no matter who does hit ner why. I learned Rosie allers ter be good an' I lived decent afore her. Hit's her own fault if she chooses diffrunt."

Grady Rogers was impressed by the ruggedness of his principles and was certain that civilization would be further advanced if there were less compromising of right and wrong in the guise of tolerance or maudlin sympathy. Here was a man who, like Grady, placed all deeds of man in a category of good or bad and gave no concession to either.

"John," Rogers began, "Rosie is going to expose herself to all sorts of dangers. She may—"

"I knows hit, Brother Rogers. I knows hit good an' well. That's the reason I come ter see yo'uns. Hit's bin kinda long since I done much prayin'. Allers lived along peaceful-like an' didn't feel much need fur hit. An' now 'pears like I'se jist plumb shy with the Lord."

"I jist reckoned maybe yo'all could do hit heaps better'n me an' I jist thought if yo'all'd pray fer us maybe Rosie'd git over this wicked notion."

"Of course, I'll ask God's help, John. But that's your privilege and duty, too. It doesn't hurt any man to get down on his knees."

"I knows hit, Brother Rogers, an' I hain't too proud nuther, but jist 'pears like I'se stayed 'way from the Lord too long."

"An' now I best be a goin'. Hit's been right good ter talk ter yo'uns."

"I'm glad, John. Come again when you feel like it."

The two neighbors shook hands and Grady Rogers passed into his cabin. Life was becoming very difficult, he thought. First Rosie came to unburden her heart, and then her father. It wasn't as though he could help them. If by some magic sweep of the hand or by some premeditated deed or act he could relieve them of their sorrow and trouble, then his own heart would be made light. As it was, he felt depressed and miserable as if awaiting the approach of some dire calamity.

Rogers sat in a chair and thought hard and long, but when no answers came to the questions that probed his mind, he got up and prepared himself a simple meal which he ate without relish. Soon afterward, to escape an evening of entertaining the same questions that had tantalized his brain all day, he went to bed.

The sky since noon had been overcast with gray clouds and shortly after dusk a gentle rain had begun to fall. The tears of mist beating in gentle rhythm upon the low roof of the little cabin, with only the sighing of the trees for accompaniment, produced a melody that lulled the weary teacher into a sound sleep very quickly.

And so it was that he was very badly frightened when he was awakened at midnight by a voice in the room calling his name. For a time after his unpleasant run-in with Clark Harmon, Grady Rogers had been careful to bar his doors at night, but as time went on and he didn't even see Harmon again, the whole incident passed from his mind and he forgot to be cautious. Now when he was sure of the presence of an intruder in his house, he wished he had at least locked his door.

He bolted upright in bed as the voice again called in a hoarse, strained whisper. "Brother Rogers, air yo'uns there?"

"Yes," the frightened man answered. "Who is it?"

"Me, Brother Rogers, Hiram. Did I skeer yo'uns?"

"Well, you certainly did, Hiram. But I'm glad it's you. I'll light a lamp and find a place for you to sit."

"No, don't do hit, Brother Rogers. Might be somebody a snoopin' 'roun' through the woods an' see me here with a light a goin'."

"Well, then sit here on the bed," the teacher invited, pulling on his clothes. "It's a bad night. You must be cold and wet. I'll stir up a fire so you can get dry and warm."

"I jist had ter come, Brother Rogers," Hiram said abruptly. "An' I hain't got Bullet ter pertect me no more."

"Did Bullet die? Rosie told me about his being shot."

"No, he hain't a goin' ter die, but he won't be no 'count fer a long time. I come 'bout me an' Rosie."

Grady Rogers stiffened. For some reason he didn't bother to define, he was steadily becoming more resentful of Hiram's relations with Rosie.

"What about you and Rosie?" he asked, feeling if there were any manhood to Hiram, he wouldn't ask his fiancee to sacrifice her very honor under any circumstances. His mind was so completely absorbed with these recriminations that he was only faintly conscious of Hiram's reply.

"Hit's kinds hard ter talk 'bout, Brother Rogers, an'– an'–I'se shore Rosie never meant nuthin' by hit, but–but–well, she writ me a letter sayin' as how she aimed ter come an' live with me in my cave. An' I jist cain't let her do hit."

Rogers came to attention. He hadn't expected this. "No, Hiram," he said, "you can't let her do it. I'm glad to hear you say so."

"I reckon they had been plenty o' times I'd a tuck Rosie any way I could a got her," Hiram explained, "but this is diffrunt. Rosie hain't a doin' this 'cause she wants ter. She just thinks she has ter. The last time I seen her I said some pretty mean things to her."

"Yes," Rogers commented. "She told me. And you are right. She doesn't want to do this, but she thinks she has to prove to you that she loves you."

"Wal, I hain't much 'count, Brother Rogers, but I shore hain't that low-down. Rosie's a good woman an' I hain't a goin' ter drag her down."

"I'm glad to know this," Rogers repeated. "What will you tell Rosie?"

"Brother Rogers, I knows now I cain't stay hid much more 'thout Bullet. They is bound ter find the cave. 'Course, they cain't ever git ter me long as I'se inside 'cause I'll jist nacherly shoot anybody daid what comes nigh. But I jist cain't stay in there shut up all a time. I'd ruther die."

"What do you intend to do?" Grady asked again.

"Like I says," Hiram continued, "I cain't last much more an' I figgers me an' Rosie has a right ter a little bit o' each other. So when Bullet gits better so's I kin leave him – I shore felt bad ter come 'way from him ternight – then I wants Rosie ter meet me here in yore cabin an' I wants yo'uns ter marry us."

"How about license and witnesses, Hiram?"

"Does we'uns has ter have witnesses?"

"I won't perform a marriage unless it is legal," Rogers said firmly.

"Then I reckon Tobe an' his boy Steve will have ter be witnesses. They's the only ones can be trusted ter keep still."

"What about Charlie Raiford?" Grady asked.

"Charlie'd keep still all right, but he jist wouldn't do hit. He don't take no chances with nobody."

"And the license? Can you get one?"

"I'd be proud fer yo'uns ter he'p me out on that, Brother Rogers. They's a new clerk over at Hartstown what stays in the office on Saturdays, Rosie says. He don't know me but I reckon he's heerd a plenty 'bout Hiram Jackson like mos' ever'body else in this here county. But he hain't likely ever heard o' Hiram J. Pemberton. That's my real name. So I reckon yo'uns won't have so much trouble arter all."

Grady marveled at the man's astuteness. Whatever else could be said about these folk of the hills, one couldn't say they weren't smart, he thought.

"I'll do my best for you, Hiram," he said. "It will take a little while to arrange things. Probably two weeks."

"Hit'll be that long afore Bullet's well nohow. I'll be back here two weeks from ternight. Yo'uns tell Rosie an' Tobe an' Steve. I won't be a seein' nobody fer hit's too risky. Any messages yo'uns has fer me, Tobe'll take keer of."

"All right," said Grady Rogers. "I think it's well enough that you and Rosie are getting married. It's bound to be bad for her any way you look at it, but–"

"I aims ter give myse'f up arter we has been married a while. Hit'll be the best way fer her. I gotta go now. I been gone too long from Bullet. Thanks fer–fer–wal, fer ever'thin'."

"You're welcome if I've been any help," Rogers declared modestly, as his visitor slipped out into the cold, wet darkness.

Give Me Thy Vineyard

Give Me Thy Vineyard

Give Me Thy Vineyard

Chapter 32

G RADY ROGERS set out the next day to make plans for the secret wedding. First he told Rosie, who exclaimed illogically, "Oh, Brother Rogers, hain't that wonderful. Now I kin make up the weddin' dress I bought more'n four years ago an' have a shore 'nuff weddin'. I been a prayin' the Lord would forgive me fer doin' such sinful thinkin'."

From Rosie, Rogers went to enlist Tobe Alton and his son Steve whom he swore to secrecy. The matter of securing a license would have to wait until Saturday when he was free from his school duties.

Rogers felt that it would be a long, tense interval of waiting with all participants extremely anxious.

But a new bit of excitement was astir on the ridge, and all minds were temporarily occupied with it.

It all started in Sunday school when Annie Montgomery finished reading the weekly attendance record.

"Air there any 'nouncements before we all stands an' Brother Rogers dismisses us with a word of prayer?" she asked.

A young giant of a hillman arose with a clatter from the back seat and then looked bashfully at the floor.

"I reckons yo'uns knows by now what the Good Book says 'bout carin' fer widders an' orphans when 'fliction o'ertakes em," he mumbled. "Well, I'se a thinkin' o' Hank Stark's woman an' her young'uns down there in that cabin a needin'

263

what they hain't got, an' then yesterday the shuriff a postin' notices as how the bank war a closin' the mortgage on her stuff."

His weight shifted from one foot to the other as he nervously tried to fill this unfamiliar position of speaking publicly.

"Them fellers from the dam took Hank's farm fer almost nothin'," he continued after a brief pause, "but he put the money away an' started in a workin' the piece o' land that belonged ter his woman, like yo'uns knows. But then Hank – he's my uncle – he got sick an' had ter be took ter the hospital in Springfield. That tuck all the money the farm fetched an' Hank an' his woman signed some papers fer the rest o' the bill. Them papers war a mortgage. The hospital sold the mortgage ter the bank. But Thursday Hank died an' the widder cain't pay them so they's havin' the shuriff close out the mortgage. I 'lowed we ort ter do somethin' 'bout hit!"

Toward the last he had forgotten, in his sincere concern, to be self-conscious, and his words ended in a ringing challenge.

The people all looked at each other murmuring sympathetically. But what could they do? Few of them had ready cash, let alone any surplus. Finally, someone suggested a pound party and the congregation readily agreed.

Monday evening after school Grady Rogers walked to Clear Springs for some kerosene. No one was in the store except Big Dave. Rogers read the notice which the sheriff had posted announcing the sale of the Widow's goods at foreclosure.

"Is a pound party a money-raising affair?" he asked Dave. "The folks announced yesterday they were going to have one to help the Widow Stark, but I didn't want to show my ignorance by asking what it was."

"No, hit ain't that," Dave answered. "Most folks round here ain't got no money. An' even the ones which has money might say they war willin' ter do anythin' fer the Widder, but when they says anythin' they ginerlly means anythin' that won't cost 'em much."

Dave, as usual, had forgotten the subject at hand.

"But what is a pound party?" Rogers reminded.

"Huh? Oh – that's when they brings food 'n' stuff. But I war jist a thinkin', Brother Rogers, I'se got an' idea where we kin do more fer the Widder than jist give her somethin' ter eat. Yep, might even keep her stuff fer her." He rubbed his tremendous stomach in satisfaction. "Yep, ol' Dave shore hain't gittin' as old as some folks is a thinkin'."

"What's your idea, Dave?"

The postmaster's wink was lost in the creases of his fat face. "I ain't a goin' ter tell yo'uns, Brother Rogers, in case somethin' goes wrong an' you might be disappointed in us hill folks." He smiled. "But I don't 'low nuthin'll go wrong."

On the night of the pound party, Reed's Ridge again echoed with the sounds of wagon wheels and people's voices. Social events in the hills were so rare that when they did occur, everyone who could move tried to be present.

The young people had lit a huge bonfire in the schoolyard, where the party was to be held, and were gathered around it, laughing and talking. The older folks chatted with their friends, many of whom they had not seen for months, for not all of them were regular churchgoers. And the children ran wildly around, spurred on by the excitement in the air, and realizing that their parents were too busy visiting to pay much attention to them.

Soon the loud, shrill voice of Mrs. Morgan attracted Rogers' attention. She had taken charge of the party and was calling everybody into the schoolhouse. Picking up his own bag of groceries, he was jostled with the crowd into the building.

Mrs. Morgan's thin face was flushed with excitement. She clapped her hands for attention. Then she asked Grady Rogers to come forward to lead them in prayer after they sang a few songs. Sam Bates led the singing with the aid of a tuning fork. At the conclusion of this impromptu service

Give Me Thy Vineyard

Mrs. Morgan turned to the audience with these words.

"Folks, I'se jist as pleased as punch with this here big load o' grub yo'uns has brung. I reckon ever'body shore knowed what we's a tryin' ter do. Now iffn yo'all will pile yore stuff in the Squire's wagon, we'll git hit down ter the Widder's ternight. She shore will be happy ter see hit."

Back out again went the pushing, laughing crowd. Everyone lifted his contribution to the Squire's wagon and soon it was piled high with sacks of wheat and shelled corn to be ground into flour and meal; home-cured hams; slabs of smoked bacon; five-gallon stone jars of sauerkraut, sorghum and lard; canned fruits and vegetables of all sorts; bags of dried apples and pears; and miscellaneous varieties of foods, plain and fancy, common to the hill people. Rogers was sure that enough food was there to feed the Widow and her children for a year.

The party went on for another hour before the people began to get ready to leave. Rogers was continually surrounded by groups of gay, joking hillmen and women, asking him questions and telling him one story after another.

But throughout the evening Rogers noticed the peculiar behavior of Dave Gurney, who moved from one group to another speaking to each in low, earnest tones and receiving in response slow, meaningful nods of affirmation. His curiosity was naturally piqued but he refrained from asking questions because he knew full well that these people would tell an outsider like himself only what they wanted him to know. Any attempt to question them beyond that would be rewarded with evasive answers. So Rogers had no idea that the strange behavior of the group had anything to do with the auction that was scheduled for the next day at 1 o'clock. As was the custom of the schools when there was to be an auction, he dismissed school at noon that day so that the children might be free to go. And he went, too.

Almost everyone on the ridge was present, milling around and appraising the livestock. The sheriff stood on a crude platform which had been erected for him near the Widow's cabin and called, "Folks, now le's have some quiet here. First o' all I wants ter tell yo'uns that I is shore sorry that I has ter be the one ter sell this here stuff, but as shuriff o' this here county, I got ter do hit 'cordin' ter law."

His listeners looked unimpressed.

"I 'lows ter sell these three Jersey cows fust. What'll yo'uns bid on 'em?"

He looked down expectantly at the people, but no one said a word. What was the matter with them, he wondered. Didn't they know good livestock when they saw it?

"Come on, folks!" he shouted. "Le's have a bid."

"I'll give yo'uns twenty-five cents apiece fer 'em," came Dave Gurney's roar from the rear of the crowd.

"I got twenty-five; who'll give thirty?" he began to cry, only to stop suddenly. "Twenty-five cents!" he bellowed. "Dave, what's the matter with yo'uns? 'Course yo'uns means twenty-five dollars. Come on, folks. Now who'll give me thirty?"

"I said twenty-five cents an' that's shore what I meant," Big Dave bellowed right back.

The crowd looked bored and disinterested as the group maintained a stony silence. Rogers began to feel that something extraordinary was going on and wondered what it was.

The flabbergasted sheriff mopped his forehead with a grimy bandanna and roared irritably.

"What'd yo' fellers come here fer iffn yo'uns hain't a goin' ter bid on this here stuff?"

"I made yo'uns a bid," Dave returned matter-of-factly.

"But–but, Dave," he stuttered, "yo' knows well and good them three cows is worth at least one hun'erd dollars."

Dave pushed his huge bulk through the crowd to the platform, waving a handbill.

"Mr. Shuriff, in this here notice hit says the judge ordered this here sale an' that ever'thin' is ter be sold ter the highest bidder. An' I seems ter be yore highest bidder, so reckon them cows is mine!"

The sheriff, sensing a trick, begged, pleaded and even cursed for other bids. But the people of Reed's Ridge kept their word to Dave Gurney. No more bids were made, and so, after yelling himself hoarse, the sheriff was forced to sell the cows for 75 cents; the mule team for a dollar; the big black sow for 10 cents and seven pigs for a nickel each; and the 50 chickens for 50 cents.

Grady Rogers smiled from his place in the crowd. Dave certainly knew his friends and neighbors.

The sheriff felt like a fool and there was murder in his eye as Dave handed him the total amount of the sale in silver and drawled, "Shuriff, 'cause I hain't got no reason ter trust yo'uns I'm askin' yo'uns ter give me a written receipt fer havin' paid fer this here stuff."

The irate officer motioned with his chin for Dave to follow him, and the large man waddled into the cabin. After reading aloud the receipt, Dave turned to the puzzled Widow Stark who had witnessed the strange auction without suspecting what was happening. He scratched his head as if he were completely bewildered.

"Miz Stark," he said, "I seems ter have bought up all yore stuff, but I shore hain't got no place ter keep hit. Will yo'uns take keer of hit fer me an' use hit iffn I pays yo'all a dollar a month?"

Then the Widow caught on. With a shriek of delight she threw her arms around Big Dave Gurney and kissed him again and again on his chins. He pushed her away in embarrassment.

"Come, come now, Widder Stark, they hain't no sense in carryin' on like this. This air a business deal, pure an' simple. Now listen, the bank'll hold judgment agin yo', but they cain't take yore stuff. I 'lows iffn yo'uns sells a few calves an' pigs ever' year, yo'll git paid up arter a while."

He backed quickly toward the door, frightened by the look of gratitude which again lit up her face.

Give Me Thy Vineyard

Give Me Thy Vineyard

Chapter 33

THE SECRETLY GUARDED PLANS for Rosie and Hiram's wedding were never completed. On the Thursday before the teacher was to go on Saturday to Hartstown to try to get the marriage license, a storm invaded Reed's Ridge. Thunder reverberated from one hill to another; lightning blazed down, tearing huge trees to pieces; and a shrieking wind drove a downpour of rain wildly about. Not an unusual storm, but it played an unusual part in the lives of several people.

Rogers' pupils huddled around the little black stove in the center of the schoolroom, more frightened than cold. Several of the smaller children were crying, and though the older boys blustered, there was fear in their eyes when the lightning came too close. Suddenly a terrific crash shook the building as though it were being lifted from its foundation and the children buried their heads in their arms. The blast shattered two windowpanes.

Quickly, the teacher and some of the calmer boys and girls stuffed the empty frames with coats and then fought to stifle the rising panic among the other children by playing games.

I wish we had a storm cellar, Rogers thought in anger, remembering the countless times he had vainly asked the school board to have one built.

But as abruptly as it had begun, the storm let up. An hour before the end of school, a pale sun appeared, looking as if all the color had been washed out of it. The countryside was a distorted mess of drenched earth, torn and broken timber and careening rivulets.

Rogers felt inclined to dismiss school early because their nervousness over the storm had made the children unfit for study or learning, but he changed his mind. He knew that most parents would be anxious about their children and would come for them for there were many streams to ford and these were too dangerous for youngsters to cross alone. Therefore he kept them there until they were called for.

But long after all the other children had gone, a little boy and girl who lived two miles from school still waited. No one had come for them.

"Reckon Pa ain't feelin' good, Mr. Rogers, so he figgered we could git home by ourselves someway," the boy said at last.

The teacher sighed. *Some parents treat their children's lives lightly*, he thought, remembering Tom with a stab of pain.

Aloud, he said, "I'll go with you, then, at least to the other side of the creek."

After helping them on with their coats and mittens, he took each one by the hand and started up the trail. Walking was difficult, for frequently they had to crawl over trees which had fallen across the narrow paths.

As they approached the foot of a hill a mile from the school, they saw a tremendous oak sprawled across a caved-in double-rail fence between the Harmon and Reeves farms. Its roots were just inside the Harmons' fence, but its branches were spread all over Buck Reeves' field of fodder. The three walkers stopped to look at it.

"Look!" exclaimed the little boy. "Right across the devil's lane!"

"The what?" Rogers asked.

"The 'devil's lane,' I said. Ain't you never heard of a devil's lane?"

"No," answered Rogers, deciding this was not the time to correct the child's grammar. "What is it?"

The little boy felt important. Now he could tell teacher something.

"Well," he began, "when two fellers has a farm next ter each other an' neither of 'em knows jist where his farm ends, they makes a devil's lane between 'em."

"Four feet," the silent little girl suddenly broke in.

"That's right," conceded her brother. "Both fellers moves their fences four feet over. The place between the fences is the devil's lane." He eyed his teacher proudly and received a smile of admiration that was satisfying, and Rogers realized that he still had a lot to learn about the Ozarks.

Slowly walking around the fallen tree, the three paused to look into the deep pit which it had gouged out. More than a cubic yard of earth and stones, still held together by roots, now stood on the edge like a giant lid, ready to close the pit when the roots would be sawed free from the trunk and permitted to fall back into place.

Something imbedded in this lid of earth glistened in the sunlight. They bent over and peered at it.

"What yo'uns 'spose is in that air fruit jar?" the little girl asked.

Rogers leaned down to look more closely. It was indeed a half-gallon fruit jar. He tried to pull it out, but it was stuck fast.

"Maybe we'd better not get mixed up with it," he said finally, straightening up. "It's probably moonshine."

The children nodded. They knew the customs of the hills.

"Now come on," Rogers urged. "The sun will go down pretty soon. Let's get across Cricket Creek. I think you can make the rest of the way by yourselves. This is the only place where there's any danger from high water."

At the edge of the stream Rogers removed his shoes and socks and rolled up his pants as far as he could. Then pushing hard against the swirling, muddy current, he carried the children one at a time across the water which came nearly to his hips.

"Run on home now," he called as he recrossed the stream.

Breathing heavily, he sat down on a rock and put on his shoes and socks. It was cold out and the water clung to his legs like a sheath of ice. Shivering, he walked as quickly as he could back along the darkening, treacherous trail.

But as he hurried through the devil's lane, curiosity made him stop again at the fallen oak. *Now who could have hidden moonshine in those roots?* he wondered. They were on the Harmons' land, but he didn't know they were moonshiners, too, along with their other nefarious activities. But maybe the Harmons were customers for this jugful, and would pick it up later.

I think I'll dig it out, he thought mischievously, *and then when they come to get it, they'll think whoever sold it to them didn't put it there at all. What a wonderful fight there will be!*

Ignoring his cold, damp legs, Grady opened his penknife and dug the jar out of the uprooted soil. Through the caked mud he could see something shiny inside. Something that wasn't liquid at all, but rattled like coins. With a mighty twist he loosened the top of the jar and turned it upside down. A stream of gold coins came tumbling out.

Rogers was stunned. Where had the Harmons gotten a cache like this? He picked up one of the pieces from the ground. It was a $20 gold piece. He picked up another and another. More $20 gold pieces. He shook his head dazedly. What should he do with this find? Put it back, naturally. It belonged to the Harmons. But where had they gotten all this money? Money – The gold – That was it – The gold. The gold that the electric company official was bringing to Hiram Jackson before he was killed. Of course! And the Harmons would be coming to get it as soon as they found out about the tree. Maybe any minute.

Give Me Thy Vineyard

Quick, get out of here. Then his eyes lit on a clump of bushes on Buck Reeves' land about 20 feet from the tree and he got a better idea. Hide there. Then when the Harmons came for the money, confront them – No. He shook his head. That would be stupid. They would shoot him right on the spot and bury his body the way they had the gold. He shivered. Another idea came. Hide anyway and watch them dig out the gold. Then tell the sheriff. It would be his word against theirs but maybe he'd hear where they were going to hide it again, and the sheriff could search for it.

Quickly, he put the jar in the hole, covered it with dirt and crawled into the bushes.

The Harmons had better come soon, he thought. He was very cold.

It was already dark when he discerned three forms with lanterns moving over the rise in the rough clearing which was the Harmon farm. Nervously, he curled his numb legs up tight against his body and flattened himself against the ground. He wished he could stop shivering.

Ray and Clark Harmon, hulking, unshaven men, and their grotesquely short, skinny father, approached the devil's lane. Rogers could hear them swearing even at a distance.

Old Lige Harmon growled. "Look what that tree done ter our fence. Caved hit plumb in!"

They looked it over, holding their lanterns above the hole.

"Look what a hole," Ray said. "Hit mus' be three feet deep." He peered into it and shook his head.

His brother pointed to Buck Reeves' farm and laughed.

"Look what hit done ter ol' Buck's fodder shocks. An' him a makin' brags all over 'bout what a good farmer he is."

The other two men looked and smiled at the crushed, broken tepees of corn stalks and the section completely buried by the oak tree's sprawling branches.

"Well," said Lige, "'tain't as bad as hit might o' been. Tomorrer we'uns'll saw them roots offn the trunk ter fill up the hole an' fix the fence right over hit." He winked. "We'll let Buck worry 'bout gittin' the rest o' the tree outen his field."

The Harmons were in better humor as they went back across the clearing, swinging their lanterns. But Rogers, lying in cramped agony in the bushes, was baffled.

Why hadn't they dug out the gold? Were they deceiving each other? Maybe the sons were hiding it from their father. Ray had looked long into the hole. Maybe later he would come back to take the jar. But how long could he, Rogers, wait? He was freezing. This playing detective wasn't worth pneumonia. He'd better just take the gold and tell the sheriff where he had found it.

With a groan he tried to straighten out his legs. But before he had gotten into a standing position, rapid footsteps along the devil's lane frightened him back into a crouch. Someone else was coming. The moon had gone down and now he could see nothing.

Rogers heard the footsteps stop by the tree and he leaned forward, straining to pierce the darkness. Who was it? Had Ray come back so soon? He heard scraping noises and he knew that the person was digging. Then silence, followed by sputtering sounds. And suddenly a lantern light lit up the face of—

"Tobe Alton!" The words were out before Rogers knew it.

The big mountaineer jumped and almost dropped his lantern. Rogers was so surprised that he forgot to be careful.

"Why, Tobe!" he exclaimed, staggering forward on his stiff legs. "What are you doing here?"

The man looked at him strangely, his frightened, bloodshot eyes magnified by the lantern light.

"Why, I war a lookin'—er—I war a—what air yo'all doin' here, Brother Rogers?"

Rogers hesitated. He was all mixed up. But Tobe was his friend. He knew that. Quickly he told him about the jar of gold coins, the Harmons' coming to look at the tree, and his plan to turn them in. But when Tobe did not comment, but continued to stare at him, he asked again, a little nervously, "What are you doing here, Tobe?"

The big mountaineer seemed to shrink as Rogers' curious eyes probed him. He looked wildly about, as if trying to find a place to hide. But suddenly he sat down on the fallen tree and buried his face in his hands.

"'Tain't no use me hidin' hit no more," he mumbled. "I done hit, Brother Rogers."

"You done – did what?"

"The killin' an' the robbin' o' that air company man."

Give Me Thy Vineyard

Give Me Thy Vineyard

Chapter 34

ROGERS NEVER KNEW how long he stood there looking down at Tobe Alton. His mind would not absorb what he had just heard. How could it be possible? He tried to analyze the situation. Tobe was a simple person. He was a moonshiner. He never went to church, but he was not mean or two-faced. Rogers had learned from experience that Tobe was goodhearted and kind and completely devoted to Hiram. How could he have done a thing like that? No. There was something wrong. He sat down beside the big hillman whose face was still buried in his hands.

"Tobe," he began softly. "Tobe. Look at me. Did I hear you right? Did you really say that you had killed the company man and robbed him?"

Tobe nodded but did not look up.

"But, Tobe," he persisted, "how could you possibly? Why? And why did you let Hiram–"

Tobe looked up at him. His eyes flamed in the lantern light. Rogers edged back, frightened.

"Shore, I done hit," he repeated, his voice shaking. "'Most five years ago, hit war. I kilt that air compiny man when I seen him a comin' down the road with the shuriff. An' when he dropped the gold an' the shuriff run away, I picked hit up an' hid hit. But I didn't mean hit! Honest! You gotter believe me, Brother Rogers. I didn't mean hit!"

His voice was unnaturally shrill and when he suddenly

grabbed Rogers by the lapels of his coat, the teacher wanted to run like mad. But he pulled himself together and broke Tobe's hold on him.

"Tell me about it, Tobe."

Tobe sighed heavily and dropped his hands into his lap.

"I'll tell. I don't keer no more," he muttered. "I'se stood enough." He stared vacantly at the ground.

Rogers waited.

"I war a walkin' up the trail that day," Tobe began at last, "sick and drunk as I could be an' a tearin' mad 'sides. The company had took my farm early that month, an' me an' Sary couldn't do nothin' with our new place. Us an' the kids, we war all hongry an' sore an' yellin' at each other till I couldn't stand hit no more. I went down ter the still an' drank till I fergot 'bout ever'thin'."

He stopped and began to break some twigs between his fingers.

"Then what happened?"

"Well, finally I got so hongry I felt like ter die, so I started on home. I kept a fallin' an' a throwin' up an' a fallin' over an' over agin. Onct I tripped over my gun an' hit went off. Jist missed my head. Scairt me so I got sick agin. When I got ter the main trail I could hardly stand up. An' then I seen the shuriff an' a man dressed like a city feller a headin' toward Hiram's place. I knowd hit war the compiny man, cause Hiram had tole me 'bout how he war a makin' that air compiny man bring him gold.

"Then all of a sudden ever'thin' started ter jump in front o' my eyes, an' my head hurt an' I hated that air compiny man so much fer all he had did ter us folks that I felt as how I jist had ter kill him – so I shot him. But I warn't a thinkin', Brother Rogers. I wouldn't o' done hit iffn I war a thinkin'!"

Tobe emitted another rasping sigh and put out the lantern.

"Someone might come," he muttered, as Rogers' heart leapt. He felt unsafe, sitting there in the blackness with Tobe Alton.

But he said, "Go ahead, Tobe."

"Well, the shuriff never even turned aroun'. Reckon he war as scairt as his horse. The two o' 'em jist bolted down the trail as quick as they could go. They looked so funny that I started in a laughin'. I sat down in the road an' laughed an' laughed till I had ter throw up agin.

"Then I wanted to go home real bad, but first I had ter look at that body. I jist couldn't he'p myse'f. His clothes war all wet with blood an' they war a puddle o' blood on the ground. He war shore dead. An' then I seen the pouch a hangin' out o' his pocket an' I knowed they war gold in hit an' I knowed I had ter have hit. So I took hit an' started on home. An' then hit come ter me what I done an' I ran plumb inter the woods without lookin' back onct. I couldn't go home, but I had ter go someplace where I could figger out what ter do. I fetched the gold here an' hid hit in this tree where Steve an' me used ter hide jugs o' likker fer folks till the Harmons caught wise." He took a deep breath. "Then I went back up inter the hills an' then I must o' passed out. I don't 'member nothin' very clear right arter that."

Rogers felt as if he were dreaming. He shook his head wonderingly as he asked, "But, Tobe, what about Hiram? Think what he has been going through–"

"I knows." The words were sharp. "I'se a fixin' ter tell yo' how hit happened, Brother Rogers. I hid out in the hills fer days, livin' on squirrels an' roots an' things, an' tryin' ter make myself give up. But I couldn't. I jist couldn't. Then I reckoned I'd best come down er folks'd start wonderin' where I war an' start suspicionin'. When I come down an' found they had ketched Hiram fer the murder an' the Harmons had said they had seen him, I war really a goin' ter give myself up right then. But some o' the fellers told me how they war a fixin' ter git him out o' jail, so then I thought he'd git out an' ever'thin' would be all right an' I wouldn't have ter say nothin' 'bout myself. So I he'ped with the escape. I war sure that arter Hiram had hid out in the hills fer a couple o' months the company would stop lookin' fer him, cause the shuriff started in a sayin' that he war on our side. But that hain't never happened."

Tobe came so close to Rogers that he could feel his breath on his face.

"I tell yo', Brother Rogers, hit shore is right good ter be a tellin' this stuff," he said wearily, "even though I knows yo'all'll be a turnin' me in. I war like ter bust with hit inside me all these years."

And then Rogers knew that Tobe would never hurt him, and was ashamed of his fear. With more courage he asked, "But when you saw that the company would never stop looking for Hiram, why didn't you give yourself up?"

The big man shook his head sadly.

"Hit's like I said afore, Brother Rogers. I jist couldn't. I'd git cold all over a thinkin' 'bout bein' hung er spendin' the rest o' my life in the pen, where hit's so dark an' they hain't no air an'–"

"But would you let Hiram get–"

"I know what yo' is about ter say, Brother Rogers. I shore didn't want Hiram to go through that neither. Why do yo'all think I watched out fer him so keerful all these years? I took good keer o' Hiram, Brother Rogers. An' he warn't livin' such a bad life out in that air cave. He always said he liked the hills. An' I did ever'thin' I could fer him. Twict the revenooers almost got my still when I went to warn Hiram that the shuriff war a lookin' fer him an' onct I war shot in the leg when I scared them Harmons away from Gobbler's Knob when I knowed Hiram war a waitin' fer me there."

He stopped as if he were waiting for Rogers to say something, but the teacher was still dumbfounded. And then Tobe's hands came at him again in the darkness and pulled Rogers toward himself.

"Brother Rogers," Tobe muttered, "say what yo're a thinkin'.

I gotter hear hit. I gotter. I done a terrible wrong, hain't I? I'll go to hell shore, won't I? Won't I?"

Abruptly he let go of Rogers and again buried his face in his hands. The teacher heard him crying. "What kin I do? What kin I do now? Cain't yo' say somethin'?"

Rogers pitied him with all his heart. He said brokenly, "I don't know what to say, Tobe. I'm all mixed up myself. I can see what you've been through, but I still can't understand how you could let the years go by and see Hiram suffer this way without—"

"Why cain't yo' understand, Brother Rogers?" Tobe interrupted fiercely. "I jist didn't have the nerve ter tell the truth."

How it hurt him to admit this.

"I'd start in a thinkin', *What would Sary say, an' my boys – Steve an' Jack an' Pete – an' the other kids? Their pa a murderer – a critter what would shoot a man in the back!* Don't you see, Brother Rogers? I been sufferin', jist as much as Hiram. More. I thought times I'd go plumb crazy. For two years I didn't go near this tree. I war skeered – skeered that God would punish me right on this spot. An' then one night I jist had ter look. I tried ter keep away, but somethin' war a draggin' me here. So I dug away the dirt an' retched in – an' the pouch gived away in my hands an' them gold coins started a pourin' out all over the place. I didn't know what ter do. I jist know'd someone would come by an' see me a standin' there with the gold in my hands. So I throw'd ever'thin' back in the hole an' run home an' stole a jar offn the shelf an' come back an' put the gold in hit an' buried hit jist as deep as I could. I never looked at hit again, Brother Rogers, till ternight.

"When my young'uns come home from school terday they tole me 'bout how this here tree had blowed down acrost the Harmons' an' Reeves' devil's lane. I almost jumped plumb outen my shoes. I wanted ter run right then ter see what had happened ter the gold, but I made myse'f wait till hit got dark. I never reckoned that yo'd git here first, Brother Rogers."

For several minutes the two men sat silently staring into the darkness.

Rogers' mind turned and twisted. What should he do? What could anybody do? Ah, if he could only go away, far, far away from all this, and cover up his head and let things slide indifferently on. But life was not like that.

"What do you want to do, Tobe?" he asked at last.

"I don't know. I reckon I better give myse'f up. I've suffered so much these last four years that livin' in the pen or even gittin' hung will be like nothin'. Wisht I could tell yo'uns jist how turrible I'se been a feelin'. My good ol' mother shore warned me what corn liker would do fur a body. Reckon I'se done the turriblest thing a feller kin do – betrayin' a friend. Hiram's been hurt bad – hidin' out, folks a waitin' ter kill him fur the reward on me, a knowin' all the time it war me an' this drinkin' corn liker. I'se a goin' ter the sherruf an' give myse'f up, Brother Rogers." His voice was hoarse.

Rogers felt like crying himself. But Tobe was expecting him to be the preacher and to give him comfort. Wearily he stood up.

"Tobe, the Bible says, 'And be sure your sin will find you out,' and your sin has found you out. But the same Bible also says, 'Though your sins be as scarlet, they shall be as white as snow,' and that 'God so loved the world, that he gave his only begotten Son, that whosoever believeth in Him should not perish, but have everlasting life.' You have suffered a great deal, Tobe, as every sinner does, and the fact that you now condemn yourself so bitterly is the first step toward Christ. You feel now that you are not worthy to be a Christian even though you accept Christ. You are not worthy, Tobe. Neither am I. Peter even denied his Lord, but was forgiven."

Give Me Thy Vineyard

"Brother Rogers," Tobe answered, "I shore hain't fittin', fer I'se jist nacherly bound ter be a turrible Christian. Folks'd say I'se jist a bein' a hypocrite."

Grady repeated, "No man has ever been worthy to be a Christian. We are saved not by works, but by God's grace. The poorest kind of Christian is stronger than the best sinner. The poorest Christian has hope. The best sinner has none. You cannot give back the life you have taken. You cannot ease the suffering you have caused Hiram. The only way you can receive peace is to accept Christ as your Saviour. Why don't you pray to God for His forgiveness now and become His child?"

"Brother Rogers, let me think this here over. Reckon I orter talk ter Sary first."

"Go on home, Tobe," Rogers replied wearily. "You don't have to rush to the sheriff right away. Tell Sarah first. And I'll tell Hiram and Rosie. They'd better be prepared for the shock. You can go to the sheriff tomorrow or the next day. And I'd better take that cursed gold home with me in case somebody else finds it."

• • • • •

But Tobe Alton never got home. How can a man tell his wife and children that he is a murderer and about to give himself up to be hanged? Five days later Charlie Raiford found his body near their still, a bullet hole through his head.

Give Me Thy Vineyard

Give Me Thy Vineyard

Chapter 35

ROGERS LEFT TOBE and the fallen tree and hurried back to his cabin. His head throbbed and his throat was sore and he knew he must have caught cold, but there was no time to doctor himself. He had to get to Rosie and Hiram and tell them what had happened.

When he reached the cabin he quickly lit a kerosene lamp. Then he looked around for a place to hide the gold. The dresser. Good. Opening the bottom drawer, he shoved the jar under a thin pile of linen. It would be safe there, for a while anyway.

Now what? Supper. Rapidly he warmed up some leftover meat and potatoes.

While they were heating, he peeled off his damp, cold socks and hung them over the stove to dry. He put his shoes under the stove.

Suddenly he was convulsed by a tremendous sneeze. This was a bad cold, no fooling. There were some pills on the shelf left over from Tom's last illness. Maybe they would help. He put two in a glass of water and quickly drank them down.

After putting supper on the table he bowed his head. But this time he forgot to thank God for his food. Instead he prayed earnestly for help and strength and wisdom.

Leaving the dishes unwashed, he put on the now dry and warm socks and shoes, wrapped a scarf tightly around his sore throat, took out his heaviest coat and a hat, which he seldom wore, and started on the trail to Clear Springs.

Near the village he left the main trail and took a shortcut through the woods. When he finally arrived at the northern edge of town opposite the mill, he made his way through the darkness to John Gurney's cabin.

John's voice answered his knock, and in a second the black-bearded miller was at the door.

"Why, Brother Rogers!" he exclaimed. "How nice of yo'all ter drap by. Come on in."

"Thanks, Mr. Gurney. Is Rosie home? I've got something important to tell you both."

John peered at him curiously and led him to a chair.

"What's the matter? Yo'uns shore is out o' breath." Had Grady Rogers finally gotten up enough courage to court his daughter? he wondered. He had never come before. Why else was he so flustered?

"Rosie's purtyin' up arter supper. She'll be right out. I'se shore she heard yo'all come in. But set down, set down." John smiled. He remembered his own courting days.

Rogers felt vaguely uncomfortable under Gurney's beaming gaze. He had a feeling that Rosie's father was unduly happy to see him.

"I made a terrific discovery, Mr. Gurney," he began. "It's about Hiram."

John stared at him.

"I found out definitely that Hiram is innocent. And I can prove it, too."

John Gurney sat down heavily. "What?" he gasped.

"What did yo'all say, Brother Rogers?" Rosie was standing in the doorway, her face white. "Did I hear yo'uns right?"

"Yes. Better sit down, Rosie. This is a long story."

And while John Gurney and his daughter stared unblinkingly into his face, Rogers told them about the storm and the fallen tree and the gold and the Harmons. When he came to the part about Tobe Alton, Rosie stammered, "No, Brother

Rogers. It jist cain't be true. Tobe is Hiram's friend an'–"

"I know, Rosie. That's what makes it so hard to believe. Now let me tell you why he did it exactly as he told it to me."

And again the girl and her father gazed fascinated at him as he told of Tobe's crime and his mental agony. When he finished, both were silent. Finally John stood up and began to pace the floor.

"I could kill Tobe Alton fer what he's done. But he's paid. He's paid plenty. An' he'll pay a good piece more when the state gits arter him. But yo' know, Brother Rogers, I kin jist feel what's been a goin' on in his heart all these years. Deep down Tobe is a plumb nice feller. He's done plenty fer me in his time." He stared vacantly ahead of him, momentarily paralyzed with shock and mixed emotions.

Rogers looked at Rosie, expecting her to collapse. But she remained sitting stiffly in her chair, hands clenched in her lap, dark eyes blazing.

"What's Tobe a goin' ter do?" she asked quietly at last.

"First he's going to tell his wife. Then, probably tomorrow, he'll give himself up to the sheriff." He walked over to her and said sympathetically, "How you must hate him for what he's done to you and Hiram!"

For a long while Rosie did not answer. Then she said in a tired voice, "I should, but I cain't. I guess there jist hain't no more hate left in me, Brother Rogers. Fer so long I been hatin' the 'lectric company, an' hatin' the shuriff an' hatin' the Harmons – I war sartin that they done hit an' war lyin' – now I jist hain't got no power left ter hate Tobe. I jist feels orful sorry. That's all." She shook her head slowly and started to stand up, but quickly sank back in the chair. "I wanted ter go tell Hiram 'bout this right away," she said with a wry smile, "but I hain't got no power ter move, neither."

"Better wait a while, Rosie. This has been a shock."

"Hit shore has. But I'se got ter go as soon as I kin."

"Do you think Hiram should go right ter the shuriff now

an' tell him 'bout Tobe?" John Gurney asked.

"No," Rogers replied. "If he's lived in the hills for more than four years, he certainly can wait another day or two. Let Tobe confess first and let everybody know about it. Then Hiram can come out. Otherwise somebody might shoot him."

John nodded, thinking, *I could figger things out right clear like that, too, iffn I warn't so excited!*

At last Rosie stood up. "I'se a goin' ter Hiram now," she said. "I hain't seen him fer more'n two weeks. I'se been a leavin' messages fer him with Tobe." She grimaced.

"You don't dare go to him, Rosie," Rogers warned. "He told me he would shoot anyone who came near his cave."

"That's right, he would," Rosie gasped. "I never thought. But how'll we'uns git a message ter him?"

"Do you know the tree where Tobe puts his stuff he takes to him?"

"Yes, hit's a old oak up on Gobbler's Knob," the girl replied.

"Good. Then you'll have to take a note up there and wait until you are sure Hiram has obtained it before you can risk seeing him in his cave."

Rosie agreed with Rogers and her father that this was the safest way, but she didn't see how she could wait so long.

Give Me Thy Vineyard

Give Me Thy Vineyard

Give Me Thy Vineyard

Chapter 36

ROSIE INSISTED upon taking the message to Hiram that night, for she knew that once every 24 hours the fugitive went to the old oak tree that none but she and Tobe knew about. In the missive she told Hiram that she was coming to his cave as soon as she found this note missing from the tree. That she had very important news about who the real murderer was.

Hiram, however, when he came to the tree and found the message, decided to wait for Rosie, and so it was when she came to the old oak after returning from delivering the mail the next day to see if the message had been received she found Hiram waiting nearby, securely hidden by a clump of thick bushes.

When she told him that Tobe Alton was the cause of all their troubles, his head snapped back as if he had been struck. He looked at her, disbelief clouding his eyes.

"But is yo'all shore, Rosie? Couldn't Brother Rogers o' made a mistake? Look at the way Tobe has pertected me all these years!"

"That's *why* he pertected yo'uns, Hiram," and she repeated to him what Tobe had told Grady Rogers.

Hiram was deeply shaken. He failed to grasp the significance of the good news. His thoughts were all on Tobe. How could it possibly be Tobe? Tobe who had brought him food, who had gotten shot because of him and who came nearer having his complete confidence than anyone except Rosie. No. It just didn't make sense. He knew Tobe drank too much, and that when he was very drunk he was capable of anything, but how could Tobe keep this thing a secret for so long? He tried to put himself in Tobe's place. But he, Hiram, could not have stood by and let his friend's life be ruined just because he was afraid to die – but wait a minute – why couldn't he? What if he had killed a man in a fit of drunken anger? What would he–

"An' don't yo' see what this means, Hiram?" Rosie was saying.

How long had she been talking? he wondered, with a start.

"Hit means that yo're free, an' that we kin go down an' git married an' live on the ridge with all the other folks an' have a home an'–an' ever'thin'–an'–" and suddenly Rosie felt tired and anxious to be held in Hiram's arms. She ran to him and curled up tight against his chest. Oh, it was so wonderful to feel safe and warm and protected, and to know that pretty soon your dreams were going to come true.

Hiram held her close, kissed her and wondered if loving made all women forget their troubles the way it did Rosie. But his mind was still trying to grasp the new situation. He wanted to feel murderous toward Tobe, but somehow he couldn't. He couldn't figure out just what his feelings were toward the man.

"When is Tobe a goin' ter give hisse'f up?" he asked at last.

Rosie's answer was muffled in his shoulder. "He didn't say, but I reckon real soon. He's got ter tell Sary first."

Hiram shook his head, thinking of stern, tight-lipped Sarah Alton. "I shore hain't jealous o' Tobe right now. I kin jist see Sary. She won't say nothin', only she'll break a chair over his head."

"Brother Rogers said yo' should wait till ever'one on the ridge knows Tobe done hit afore you comes down, otherwise you might git shot."

Give Me Thy Vineyard

Hiram smiled a slow, thoughtful smile. "Yo' know, Rosie, now that all this air over an' I kin start livin' like folks should, I'se skeered. I'se skeered stiff. I don't reckon I'll ever git outta lookin' back over my shoulder ter see iffn anyone's a follerin' me – an' I'll have ter teach Bullet all over agin, er he'll kill ever'body on the ridge."

Give Me Thy Vineyard

Give Me Thy Vineyard

Chapter 37

WHEN GRADY ROGERS woke up to go to school the next morning, there seemed to be a ball and chain tied to each of his legs. He had to use all his strength to push back the covers and put his feet on the floor. But everything danced before his eyes and his mouth seemed full of cotton batting. He shook his head weakly and pulled his feet back into the bed. It was either the grippe or the flu. There was no point in even trying to go to school. With a shiver and a groan, he buried himself under the covers and waited for someone to come and do something for him.

He knew that when the children got to school and waited for about an hour without seeing him, they would go home. Then they would tell their parents and those near enough and interested enough would come by to see what had happened to him. Cliff and Annie's three boys were his pupils. He could count on Annie's coming.

He tried to figure out how long it would take the boys to get to school, get back home again, and, finally, how long it would take Annie to hustle over to see him.

But some of the other children, like the Barneses', lived closer to the school than the Montgomery kids. Mary and Martha Barnes would probably be the first ones home. Therefore they would be the first to tell their mother that Brother Rogers had not come to school.

He pictured a waddling race between fat, kindhearted

Give Me Thy Vineyard

Ruthie Barnes and fat, kindhearted Annie Montgomery along the trails to his cabin.

Then he remembered Tobe Alton and the events of yesterday. Was Tobe already on his way to the sheriff? What would the sheriff do when he heard the news? He had such a one-track mind. He probably would argue with Tobe and try to talk him out of it!

Rogers thought of the gold. Hiram would be a rich man now. He did not remember exactly how much gold was supposed to be in that jar, but it was somewhere around a thousand dollars.

He sat up with a start. The jar!

His teeth chattering, he bounced out of bed and dragged himself across the room to the dresser and opened the bottom drawer. There was a noticeable bulge in the thin pile of linen. Annie or some of the other women would be sure to find it, and then – oh, no. He was in no condition to tell a crowd of eager listeners what had happened yesterday. Let them find out for themselves, after Tobe had made his confession. He picked up the jar and looked blearily around the room for a place to hide it. But the cabin was so small and bare that everything in it showed. He focused his eyes along the shelf. There were a few jars of preserves, some cans, and – the flour tin – that was it! Shivering, he emptied the gold pieces into the big tin and covered them over with flour. He prayed that the good women wouldn't decide to make him biscuits or a pie while he was sick.

And then he crawled back into bed and lay there shivering and miserable until help should come.

When Annie and Cliff Montgomery arrived three hours later, they hardly knew what to do first. The cabin was a mess, the fire was out, and Rogers was tossing feverishly on the bed. Cliff ran home to get the medicine they used for their own children's rare illnesses and came back on horseback, carrying food and extra blankets.

Give Me Thy Vineyard

By the time they had straightened everything out and poured some hot soup and medicine into Rogers, three more women and two men arrived. They agreed that two of the women should spend the afternoon there, that a man and his wife would spend the night, and that Cliff and Annie would come back in the morning, and so on, until the teacher was able to take care of himself.

Rogers was unaware of what was going on. Partially drugged by the medicine and exhausted anyway, he slept through that day and night until just after dawn the next morning.

When he woke up he looked queerly about him, and it took Zeke and Ruthie Barnes a long time to convince him that it was today and not yesterday, but that today was a different "today" from the one he remembered, and that actually, from his point of view, it was tomorrow!

Soon afterward, Annie and Cliff came to relieve the Barneses. Rogers could hardly lift his head to eat the thin gruel which Annie made for him. He was still feverish, but his mind felt a little clearer than it had the day before.

"What's happening on the ridge?" he feebly asked Cliff. Had Tobe told yet? he wondered. He must have by now. The ridge must be leaping with excitement.

But Cliff sat back in his chair and waited a moment before answering, "Nothing much, Brother Rogers. We'se a closin' the school till yo'uns gits better. But don't yo'all worry none. Yo' been a workin' them kids purty hard nohow. They kin use a little loafin'."

"Is that all? Isn't there any other news?"

Cliff shook his head. "Nope. Not that I kin think of."

He smiled at Rogers. "Sick people is always like that. They think jist 'cause they is stuck inside, big things is a happenin' outside."

His wife eyed Rogers. "You might be intrusted in knowin' that Rosie Gurney war in ter see yo'all last night – an' lookin' mighty anxious, too, Ruthie Barnes told me."

"She was!" Rogers nearly leaped out of bed.

"Yep. Told Ruthie she'd be by agin ternight."

Tonight. By tonight the truth would surely be out. Rogers became more and more excited as he pictured how everything would explode.

In the afternoon Mrs. Morgan came in and he tried to listen politely to her as she began to pour out all the news, public and private, from Lake City to Clear Springs. *Guess Tobe's confession hasn't come through yet,* he thought, *or this little river of gossip would surely know about it.* But he chided himself for his impatience. How could he expect Tobe to hurry over a thing like that? No man would rush to give up his life. He uttered a silent prayer for Tobe as Mrs. Morgan gabbed on.

His heart almost came up into his mouth when she stood up, went over to the shelf and began to snoop among his jars and cans.

"What are you looking for, Mrs. Morgan?" he asked sharply.

She whirled around surprised at his tone.

"Why, lan' sakes, Brother Rogers, I was jist lookin' ter see iffn yo'uns had any chicken soup. I was a goin' ter heat up some." She shook her head sympathetically. "Yo'uns shore must be sick, Brother Rogers. I hain't never heered yo' talk like that afore."

"I'm sorry," he said. "I guess I'm just – nervous. Anyway, I have no chicken soup, just tomato and vegetable. Annie left some prepared soup in the pan, didn't she? I don't know what kind it is – I can't taste."

He sighed with relief as she walked away from the shelf and toward the little stove. He wondered how much more of this he could stand. His weak head was beginning to beat violently. He turned over and tried to sleep.

Rosie came to the cabin late that afternoon. Rogers knew at first sight of her that something was wrong. Instead of the radiance he expected to see in her face she looked tired and distressed. Rogers was so eager to question her that he could scarcely control himself. He wondered how he could have a word alone with her when Annie Montgomery spoke up.

"Rosie, do yo'all 'spose yo'uns could sit with Brother Rogers a little bit whilst me an' Cliff goes home ter chore?"

Rogers felt he could hug her.

"I got ter be a goin', too," Mrs. Morgan said airily. "I cain't no more'n git home by dark. I'll be back agin tomorrer."

The door had scarcely closed on them when Grady sat up in bed and said, "What is it, Rosie? What's gone wrong?"

"I don't know what ter think, Brother Rogers," she said. "Tobe hain't gone ter the shuriff yet, an' his boy Steve says he hain't been home fer two days. I met Steve on my way back from Oakridge an' I asked him keerful-like what Tobe war a doin'."

"'I hain't a knowin',' he says. 'Pa hain't been home since Monday night.'"

"'Air he at the still?' says I."

"'I hain't a knowin',' Steve repeats, an' looks at me real suspicious-like. 'What do yo'all want Pa fer nohow?'"

"I jist couldn't bring myself ter tell him, Brother Rogers, so I didn't say nothin'."

Give Me Thy Vineyard

Give Me Thy Vineyard

Chapter 38

THE NEXT DAY Grady Rogers was sitting up in bed. His fever was gone and he was eating solid food. But his legs still felt like paper when he tried to stand on them. Now his mind was perfectly clear, and he was using it to plan with.

While Annie Montgomery sat beside him and talked, he tried to figure out what he and Rosie and Hiram could do about Tobe Alton.

Rosie had come to see him every night, looking thinner and more anxious. Tobe had not confessed. No one had even seen him. And Hiram was going crazy.

What should they do? Should Rosie go and tell the sheriff Tobe's story? Should she bring the sheriff to Rogers' cabin so that the teacher could back her up? But would the sheriff believe Rogers? He had a head of granite. New ideas had to be drilled into it over a long period of time. It was so much simpler for him to believe that Hiram was the guilty one. Rogers could show him the gold, but the sheriff could just say that Rogers had found it and nothing would be changed. No. They would have to wait a few days longer. Some news of Tobe Alton was bound to come. How could the big moonshiner disappear like that?

Then he realized that Annie was telling him that her boys were hanging uselessly around the house, wanting to go back to school.

"I never thought I'd see the day, Brother Rogers!" she exclaimed. "They really misses school, honest to Pete. They was even fixin' ter play school this mornin', an' that's onusual fer my boys!"

Rogers smiled, vaguely pleased, but too distracted to pay much attention.

Suddenly they were both jolted by a loud succession of knocks on the door.

"Come in!" Annie shouted.

It was Pete Alton, Tobe's youngest boy. His face was chalky white and he was so out of breath that no words could come out of his open mouth. His chest heaving, he stared at Rogers.

"Sit down, Pete, and get your breath," the teacher said, fearing he did not know what. "What happened?"

It was more than a minute before Pete could gasp, "Hit's Pa. They found him. Up by the still. Shot plumb through the head. Kilt hisse'f!"

"How do you know he killed himself?" Rogers asked in a taut voice.

The boy felt so full of importance at being the bearer of startling news that the tragedy of it escaped him completely.

"Ma an' Charlie Raiford thought he war murdered at first," he began eagerly, "so after they laid him out they sent Bob ter git the shuriff. But the shuriff said the way his head was blowed clean open from the front an' the way his hands war an' ever'thin', hit meant he jist up an' shot hisse'f. Then Charlie showed him how the gun war a layin' nigh, an' the shuriff said that proved he done hit hisse'f. Said he's been dead a couple o' days a'ready. He's stiff as a frozen fish. They is a goin' out purty soon ter look at the place where Charlie found him."

Annie and Rogers stared at each other. The boy, sensing the impression he had made, continued importantly, "Ma wants fer the funeral ter be tomorrer an' fer yo'uns ter preach hit,

Brother Rogers. That's why she sent me ter see yo all."

But Rogers hardly heard him. The drums in his brain had begun to beat again. So Tobe had committed suicide. Maybe now, with the moonshiner's dead body before him, the sheriff would believe the real story. But what if he didn't? Well, it was certainly worth a try.

"Is the sheriff still in your cabin?" he asked Pete.

"He shore war there when I left out."

Rogers leaped out of bed and, before Annie's startled eyes, began to pull on his trousers.

"Why–why, Brother Rogers," she stammered, "what yo'all a aimin' ter do?"

"I have to see the sheriff." He was dizzy and his legs felt dangerously weak. But he reached for his coat and scarf.

By now Annie was on her feet.

"Brother Rogers, is yo'all plumb crazy? Yo'll die shore iffn yo'uns goes out inter the cold now arter bein' so sick. Yo' ain't well yet."

She reached out to hold him back, but he shook her back off.

"I'll be all right," he said, and pulling the dazed boy after him, ran out of the cabin.

They covered the first two miles in silence. Then when Rogers had slowed down to a dragging walk, he asked Pete, "Where did you say Charlie had found your father?"

"Right next ter the still."

So Tobe probably drank himself into a half-stupor before he shot himself, Rogers thought bitterly. Then a new thought struck him. "Say, what about the still? Won't the sheriff find it when he–"

"Charlie a'ready took keer o' that," the boy interrupted with satisfaction. "Before he fetched Pa home, he went ter his own cabin first an' tole three o' his boys ter come an' move the still. Hit's 'bout five mile off by now."

When they finally arrived at the Alton cabin, it was full of unwashed Alton children sitting and standing quietly, their eyes held fast by a figure covered with a grimy sheet. Sarah and the sheriff were seated in a corner near the fireplace, their backs to the door. Charlie Raiford was nowhere to be seen.

Probably gone back to the still, Rogers thought.

The only sound in the room was Sarah's slow, harsh voice. She was talking to the sheriff. "He's daid by his own hand. Kilt hisse'f. He's done a turrible lot o' sufferin' like all sinners does in this life."

Grady Rogers' cough caused the sheriff to whirl in his chair.

"Oh, hit's yo', Brother Rogers." He didn't like the teacher. He had always been too close-mouthed about Hiram Jackson.

Sarah got up and moved painfully toward him.

"I'se shore tickled ter see yo'uns, Brother Rogers, though I warn't 'spectin' yo'all till tomorrer. I heered yo'uns war sick."

Rogers wanted to say something proper and sympathetic, but words failed him. What could he tell this unhappy woman just before he would speak out about her husband's crime and make her more unhappy? He stared at her, thinking.

Quick, let's get this thing over with. Tell her now. Now.

The sheriff was looking inquiringly at him.

But suddenly his mind heard his mouth say, "I'm terribly sorry, Mrs. Alton. I was shocked when Pete told me the news."

Then came the sheriff's reply. "Yo' ain't heered nothin', Brother Rogers, iffn yo'uns thinks yo're shocked now. Yo'uns know what Sary jist tole me? Tobe war the one what kilt that air comp'ny man more'n four year ago! Yo'uns 'members, the one we'uns thought Hiram Jackson kilt."

Rogers remembered and felt like murdering the blundering officer while colored lights flashed through his head. "Then you knew, Mrs. Alton?" he gasped. "About the murder and the robbery and everything?"

She looked away from him and muttered, "Shore I knowd.

I knowd fer more'n two year. Like I jist tole the shuriff, when Tobe uster come home drunk, he'd fall inter bed an' say all sorts o' things. It didn't take me long ter figger out what he done."

"But why didn't you tell, or make him tell?"

"Tobe never even s'picioned that I knowd. I don't know what he would o' did iffn he had. But like I jist said, it warn't my duty ter say nothin'. But I kep' a hopin' and a hopin' that he would make his peace with God and get fergiveness fer his sin. But now that he's gone, I kin tell o' his sin. An' I jist tole the shuriff ever'thin' I knowd."

Rogers shook his head wearily. "That's what I came here for, too, sheriff. Tobe confessed the whole thing to me Thursday night."

"What?" Sarah, the sheriff and the brood of Alton children gasped at him.

Quickly he told them of his meeting with Tobe near the fallen tree. The sheriff was silent, laboriously digesting this information.

Sarah's eyes filled with tears. "I'se right glad he done tole yo'all 'bout hit afore he died, Brother Rogers."

Gradually a thought penetrated the sheriff's mind.

"All that air gold yo'uns got," he began, "hit belongs ter Hiram Jackson. An' he shore ain't no outlaw no more. Tsk. Tsk. Ter think that all this time that air reward out fer the wrong man. An' now hit's gone ter waste."

But Rogers paid no more attention. He was feeling weak.

Give Me Thy Vineyard

Give Me Thy Vineyard

Chapter 39

G RADY ROGERS never got to preach at Tobe Alton's funeral. He had caught pneumonia. Sarah reluctantly called in the preacher from Hartstown to take charge of the service.

For 10 days afterward, the life of Grady Rogers tottered between this world and the next. The days dragged by, darkened by unconsciousness and delirium, and brightened only by flashes of lucidity. He never knew how sick he really was. His mind was full of strange, heavy images.

He saw Rosie, her beautiful face distorted and big, looking down at him. Then her face would become part of the logs in the ceiling, which always seemed to be falling on top of him. Or her face would turn into a large white sofa pillow which stifled and choked him until he gasped for breath.

Tom was with him most of the time. Occasionally he looked as he did before his fatal illness, and Rogers was pleased.

The boy would always say, "We are all proud of you, Dad, for the way you helped Hiram and Rosie."

Rogers would be glad but puzzled. Who were the other people who were proud of him? He asked Tom, but the boy did not seem to understand.

Tom told him repeatedly that he was all better because he had a mother to take care of him now.

Who was his mother? Tom would tell him a familiar name

that he could not quite place – Jean or Joyce. He knew he should know her. Tom would always promise to bring her but he never did.

Then Tom would seem to fade into a big choking cloud and Rogers wanted to push him away, but how could he push his own son away? But it wasn't his son, it was a cloud and it was strangling him – but it *was* Tommy, it was …

One afternoon Grady Rogers opened his eyes and saw Hiram Jackson looking down at him. He had never seen the outlaw in his dreams.

"Hiram," he began in a faraway voice which was surely not his own. "What are you doing here?"

The man smiled broadly and his tired eyes seemed to fill up.

"Brother Rogers," he said, "yo'all must be all right now. This air the first time yo'uns knowed who I war in 10 days."

"Ten days?" The teacher looked about him at the bed and the darkened cabin. Then he remembered. "Hiram, have I been sick?"

"Yo'all shore have. Matter o' fact, hit's been close ter two weeks. Fer a spell we didn't think yo'uns war a goin' ter pull through atall." He laid a rough hand on Rogers' forehead. "Yo'all air plumb cool now, Brother Rogers. Ever'one shore will be glad ter hear 'bout hit."

The teacher's eyes roamed haphazardly around the cabin. Somehow it seemed unfamiliar. Fearfully he glanced up at the ceiling. But the logs weren't falling down. He ran his hand weakly through his hair. Had he dreamed that? But it had seemed so real. Then, as his eyes became accustomed to the dim light, he noticed a pile of bedclothes on the floor. He stared at them.

"What's all this, Hiram?" he asked feebly. "Have I been sleeping on the floor, too?"

Hiram laughed. "Yo'uns shore ain't, Brother Rogers, though a couple o' times yo'all tried to. I been a sleepin' there whilst I war a lookin' out fer yo'uns."

Rogers shook his head, trying to arrange his thoughts.

"Oh," he groaned, "I'm all mixed up. What's been going on? What day is it? What time is it?"

Hiram beamed at Rogers. His long vigil was over. The teacher's mind was clear. Better get some food into him quickly and make it strong.

"Hit's March 10," he answered, "an'–" he peered behind the sheet which hung over the window – "hit's 'bout 4 o'clock, 'cordin' ter the sun. Rosie'll be here purty soon. Boy, will she be tickled ter see yo'all like this!"

Rogers sank back and shut his eyes. He was so tired.

Hiram busied himself making squirrel soup, the aroma of which soon filled the sick man's nostrils and made his mouth water. Slowly he opened his eyes again.

"What are you making, Hiram?"

"Squirrel soup. Yo'uns has gotter eat an' git back ter yorese'f, Brother Rogers."

"It smells good." He felt empty. "While you cook it, tell me what's been going on." He smiled a little. "Honestly, I feel so weak I won't be able to ask you many questions."

"Yo've been sayin' too much a'ready, Brother Rogers. Yo'uns jist shut yore eyes an' let me talk. I'll tell yo' ever'thin' jist like it war."

And while the teacher relaxed, and the smell of the soup grew stronger and more tantalizing, Hiram recounted the story of the things that had been happening on the ridge since Tobe Alton's body was found.

Give Me Thy Vineyard

Give Me Thy Vineyard

Chapter 40

THE FORMER OUTLAW began at approximately the point where he knew Rogers had lost track of events.

When Rogers had almost fainted in Sarah Alton's cabin, the sheriff and two of the Alton boys had half carried him home.

It was late by then and Rosie had already arrived at his cabin. Annie Montgomery had just finished telling her how Rogers had rushed out of the house with little Pete Alton. Annie was so curious and worried about the teacher that she didn't want to go to her own home. She told Rosie she was going to stay until Rogers came back.

"I jist know he won't be able ter make hit alone," she said.

Rosie was leaving to ride over to the Alton cabin herself when the door burst open and the sheriff, his arm around Rogers' waist, and the two Alton boys came in. The women took one quick look at the half-conscious teacher and put him to bed. Rosie told Steve Alton to take Fred and ride to Hartstown for the doctor – and not to come back without him. Steve's brother Jack hung curiously around, but Annie soon sent him packing.

While Rosie piled all the clothing and blankets she could find on the shivering Rogers, and Annie heated a brick to warm up the sheets near his icy feet, the sheriff began opening drawers and throwing things all over the floor.

When Annie noticed him, she growled angrily, "An' jist

what do yo'all think yo're a doin', Shuriff?"

Even her murderous tone did not make the man of the law look up.

"I'se a tryin' ter find the gold, Miz Montgomery," he said, heaving a pile of books to his feet. "Brother Rogers said he hid hit in this here cabin, but he didn't say where."

Rosie swung around. "What gold?"

"Yo'all ort ter know what gold, Rosie Gurney. The gold what belongs ter Hiram Jackson."

Rosie stared at him. Then Rogers had told him about Tobe. This was why he had rushed to Alton's cabin. But did the sheriff believe it? Or was he still pigheaded enough to think Hiram was guilty? She'd have to be careful.

"What does yo'all want ter do with the gold, Shuriff?" she asked.

"Well, first I wants ter see hit. Then I wants ter count hit ter make shore hit's all there an' Tobe er Brother Rogers ain't took none o' hit. Then – well, then I reckon I'd best bring hit over ter the 'lectric comp'ny an' see iffn they wants ter give hit ter Hiram. Hit's his 'cordin' ter law."

Rosie walked over to him and looked hard into his eyes.

"Then you don't think Hiram done hit no more, Shuriff. Yo' knows the truth now."

"I reckon so, Rosie. An' I shore war surprised. But say, gal, how do yo'all know? Did yo' know Tobe done hit, too?"

"I got ways o' knowin', Shuriff. Hain't I been tellin' yo' an' yore deputy all these years that Hiram war innocent?"

He nodded as she continued, "But I shore didn't know hit war Tobe till last week, I kin tell yo'uns that. What is yo'all a goin' ter do now, Shuriff? Is yo'uns a goin' ter take them notices down an' let ever'body know jist who done that murder?"

But before he could answer, Annie was upon them, her eyes wide with curiosity and the sick man momentarily forgotten.

"Now jist what's a goin' on here?" she asked. "What murder is yo'uns a talkin' 'bout? What gold? Tell me afore I bust open!"

314

Quickly, Rosie told Annie what had happened. With a tremendous gasp, the school board chairman's wife flopped into a chair.

"An' here we'uns war so sartin hit war them Harmons," she said. "Cliff has been a keepin' his eye on 'em all this time, a tryin' ter catch 'em in a mistake, so's they'd give away that they war guilty."

"Aha!" The sheriff had stuck his hand into the flour tin and found something harder than flour. "Aha! Here 'tis!"

And while Annie threatened to hit him with a hot poker, he dumped the contents of the tin on the floor and eagerly separated the gold from the flour.

Laboriously he counted and bit into each piece. When he was finished he shook his head in surprise.

"Hit air all here," he said, "ever' cent. Forty-eight golden eagles. Nine hundred an' sixty dollars. Hit hain't been touched."

Rosie and Annie gazed fascinated at the mess of gold and flour on the floor. But a groan from Rogers snapped them back to the problem at hand. Annie quickly took the hot brick from the fire, wrapped it in her apron and placed it near his feet. Rosie dipped a rag in a pan of water, wrung it out and squeezed a few drops on the teacher's dry, burning lips.

The sheriff watched them curiously.

"Reckon Brother Rogers'll die?" he asked in a hoarse whisper.

"Iffn he does, hit'll be yore fault an' ever'body'll know hit."

The sheriff was agitated.

"But, Rosie, why does yo'uns say hit's my fault?" he asked.

"Youns knows why! How kin yo'all even pertend yo'uns don't? Iffn yo'all hadn't a been so set on gittin' that reward fer Hiram, we could o' tole yo'uns 'bout Tobe a week ago. But knowin yo'all like we does, me an' Brother Rogers war both sartin yo' wouldn't believe the truth. That's why this pore man got outen a sickbed an' walked all the way over ter Tobe's ter catch yer right there, so's yo'all could see the truth right in front of yore big nose!"

Rosie's voice had risen in anger and Annie cautioned her to be quiet. The sheriff scratched his head nervously and began to pile the gold on the table.

"Reckon I'll put this here gold back in the flour tin an' take hit ter the jailhouse. I'll see the comp'ny man termorrer."

But Rosie was not yet through. She shook her finger at him.

"Yo'—yo' big polecat! Oh, iffn I only dared call yo'uns what I'se a thinkin'! 'The jailhouse' an' 'the comp'ny man'" – she mimicked him hoarsely – "that's all yo'uns kin think 'bout. Don't yo' reckon yo' owe me an' Hiram somethin'? Look what yo'uns made us go through all these years. Why not first see 'bout gittin' them reward notices down so Hiram can come home 'thout gittin' shot?" She came so close to him that he could feel her warm breath on his face. He tried to back up but the table blocked his way.

"Hiram's a comin' ter the jailhouse day arter termorrer mornin' ter see yo'uns," she continued, "'cause I'se a goin' ter tell him hit's all right ter come down. Iffn anyone tries ter nab him er iffn yo'uns lays a hand on him, Shuriff, they'll be some killin'. I'se warnin' yo'. We has all stood all we kin from yo'uns an' yore 'lectric comp'ny."

Rosie sat down, spent by her outburst, and hardly knowing what she had said.

But she had touched the sheriff's conscience. Or maybe it was the way her eyes flamed and her bosom heaved that affected him. But whatever it was, he said, "I know we done wrong ter Hiram, Rosie, but hit shore warn't no fault o' ourn. Nohow them reward notices'll be down termorrer, first thing in the mornin'. Hiram kin come ter see me safe an' sound arter termorrer."

Give Me Thy Vineyard

Give Me Thy Vineyard

Give Me Thy Vineyard

Chapter 41

WHEN ROSIE saw Hiram that night and told him that the next day he would be free, he sat down and cried like a little boy. Rosie had never seen him cry, and she did not know what to do. Even Bullet cocked his head to one side and looked at his master wonderingly. But Hiram's taut nerves needed the soothing tears. He forgot his embarrassment at breaking down before her in the wonderful relief it brought.

The next day, all along Rosie's mail route, people stood by their boxes to tell Rosie how tickled they were by the good news. The word had gone completely around that Tobe Alton, and not Hiram, had shot the company man. Even the little post office in Oakridge was crowded with well-wishers. To a man, the people said they knew all time that Hiram was innocent and several declared they had suspected Tobe all along. Rosie knew that many of them would have gladly turned Hiram in for the $2,000 reward, but she held her peace. Why not forget all that now?

The girl wished that she could tell Granny Smith of all this, and maybe cry a little bit on her lap as she had done when she was a child. But the old woman had died last August.

Many of the ridge inhabitants had attended Tobe Alton's funeral. They told Rosie that Sarah had stood straight and unmoving through the whole service.

"She didn't carry on one little bit," they said and shook their heads sympathetically. Things were going to be hard for

Give Me Thy Vineyard

Sarah now.

When Rosie passed the big oak trees along the main trail into Clear Springs, she noted with grim satisfaction that the reward notices had been removed from them. At last the sheriff had shown that he could keep a promise.

As she started into the clearing in front of Big Dave's store, loud shouts made her rein up Fred in surprise. There was a crowd of people on the porch and they were calling her name and waving to her. Some of them even started across the clearing to meet her. Someone was shouting, "Say, honey, when is that air Hiram a comin' back?"

"Ternight!" she shouted in reply, as the hill folk became delirious. They were all for going with her when she started off to get Hiram, but she put her foot down.

"Does yo'uns want ter scare him ter death?" she asked. "He hain't been roun' a lot o' folks fer 'most five years. Let him come back ter our kind o' life quiet-like."

Three hours later she and Hiram entered Clear Springs by way of Gurney's Mill. Hiram had decided not to bring Bullet into the village with them. The dog was not ready for the changed situation. He had been taught to hate and fear all but a few people. Hiram was afraid to think of what might happen if Bullet were suddenly surrounded by his erstwhile enemies. So they left him at Gurney's Mill.

The next day she and Hiram rode from Clear Springs to Hartstown, to the sheriff's office, where that officer and Clarence West, the lawyer from the electric company, were waiting for him.

Hate seared Hiram as he looked at the two men who could have killed him yesterday. But he managed to control himself and listen in grim silence as they apologized profusely. Then the sheriff handed him a full leather pouch.

"This air the money that the company man fetched yo'uns ter pay fer yore farm, so the money shore air yo'rn."

The former outlaw snatched the pouch without a word.

"And, furthermore, young man," the lawyer said, "United Electric wants to prove to you that it never had anything against you, personally. Our officers decided this morning to give you the reward of two thousand dollars, to use as you wish. Here is a check. I hope you won't want gold this time." He laughed thinly, as he laid the check on the table.

Hiram towered above the men, breathing hard and clenching and unclenching his great fists. Rosie held her breath and wished the earth would open and swallow them before Hiram did something to spoil everything. At last the young hillman opened his mouth to speak, every word poisonous and meaningful.

"Yo'uns kin keep yore money," he said. "I never asked fer nuthin but the worth o' my farm. That air reward money belongs ter Brother Rogers nohow. He's the one what found the killer."

"But he refused it once," the lawyer began.

It was now Rosie's turn to explode.

"Shore he did," she hissed, "'cause he warn't willin' ter guess at things like the rest o' yo'uns done. Hiram never war proved guilty, but plenty o' yo'uns made out like he war. S'pose Brother Rogers had a lissened ter yo'uns an' a tuck that air money. Where'd Hiram an' me be now?"

"I'm sorry, Rosie," the lawyer replied. "We made a mistake, but there is nothing we can do now to change it. If the company feels that Mr. Rogers is entitled to this money, I'm sure he shall have it since Hiram wants it that way."

From the sheriff's office Rosie and Hiram were taken to the judge to see about Hiram's pardon. They were told something which neither of them understood about a writ of habeas corpus. When it was fully explained to them they gathered that Hiram would be given a full pardon by the governor and that all his rights would be restored.

After returning to Clear Springs they visited Grady Rogers' cabin where Hiram decided to stay and do everything he could for the still unconscious man until he either died or got completely well.

• • • • •

Rogers was listening to Hiram's story in a half-daze, his imagination filling in what the young hillman had left out. So absorbed was he in the tale that he did not realize that Hiram had finished. When his voice stopped, Rogers opened his eyes and said irritably, "Well, go on. Then what?"

Hiram was cheered by the irritation in his tone. He knew it was a good sign when a sick man was grouchy.

"That's all there air to hit, Brother Rogers, 'ceptin' that hit shore air time fer yo'uns ter eat yore soup. Here."

And blowing on it first to cool it off, he gently fed the brew to Rogers, a spoonful at a time.

Give Me Thy Vineyard

Give Me Thy Vineyard

Give Me Thy Vineyard

Chapter 42

CLARENCE WEST carried the news to the Electric Company that Hiram had refused the reward money, saying it belonged to Grady Rogers. The company men decided, while they didn't feel Rogers was entitled to the money, maybe if they proffered the beneficent sum to him that it would put them in better grace with the community.

However, they learned from the sheriff that the teacher was very ill and they decided to wait until they heard he was better.

So it was that the lawyer made his uncomfortable way the second time to the little cabin in the woods to offer Grady Rogers the $2,000 reward. This time, however, West knew the teacher would have no reason to refuse.

Therefore, he was not surprised as he sat by the sick man's bed to hear him say as he reached for the check, "Yes, Mr. West, I think I have this reward coming to me. I did find the murderer and turned the information over to the county sheriff. Those were the terms. Thank you very much."

When Hiram had told him he probably would receive the reward, Rogers had said, "But, Hiram, I don't want it. I couldn't enjoy a penny of it, knowing it was the price on poor Tobe Alton's head. I'm going to ask them to give the money to Sarah Alton. She really needs it."

"Oh, no, Brother Rogers, don't do that," Hiram objected. "That air comp'ny never would give it to Sary. Her own husbin a killin' one o' their men."

"I guess you're right, Hiram. But I'd like for Sarah to have it."

"Then yo'uns let on like yo're glad ter git hit. Thank 'em an' be perlite till yo'uns gits hit. Then I reckon they hain't nuthin' ter keep yo'uns from givin' hit ter Sary er anybody else yer a mind ter."

And that was how the sum of $2,000 eventually came to be placed in trust for Sarah Alton and her children.

But still another two weeks lapsed before Grady Rogers was able to take care of himself. Hiram continued to stay with him at night, but Annie Montgomery and Ruthie Barnes and their husbands took turns through the day.

Hiram and Rosie had announced that they would be married as soon as Brother Rogers was well enough to perform the ceremony, so the womenfolk told Hiram it was time he was getting a place fixed up for them to live in. He found a good piece of land and bought it with the money that had been turned over to him. John Gurney and other neighbors took logs to the mill to be sawed into lumber. Then they all helped clear the land and put up the cabin.

Hiram spent most of his days finishing it and getting it ready to move into, and breaking the soil for cultivation. He relaxed by patiently teaching Bullet to get used to people. This promised to be a long and difficult job, but his sensitivity to the dog was gradually helping to bring him around. Hiram himself still had to fight the desire to run when there were more than two persons with him in a room, and he was stricken dumb in crowds. But Rosie, quietly watching, knew that before long both her man and his dog would win their battle.

As Rogers began to get better, he became concerned about the missing days of school. At last the day arrived when he could leave his cabin and he asked Cliff Montgomery to call the school board together. School had been within two weeks of the term's close when he took to his bed. He told the president of the board he was ready to make up the lost time.

Cliff announced the hour of the meeting to be held at his house. It was a balmy spring day in mid-March. As the teacher walked up the path to the brownstone cabin, he recalled the first hot day he had walked up this same path, nearly a year ago. How eager he had been to make a favorable impression. With a pang he recalled that his eagerness had been for Tom's sake. He had been so sure that a couple of years in the Ozarks would cure Tom's illness. A deep sigh escaped him as he entered the house.

"You boys remember that when I came here I told you I wanted a place where my boy could–could–" He seemed unable to go on. The men waited respectfully. "Could get well," the teacher finished. Then went on, "But God in His wisdom and mercy took him Home. My whole life was in my boy. Now I feel lost and out of place. I no longer feel there is any reason for me to stay here. You people on this ridge have been very good to me, and I can't tell you how I appreciate it. But I feel now that I must get away."

Grady Rogers found much difficulty making his argument convincing, chiefly because he wasn't convinced himself. Something within him kept repeating that there was a great reason for him to stay on Reed's Ridge, where God had given him much work to do. But at the same time he felt the urge to get away from it all. In spite of the graciousness of his neighbors he had seen much trouble since coming here. He was very tired and very, very restless. Surely he could find peace someplace. Where, he didn't know.

"Where air yo'uns a aimin' ter go?" Sam Bates asked.

"I thought I'd travel. Maybe go East. I've always wanted to go there. Perhaps I can get a job and do some studying in college at night. I've only half finished college, you know."

The men blinked at this. Grady Rogers was the best-educated man they had ever known. They couldn't see the sense of his wanting more learning.

"But, Brother Rogers," Cliff Montgomery protested thoughtfully, "hit 'pears ter me like maybe God wants yo'uns ter stay here on the ridge. Yo'all shore done a heap o' good roun here."

"I know," Rogers started to answer, "but–"

Cliff paid no heed to him, but continued, "Yo'uns has gave the young'uns in these parts the best schoolin' they has ever had. Yo'uns has fetched prayer meetin' back reg'lar an' they war plenty o' sinners a needin' hit bad. An' look what yo've done fer Rosie an' Hiram."

"That's right," Zeke Barnes interjected heartily. "Hit's right plain ter see the Almighty wants yo'uns ter stay here, Brother Rogers. We'uns needs yo'all an' God knows hit."

Grady's eyes filled with tears and his voice choked. "You are making it very hard for me," he remarked sadly. "Please give me a few days to think it over. I can't say for sure now."

This seemed fair enough to the sincerely anxious men and they got on to other matters at hand. It was decided that the teacher and pupils would spend only one more week in the schoolroom. That would give them a chance to bring their work to a close and prepare a program for the closing day of school, an occasion of such primary social importance in the community that it could not be deleted from their life even for one season. Ever since anyone could remember there had been a basket dinner and last-day program to end the school year. Nothing else would make it official.

Give Me Thy Vineyard

Give Me Thy Vineyard

Give Me Thy Vineyard

Chapter 43

G RADY ROGERS felt much relieved to get the details for the close of school planned out and set about the following Monday to get everything in readiness.

That left for him just one more bit of service to do before leaving the community. That was to perform the marriage ceremony that would link Rosie's future with Hiram's.

Hiram let Rosie make all of the plans to suit herself. He was fully occupied and contentedly so, building a place for them to live in. Besides making the cabin comfortable and handy, he fashioned many of the furnishings with his own hands – tables, chairs, benches, shelves. Rosie proudly admired it and thrilled him with her appreciative words of praise.

Her time was divided between helping Annie Montgomery and Ruthie Barnes with her wedding dress and talking over the plans in detail with Grady Rogers. She even had him measure Hiram for a new suit of clothes which she ordered for him, along with shoes and a shirt, from a mail-order catalog. She wished she dared order him a tie also, but she was afraid the idea might frighten him so that he wouldn't even consent to the new suit. The covers of the catalog closed with a bang and she sighed audibly as she thought how nice and distinguished Grady Rogers looked when he stood in the pulpit.

The wedding was to be held in the schoolhouse at the

conclusion of the morning service on the Sunday following the close of school. Tim McGonagle and Sally Bates were to be their attendants. Grady told Hiram that women appreciated flowers for special occasions and suggested he pick Rosie a large bouquet of the lovely violets that were growing in such profusion in the woods. He himself provided a small white Bible that had belonged to his mother for the bride to carry in her hand.

The eager, excited crowd gathered early on the day set for the marriage. All were able to get inside because families are large in the Ozarks and it takes a large building to accommodate the great enrollment of children going to school.

Everyone was dressed in his best for this momentous event. Few of them had ever attended a wedding other than their own. Grady preached a farewell sermon, telling the folk that he felt he must leave the ridge because there was now no reason for him to remain there. Even as he spoke these words his conscience seemed to experience twinges of regret. He thanked them all for the kindnesses they had shown him at all times. He would hold dearly always the memory of the year he had labored with them.

Grady took his text from the 11th chapter of John, the command of Jesus at the tomb of Lazarus, when He said, "Take ye away the stone." The minister spoke softly but his voice was vibrant with sincerity.

"Jesus always had a reason for everything He did," the sermon began. "He had a very great lesson to teach these people, for you know, as I know, that Jesus could have cried, 'Lazarus, come forth,' before the stone was rolled away from the grave and the stone would have rolled itself away, as the dead was resurrected. Since Jesus did not do it that way, He had a reason. Let us think this morning of that reason. The sinner is as dead spiritually as Lazarus was physically.

"When the sinner recognizes he is lost, then by God's grace rolls away the stone of his own stubborn refusal, the Holy

Spirit will guide to the blood of Christ, that washes away all sin. If you are a sinner this morning, will you respond to the invitation of the gentle loving Jesus who said, 'Him that cometh to me I will in no wise cast out'?"

Annie Montgomery took her place before the congregation to lead them in song. Following the usual custom, she chose a song designed to lead sinners to repent and accept Christ. Hiram and Rosie sat together near the front of the room. During the singing of the first stanza Rosie slipped her small hand over to rest gently in Hiram's great one. She felt his grip tighten and he seemed to tremble all over. Before she knew what was happening he was on his feet, moving toward the front.

"Folks," he began, as the last note of the singing died away, "if it's all right with Brother Rogers, I'd like ter say somethin'."

Rogers nodded his assent, trying to guess at what might be on Hiram's mind.

"Folks," he began again, "I reckon I cain't say very well what I'se a thinkin', but hit jist 'pears like I'll plumb die iffn I waits 'nuther day ter git right with the Lord."

"Amens" arose prayerfully all over the house. Rosie was overcome with joy but remained quiet and speechless.

Rogers nodded encouragingly as the confession continued.

"I'se done a heap o' sinnin' in my day like all o' yo'uns knows 'bout. God's been powerful good ter Rosie an' me a watchin' over me all the time I war hidin' out from the law. I'se shore hit's 'cause Rosie an' yo'uns been a prayin' He would. I shore believes Brother Rogers war right when he said last Sunday, 'Christian home raisin' is the only hope of this here world.' Me an' Rosie shore don't want our home to be a house divided agin itself 'cause the Good Book says sich won't stand. Pray fer us, folks, an' we'll do our level best – the Good Lord a he'pin' us."

So deeply moved he could scarcely control his voice, Hiram bowed in silent prayer. Grady Rogers and the congregation realized the sacredness of the moment. Presently Grady moved forward and took Hiram's hand.

"Hiram Jackson," he asked, "do you believe with all your heart that Jesus is the Christ, the Son of the living God, and do you accept Him as your personal Saviour?"

"Yes, Brother Rogers. I shore does."

"Then, folks," Rogers announced, "let us meet this afternoon at 3 o'clock for the baptizing."

Turning to Rosie, he said quietly, "Take your places for the marriage, please."

After the last service of the day was finished, Grady Rogers returned to his cabin and finished packing his things for tomorrow's departure. He had given Tommy's things to children who could use them. All that was left were his personal belongings. Since he didn't know for sure where he was going, most of these things were being stored at the Montgomerys'. He had only a small bag to carry with him.

His task finished, he turned from the bare little room and walked over the hills to the little graveyard. He had not been there since his illness. The bare little mound that he had seen on his last visit was now carefully sodded. It was covered with soft green grass. The top of the mound was bordered with a perfect oblong of pure-white mussel shells. Two great bouquets of wildflowers were vased in water-filled fruit jars atop the mound. At the head of the grave rested a large, brown, smoothly cut slab of sandstone on which was neatly chiseled this inscription:

TOMMY ROGERS
EVERBODY LOVED HIM

"Oh! Tommy!" Rogers sobbed, "look what Hiram made for you." The grieving father dropped to his knees and remained for long moments in prayer.

At last he arose and whispered softly, "Our friends did this and I have told them I was leaving. I couldn't go away now if I wanted to. Life's happiness, born only of the opportunity to serve, is here. The roots have grown deep and strong during the last 10 months, Tommy.

"I was so lonely without you. Selfishly I wanted to go away to be part of the rush of the city, there to forget. Now I'm going back to the cabin and unpack. These beautiful, blue, misty hills have something much bigger than self. I know now I belong here, for belonging is only the right to serve. I'll be back, for I need your nearness."

Turning, Grady walked, whistling softly, down the long slope as twilight cast its spell of enchantment across the mountains, like a soft benediction at the shut of a turbulent day. Grady Rogers walked victoriously, for he walked with God.

Give Me Thy Vineyard

About the Author

Guy Howard walked nearly 4,000 miles each year over the highways and backwoods roads of Missouri and Arkansas to preach in meeting houses, schools and churches. Pastor, teacher, confessor and general adviser, he was beloved by the mountain people about whom most Americans know little.

Howard, who died in 1966, was honored by the University of Missouri School of Journalism as a "notable Missouri author."

Give Me Thy Vineyard, first published in 1949, won the Zondervan International Novel Contest. Howard also wrote *Walkin' Preacher of the Ozarks* in 1944 and *Wings of the Dawn* in 1953. His books are available from Ogden Publications, 1-800-678-5779.